*P*etrovich walked her to the front. Her coat was still crumpled beside the door. The principal's office door was open, which looked odd. That door was never open, not even during school hours.

Lights were on inside, and drop cloths covered the carpet, the furniture, and the computers.

"May I ask you a personal question?" he said.

Larissa crouched as she reached for her coat. She mentally braced herself.

Everyone asked why she quit her high-profile job to teach high school in rural Minnesota. She had a pat answer for it, but she wasn't sure she wanted to use that answer with Petrovich. He had been honest with her all day.

She owed him the same.

She grabbed her coat, folded it over her left arm, and stood. "Ask away."

A frown created a deep line between his eyes. "You really don't remember me?"

She used to get this a lot. People she'd interviewed years before would ask her that question, or later, when she was a regular face on CNN, people who had asked for her autograph more than once expected her to remember as well.

"I'm sorry," she said, falling back on the old answer. "I don't."

His frown deepened for a moment, then he took a deep breath, and slid her coat out of her arms. He held it open for her, a courtesy a man had not done for her in years.

She slipped into it. It was too warm for the corridor.

"It's amazing how the memory works," he said as she turned toward him. "You saved my life and you don't even remember."

Bleed Through

a novel

by Kristine Kathryn Rusch

wMg
Publishing

Bleed Through

Copyright © 2013 Kristine Kathryn Rusch

All rights reserved

Published 2013 by WMG Publishing
www.wmgpublishing.com
Cover and Layout copyright © 2013 by WMG Publishing
Cover design by Allyson Longueira/WMG Publishing
Cover art copyright © Darren Baker/Dreamstime
ISBN-13: 978-0-615-76763-5
ISBN-10: 0-615-76763-X

WMG Publishing
www.wmgpublishing.com

We tell ourselves stories in order to live…. We look for the sermon in the suicide, for the social or moral lesson in the murder of five. We interpret what we see, select the most workable of the multiple choices. We live entirely, especially if we are writers, by the imposition of a narrative line upon disparate images, by the "ideas" with which we have learned to freeze the shifting phantasmagoria which is our actual experience.

—Joan Didion
The White Album

Bleed Through

a novel

one

S he came back to paint the school as a penance. Larissa Johanssen had been in Maui during the shooting. She'd taken that Monday—Presidents Day—off so that she could have one extra day in the sunshine before returning the haze of a Minnesota winter.

She'd flown back on Wednesday, trying to stifle tears, simultaneously wishing she had been in her classroom with her students and relieved that she had been nowhere near Manatowa High School when Leif Soderstrom—a student she'd been trying to draw out of his moody shell—had brought three assault rifles, six automated pistols, and a homemade grenade into third-period lunch, and proceeded to pick off his fellow students.

Leif had killed sixteen kids, wounded ten others, and murdered the guard at the front door—a friendly man who monitored the metal detector and x-rayed every briefcase and backpack. Leif had also killed the lunchroom supervisor, a rather austere woman with the apt name of Iris Winter, and the assistant principal, Walter Haigen.

The school had been closed for nearly a week, first while the crime scene analysts mapped Leif's murderous path, and then while the crime scene cleaners tried to return everything to normal.

But the school board knew that normal wasn't possible, not anymore, and they ordered a secondary cleanup—an expenditure of funds unprecedented in the school's history. Some of the funds would go to on-site psychiatric counseling for the rest of the school year, and the rest would go toward new tables and chairs for the cafeteria, a new security system, and locks for every single classroom door.

The board also called for a completely new paint job on the interior of the building—new colors, new trim and even, in the areas coated by blood, new vinyl on the floors.

The board wanted to hire a painting firm, but at that emotional board meeting—which Larissa had missed due to a delayed flight, but saw later on Community Access Channel Five—the parents and the teachers volunteered to do that part of the job.

It makes us feel like we're doing something, said Ronald Phelps, the algebra teacher, and Larissa could hear the guilt in his voice. She recognized it because she had felt the same guilt the entire way home.

Maybe if she had talked to Leif more, drawn him out, seen how very distressed he was, not just by his father's death last summer, but by the way the kids teased him. Maybe she might have noticed that glimmer of insanity in his eyes, the edge that he balanced precariously on.

She, of all people, should have seen how close he was to falling off.

But she hadn't. And not only had she failed to see the signs of Leif's mental break, but she had been in Hawaii when it happened—ten days in the sunshine, courtesy of her flamboyant sister Nadia who wanted Larissa to stand up for her at her fifth wedding. This marriage probably wouldn't last either, but Nadia wanted to milk her newly minted husband for every single dime. The man could afford it—he was worth more than forty million dollars thanks to some patents that had something to do with genetics.

The wedding had been a spare-no-expense event at one of Hawaii's most exclusive resorts. Famous musicians provided music every single night. Each meal was catered, and the ever-flowing drinks were on the house.

Larissa hadn't even spent any of her own money getting there. Nor did she spend any money while she was there. Nadia had given Larissa an allowance—which was almost half her annual salary—and told her to have fun.

Larissa had had fun, and she had brought back nine-tenths of the money, along with a new wardrobe, and presents for the friends left behind.

Presents that now seemed frivolous, just like her tan in the middle of a Minnesota winter. She looked like a woman who had been partying while the world ended, and she felt like it too.

So she'd called the principal—Helen Meiers—and volunteered to be on the painting crew. Helen, bless her, had tried to talk Larissa out of it.

You don't want to go in there until it's fixed. Trust me on this, Larissa.

But Larissa did, and she would. It was the least she could do in this new world, where the least seemed like nothing at all, not really, not considering the bullets she'd dodged—probably literally—since she often went to third-period lunch to talk to her more recalcitrant students.

The school looked the same, looming out of the winter fog like the place she had left only two weeks before. She had been afraid it would look different, probably because it had on television.

The flat school, built in the 1970s of red prairie brick, looked both bigger and smaller when viewed from a helicopter and filtered through a television screen. She wasn't used to the angle—seeing the design of the school, five wings floating out of the center ring like spokes of a rimless wheel.

She had known the school was designed like that, and she often lamented it—especially at the beginning of the year when the freshman always got lost—but apparently the design had inadvertently saved lives.

The cafeteria was in the ring, along with the auditorium and the administration offices. When the shooting started, Principal Meiers had had enough presence of mind to hit the button that unlocked all of the outside doors. Students ran down the spokes, away from the ring, heading outside as quickly as possible.

Only those students trapped in third-period lunch had died. In her weaker moments, as the extent of the tragedy became known, she thought of it as Death by Computerized Schedule, because no one liked third-period lunch since it started at 10 a.m.

She used to hate it, too, because students who had third-period lunch always did poorly in their eighth-period classes. By then, lunch had been five hours previous. Students were hungry and cranky and tired, and they didn't want to learn. They wanted to snack or gossip or sleep—and a lot of them did, which was one of the many reasons she was usually in the cafeteria during third period, making sure her eighth-period students had finished their homework and were prepared for class.

Most teachers didn't have that dedication, but she wasn't most teachers. Even though she was in her late forties, she had only had her teaching degree for ten years. Other teachers often said Larissa hadn't had the idealism beaten out of her yet.

Or maybe, Larissa used to counter, she'd seen the worth of idealism during her stint in the real world, and clung to hers like a shield.

She pulled her silver Acura into the parking lot, bumping across rutted tracks near the teachers' parking spaces. There had been snow for two days after the shooting, and no one had plowed the driveway. The tracks had come from a series of visitors and the crime scene teams.

A barren stretch of unmarked white in the student lot accentuated the emptiness. By now, even on a Saturday in February, the lot would have had dozens of cars, most owned by the athletic students or their parents and the so-called deadbeats who got called in for Saturday detention.

But this morning, there were only five other cars and one panel van. A group of teachers huddled on the sidewalk near the front door. All of them held covered Starbucks cups, and two clutched cigarettes like lifelines.

Larissa glanced at the clock in her Acura. It was 7:57 a.m. She was three minutes early, yet the looks from her fellow volunteers made her feel like she had arrived late.

She parked in her usual spot, slung her purse over her shoulder, and got out of the car. Her boots slipped on the thin layer of ice beneath the snow. The winter had been relatively mild until mid-January. The six-foot-high mounds of snow that she remembered from her Minnesota childhood hadn't formed during a single winter since she'd returned.

As a result, she always felt like she was in a winter twilight—the beginning of the end of a season she had once professed to love.

The air was damp and cold. The fog layer held, and if she squinted, she could see ice in the fog itself. Freezing fog was rare in New York, where she'd spent the last years of her journalism career, and it was something else in Atlanta, where she had gotten her start. There, freezing fog formed ice on the roads, but not in the air. Here, the fog itself was frozen, refracting the light and making the entire world a moist, shiny gray, a color she had never seen anywhere else.

She didn't welcome the freezing fog. It made her feel sad and terrified. She wiped a gloved hand across her face and crunched her way through the ice layer on the snow to the haphazardly shoveled sidewalk.

The other volunteers watched her come. She wasn't very popular with her colleagues. They saw her as an anomaly. She wasn't married, and had no children—no obligations, someone had once said with a sneer—and she dressed up every day, because she felt it was important to look her best.

Her best outclassed the other teachers—not just in quality of clothing (she had ten times the salary as a journalist that she was making as a teacher)—but in her looks. She'd learned from years on the air how to maximize her traditional Scandinavian appearance. It wasn't unusual here for a woman in her forties to be a natural blond with high cheekbones and ice-blue eyes. But it was unusual for that woman to still be as willow-thin as she had been as a teenager, and to have soft, radiant, unlined skin.

Larissa had stopped wearing makeup, but that only served to take ten years off her already youthful face. She was good-looking, she used to be famous, and she was smart.

She could have, with only a few more years of graduate school, taught at a good university. Instead, armed with a newly minted master's, she had applied at public high schools all over the Midwest, and finally got hired at Manatowa because Principal Meiers had written enough grants to hang onto the arts program, which included the journalism department.

When most high schools no longer had a student paper and an actual yearbook staff, Manatowa had both, as well as an intern program that allowed the best students to work with the local newspaper.

Larissa had expanded that to local broadcast media, and had been writing her own grant for funding for a larger broadcast unit before the tragedy struck.

She stopped near the group, feeling oddly naked without her own Starbucks cup. Had they all met at the Starbucks half a block away before coming here? Or did they always carry their caffeine with them at this time of the day?

She didn't know and she didn't ask, even though Robyn Frye stood at the outside edge of the group. Robyn was ten years younger than Larissa, just as blond but not quite as willowy after two kids. Robyn wore a new coat—white with fake fur on the wrists and around the neck—clearly a Christmas present that Larissa hadn't yet seen.

Robyn was one of Larissa's few good friends here at Manatowa, and as their gazes met, Larissa felt her worry that everyone had gathered without her, fade.

Alan Deela, the football coach and shop teacher, tossed his cigarette in the snow. He rubbed his meaty hands together. They were red and chapped in the cold.

Larissa knew that in most school hierarchies, she wasn't supposed to like a man whose job was essentially anti-intellectual, but he kept the marginal kids interested and helped girls learn how to build things. She thought his teaching skills impressive, although she had never told him that.

"Who're we waiting for?" she asked, pulling up the cloth collar of her own coat. She should have worn a cap, but she hated having anything on her head, and she thought earmuffs looked ridiculous.

"Pete Petrovich," said Oscar Verdiecke, a too-thin man with large ears and two strips of black hair on either side of his bald head, who taught chemistry. Even though he wasn't a smoker, his fingertips were always stained yellow. Today they were covered with thick leather gloves whose fake fur lining stuck out of a crack on the back.

Larissa moved closer to the group. The fog made the air brittle and colder than it should have been without a wind.

"Petrovich," she repeated. "Is he new?"

"He's a civilian," said Darren Rivell. Darren taught social studies, and was often here on Saturdays, drilling his debate, forensic, and Model U.N. teams. He looked, as Robyn once said, like an evil German intellectual from a bad World War II film—short, with reddish blond hair, a round face, and round glasses that could have passed for pince-nez in a previous life.

Larissa would have thought painting a wall beyond him.

"He doesn't work here?" she repeated.

"The school board wanted a real house painter to supervise us," said Oscar.

"Great," Larissa said and shifted from foot to foot. "Can't we just unlock without him and go in?"

Everyone looked at her as if she were crazy, and that was when she realized none of them had been inside since the shooting. She thought she was the only one who was returning for the first time this morning.

No wonder they huddled here, clutching their hot cardboard cups of coffee and staring at the ice-filled fog. They all had their backs to the building, and even now, after she had suggested going inside, no one turned to look at it.

She was the only one who faced it. The only one who looked at the windows, tinted in the 1990s so perverts couldn't look in, and incongruously decorated with red hearts from last week's celebration of Valentine's Day.

"We have to go in sometime," she said.

"Easy for you to say," Darren snapped. "You weren't here."

"Darren." Robyn's voice held caution, as if with just a sound she could hold them all together.

"It's all right. I wasn't here. I was…" Larissa groped for a word, and doubted that any word would be right. "I was lucky, I guess."

"You guess." Darren shook his small head and his glasses slipped to the edge of his nose. "You were lucky. No one pointed a gun at you."

Not then, she almost said, but didn't.

"No one pointed a gun at me," Larissa said quietly. "I didn't hear the screams."

This time.

"And I never saw what he did. Just those endless loops on television." She shook her head. "That's why I'm here today, I guess."

"To share our pain?" Darren asked, pushing his glasses up with the knuckle of his right hand.

"To do what I can," she said.

The entire group looked away then except Robyn, who gave her a tentative smile. They were all here to do what they could. They all felt as impotent as Larissa did, maybe more impotent since none of them stopped Leif from shooting all those students.

This group of teachers gathered everyone in their classrooms and ran to the nearest exit. The smart move, the police and the commentators and the authorities said. But as guilt-inducing as not being there at all. Maybe more guilt-inducing since they probably ran not to save their students' lives, but to save their own.

A battered truck turned into the student parking lot, leaving tracks in the unbroken snow. The driver went twice as fast as he should have in the lot, just like teenage drivers did.

But as the truck pulled close, Larissa realized that the man driving was no teenager. He had blond hair that needed a trim, a silvery goatee that accented his long face, and skin that had tanned so often it had darkened over the decades. He got out almost before the truck stopped.

He didn't have a coat, just a red checked flannel shirt shiny with a lot of washings and ripped jeans that looked stonewashed but were probably as old as Robyn.

He was in his forties, like Larissa, and had probably gone to Manatowa High thirty years before. Which explained why he pulled into the student lot with such authority instead of the visitor's lot directly in front of the circle.

Or maybe no one was using that lot anymore.

"Hey, Pete," said Alan. "Glad you could make it."

He leaned forward and offered Petrovich his hand, as if he had invited the man personally.

Petrovich shook it once. "I got supplies in the truck. Let's get them inside."

His mention of *inside* didn't seem to disturb the group the way Larissa's had. Maybe because he wasn't part of the school community. Or maybe because, with those last two sentences, he had just taken on the role as their boss.

Five-gallon drums of paint sat under a tarp in the truck's bed, along with brushes, standard rollers, high-tech rollers, and some equipment Larissa had never seen before. She had painted her house when she moved to Manatowa, but she had done so slowly, with a single roller and a small brush, taking her time because she found the job healing.

This didn't look healing. This looked like work.

In the center of the truck was a machine. As Alan and Oscar removed two paint drums each and carried them to the front door, Petrovich slid some of the smaller equipment to the front of the bed and dislodged the machine.

"What's that?" Robyn asked.

"For big areas," he said. "It'll slop some paint on there, and then we'll touch up."

"Are we finishing today?" Darren asked.

"School's opening Monday," Petrovich said, sounding very knowledgeable for a civilian.

Monday. Larissa had known that, but she hadn't processed it. Monday was only two days away. In less than forty-eight hours, she would have to figure out how to conduct her classes. English would be easy enough—they had a lesson plan to follow—but on Monday, the student newspaper staff met to discuss and plan Friday's issue.

They would have to write about the shootings.

She shuddered.

Petrovich shoved a pile of rolling trays and paint rags at her. "You gonna be okay?" he asked softly.

"I'm just cold," she said.

He gave her a sad little smile. "Sure," he said, and went back to his machine.

Sure. One simple word so full of confidence and denial. Sure, you're fine. On the surface, anyway. Everyone is fine on the surface.

She took the trays, their thin metal cold, and piled the rags on top. Then she made her way to the front door, which someone had propped open with one of the five-gallon drums.

She stepped inside and the trays slid. She wrapped her arms around them, trying to keep her balance, her wet boots sliding on the tile floor.

She had been expecting the indoor-outdoor rug that lined the path through the airlock, but the rug was gone.

Someone had removed it. Because it had been covered with blood?

She caught the trays and her footing, but her heart was beating so hard she could hardly catch her breath. She felt foolish—how silly had she looked there?—and relieved she hadn't dropped anything all at the same time. The sound of thin metal bouncing off tile would have echoed like a gunshot in the small space.

Everyone would have been terrified.

She turned around and used her back to push open the inner door. The hallway's familiar smell of dry heat and chalk was overlaid with the chemical odor of disinfectants, so sharp that it made her eyes water.

The hair rose on the back of her neck. She could feel the terror still trapped inside the building. It was, as her producer at CNN used to say, one of her gifts—the ability to empathize not just with what was happening, but with what had happened before she even got to the scene.

She set the trays down on the right side of the large corridor, between the glass of the entry and the wall of the principal's office. Then she turned, and felt her breath catch.

Because the trays and rags had blocked her view, she hadn't noticed that the large metal detector and X-ray machines were gone. In their place was a gap on the floor and a thick black rectangle twice as long as she would have expected carved into the tile.

She had read the accounts: she knew what Leif had done. He had shot the security guard before approaching the machines, and then hurried down the corridor toward the cafeteria.

But she hadn't understood the accounts. There were no bullet holes in the glass that partitioned the airlock from the school corridor.

So somehow, Leif had opened the heavy glass doors that she had just pushed with her back, and then shot the guard.

The guard had been so friendly. Larissa had never known his name. She'd read it in the accounts, but even now she couldn't recall it. Although she could see him sitting at his station, a heavyset former cop with a jowly face and red-rimmed eyes that suggested a bit too much familiarity with his local tavern. He'd smiled at her every day when she arrived, flirted a little as he put her briefcase and purse on the X-ray machine's belt, then apologized as he made her walk through the detector.

The set-up was just like the ones the airlines used. The school had bought it at a discount after the Columbine massacre which, despite later misleading media coverage, wasn't the first large school shooting. It was just the first large school shooting at an upper-class white high school. The previous shootings, in Kentucky and Oregon and Mississippi, had occurred in largely blue-collar neighborhoods, which hadn't made her former colleagues in the media as afraid as Columbine had.

If it could happen in a high school like the ones they had gone to, one of the other reporters at *The New York Times* had said shortly before Larissa left, then it really could happen anywhere.

Even here.

In Manatowa. Where every day, Larissa had walked in, flirted with a man who was going to die at a teenager's hand, and thought herself safe as she walked through the wide corridors filled with the smells of bubblegum, cigarettes, and teenage lust.

For the first time in any of her jobs, she had thought she was safe.

And she had been—but only because her flighty sister had invited her to this decade's wedding at just the right time.

"It looks bigger, doesn't it?" Robyn said from beside her. Robyn had come in the door carrying drop cloths like they were costumes for the school play.

"Why'd they take out the machines?" Larissa asked.

"They say they're getting new ones, and they'll install them differently."

Something in Robyn's voice made Larissa look at her.

"What else?" Larissa asked softly.

Robyn blinked, the skin around her eyes suddenly red with strain from fighting back tears.

"He shot it up," she said. "You could hear it all over the school. It sounded like target practice against cans, you know? You ever done that? It sounded…."

She stopped, then shook her head and left Larissa's side, setting the drop cloths on top of the trays. Robyn had been far from the shootings: the language arts rooms were at the end of the fifth corridor, which opened onto the only square part of the building—the music wing, the old auditorium (now the library) and the gym complex, complete with Manatowa's pride and joy, an Olympic-sized swimming pool.

For the shootings to echo all the way down there, they had to be excessively loud.

Robyn pushed the glass door open again, then held it for Darren and Petrovich, who carried the machine in together. Actually, it looked like Petrovich did most of the lifting. Darren just held an edge of the machine as if he could keep it balanced.

They crab-walked inside and set the machine beside the black rectangle. When Darren saw where they were, he started, took five involuntary steps back, and nearly tripped on a drop cloth.

Larissa put a hand on his back to steady him. He made a small sound of alarm, almost a squeak, then flushed a dark red.

If he had been anyone else, she would have commented on how unsettling it was. But he had already decided to direct his anger at her for not being there. She didn't want to compound it.

She slipped her hand away from him, then went out through the doors. The airlock was chilly compared with the school and the outside was downright frigid. The fog seemed even thicker than before. She could barely see the truck in all the whitish grayness.

Petrovich was still inside the school, probably dealing with the machine. Alan and Oscar were taking down the remaining drums and setting them on the sidewalk. Robyn grabbed an armload of rollers.

Larissa took a drum with both hands. She moved slowly. The icy film over the snow broke under her increased weight, and she didn't want to slip again. She wasn't going to make the same mistake of expecting the rug in the airlock.

Instead, she made the transition from outside to inside with amazing ease, even though her feet had gone from the relatively stable snow holes to the wet, slush-covered tile.

The janitor, Mr. Haynes, would hate the mess they had made of his school. Mr. Haynes, who used to yell at her for tracking from the courtyard outside her classroom down the hallway, had had a mild heart attack the day of the shooting.

The police had found him inside the janitor's closet, clutching his chest and breathing rapidly. They thought he'd been shot, but he hadn't. The fear had nearly killed him.

The school district had already received word that he wouldn't return.

She would miss him. She had liked his fussy precision, his almost religious devotion to his impossible job.

She was about to set the drum down near the drop cloths when Petrovich waved a hand at her.

"Take it to the cafeteria," he said.

Bile rose in her throat, and she swallowed it back. She had hoped to make it through this day without going near the cafeteria. She had figured it would take her a week, maybe more, to acclimatize herself to that room again.

But he wasn't giving her any choice—which, come to think of it, was probably better.

The drum seemed heavier now that she was inside, or maybe just because she was walking down this part of the corridor alone. Her heartbeat was so loud, she thought the others could hear it.

The very idea made her face flush.

Leif had run down this hallway with guns slung over his shoulder like Rambo. He had had even more in his backpack, along with that lethal homemade grenade. He had never used that, which was just as well. Authorities estimate that it would have taken down the entire ring.

Even more students would have died.

She stopped, set the drum down, and wiped the sweat from her forehead. A few minutes ago, she had been too cold. Now she was sweating, her heart beating rapidly. Her hands were shaking, too—and she knew it was because Petrovich had asked her to go to the cafeteria.

She remembered this feeling from reporting: this leftover angst, as if the events that had transpired here days before were still happening, as if they got repeated over and over again, like some ghostly battle in a bad horror movie.

If she closed her eyes, she could picture it: Leif—a chubby boy with a football player's body, a boy who had never used that innate athletic ability to go out for sports, but who had, instead, slumped over and hid whenever anyone called his name. He would pretend to sleep in her eighth-period English class, but his feet would move, constantly tapping, as if he had some sort of nervous twitch.

Unlike her colleagues, she wouldn't call on him when he pretended to sleep, and over time, he would raise his head and listen, leaning back, arms crossed, studying her through half-closed eyes.

Just before Christmas, he had even started to do the reading. He still wouldn't complete his homework—although when she verbally quizzed him in third-period lunch, it became clear that he paid attention and understood the materials—but she had thought they were making progress.

He had seemed disappointed when she announced she would be gone for two weeks. He had asked her if she had to leave. She had thought his concern was about his schoolwork and the hassle a sub would automatically put him through. She had told him to hold on—she would be back and they could work together—but he had seemed so skeptical, so needy, that she had patted him on the shoulder and walked away.

One thing she had learned in her few short years as a teacher was to stay as detached as possible.

The kids, another teacher had told her, *will always break your heart.*

Larissa opened her eyes. Beside her, she heard the sound of tennis shoes scuffling against tile, faint screams mixed with some confused laughter. She turned.

Petrovich was watching her from the front door. Did he know how hard this was for her? Did he feel the ghosts in this corridor or was he as detached as he seemed? Was this just a job for him or had the horrors touched him, too?

She gave him a weak smile and continued toward the cafeteria.

This part of the ring opened into a true oval. This was where the spokes of the wheel met. Between classes, this part of the ring was always full of students, some lingering near the doors and the vending machines, others (usually boys hoping to see a flash of female flesh) lurking beneath the stairs, and the rest hurrying toward their classes.

Leif had never lurked nor had he lingered. He'd hurried through the halls, often to stay away from the so-called "cool kids" who called him names and made fun of his ill-fitting clothing or his acne-scarred face. He'd always walked with his head down and his shoulders hunched forward, like a linebacker who'd unexpectedly caught the ball and was anticipating a horrible tackle that would ruin his short moment of glory.

Had he run down the hall that afternoon with his head up? Or had he hunched, head down, terrified that someone would stop him?

She shook the thoughts away, and turned toward the cafeteria doors. They were made of glass—or they had been. Two were missing, and the remaining four doors had bullet holes that spiderwebbed, blocking any view of the interior. Someone, maybe the crime scene cleaners, maybe Principal Meiers, had taped a sign to the metal frame, warning caution near the doors and promising that they would be replaced later in the week by a local glass company.

"If the school's going to open on Monday, we can't have that," said a voice behind her.

Larissa started. She made herself exhale before she turned, a calming maneuver that almost worked.

Petrovich stood a few steps behind her, arms crossed, head tilted. His blond hair brushed the frayed edges of his collar. "I've got a buddy who can bring us some plywood. We'll cover that broken glass."

"You'd think the school would have thought of that already." Oscar had come up behind him. Oscar's coat was gone, along with his gloves, and he wore a Hard Rock Cafe T-shirt that was covered with paint stains. His jeans were as stained as the shirt.

He'd come prepared to work.

"I doubt anyone is thinking that clearly," Petrovich said. "There are a lot of holes to plug here."

Then his gaze met Larissa's. She wondered if she looked as appalled as she felt.

"Metaphorically speaking," he said.

But as she forced herself to step inside the cafeteria, she realized his words really weren't metaphorical at all. Someone had slapped spackle across the bullet holes in the walls, but there were still holes in the tile. A few were covered with chunks of wood, but someone had clearly stopped that practice. The wood chunks were more dangerous than the holes. A student could trip on a woodblock, but nothing, except maybe the smallest of high heels, could get caught in a bullet hole.

Some of the tables were piled in the center of the room, and the chairs were stacked just inside the kitchen like they often were before a dance. The dances had always been held here, and unlike the gymnasium dances of Larissa's own high school years, this cafeteria—with the right lighting and the proper decorations—could look almost romantic.

But not anymore. She wondered if anyone would want to hold a dance here, or if the athletic department would subject their precious gymnasium floor to high heels and expensive shoes.

The room still had a faint smell of cooking food. Beneath it, though, was something else, something slightly sharp. Not the scent of blood—the crime scene cleaners had obviously done their job—but the scent of fear, perhaps, or the persistent odor of trauma.

She resisted the urge to bring her hand to her mouth. Her whole body was shaking. She wasn't sure how she could spend all day in here, but she had to try.

They had to repair this room before Monday, so that the students didn't have this awful feeling that she had, this feeling of lingering disaster.

Robyn was already inside, with a drop cloth spread near the far wall. Two drums of paint held down the sides of the cloth, and she was busy laying out the rollers and brushes. Her coat was piled in a corner, and she had pulled her hair into a ponytail. That, and her ripped jeans and extra-large sweatshirt, made her look years younger.

Until she stood up. The care lines around her mouth and the deep circles under her eyes added decades—decades she didn't actually have.

"You gonna use that machine first?" she asked Petrovich.

"On the big wall." He had come up behind Larissa again. She stepped to the side. She didn't want anyone behind her, especially someone she had just met.

He was looking at the long wall that extended the entire length of the cafeteria. The posters and bulletin boards that usually covered it were gone. Large splotches of white showed where the spackle had covered bullet holes.

How many rounds had Leif shot in here? Guns shot so rapidly now that she had no idea how anyone had gotten away.

Behind her, more footsteps. Obviously Oscar had come in and, she supposed, Alan and Darren. Larissa turned slightly so that she could see them out of the corner of her eye.

They stood silently, reverentially, hands folded before them, that discomfort you saw most often in funerals reflected on their faces.

None of them had been in here, either. This was the first time all of them were facing the loss and carnage that had occurred in a place they had dedicated their lives to.

"Well," Petrovich said after a moment, "I guess we all start here, then. You want to help me carry the sprayer the rest of the way, Alan?"

Alan nodded, not taking his gaze off that badly repaired wall.

Petrovich tapped him on the arm. "Let's go, then."

Alan straightened, as if he were steeling himself, then turned and led the way out of the cafeteria.

"The rest of you," Petrovich said, "get the remaining equipment in here. We have a lot to do before the afternoon crew arrives."

The afternoon crew. Larissa hadn't been entirely clear on the concept. Apparently people were going to work around the clock until this school was ready for students first thing Monday morning.

Students and counselors and panicked parents.

How would any of them recover from this?

Maybe the Amish had been right after that horrible school shooting in their one-room schoolhouse a few years ago. They'd torn that building down. They built a whole new school.

But it was one building—a small building at that—not a state-of-the-art high school, until last week the community's pride and joy, built with grant money and the hopes this impoverished community had for the future.

"You want to help me lay out the drop cloths?" Robyn asked.

Larissa turned back, and realized that Robyn was talking to her. Everyone else had left the room.

Larissa walked to the far wall. Back here, in the corner farthest from the doors, Iris Winter had crumpled, food spilled all around her. She'd come out to talk to Leif, hoping that she could calm him and somehow stop him from shooting.

She'd stopped him momentarily—she'd surprised him, the papers said, although Larissa wasn't entirely sure of that—and then he'd shot her so many times that her body skidded backwards until it hit the wall.

Larissa stared at the spot. Robyn shoved a heavy canvas drop cloth in her hands.

"Don't think about it," Robyn said softly.

Thinking about it used to be Larissa's job. She used to, as a reporter, reimagine a tragedy so that she could communicate it to readers or viewers or both. When she spoke the report before a camera, she had to have the right tone in her voice—a mixture of professional detachment and regret or, in this case, sorrow, feelings that she often never had.

Here, though, here she had the regret, and the sorrow, and the remnants of fear.

Larissa didn't answer Robyn. Instead, Larissa spread the drop cloth over the clean floor. Her fingers brushed the cool tiles, and she found herself hoping that Iris hadn't felt much more than momentary shock.

Then Larissa rose and got another drop cloth. Robyn was holding masking tape and staring at the doorframe, apparently trying to decide if it needed to be taped off.

"How do you not think about it?" Larissa asked. "It's why we're here."

Robyn swallowed, but didn't look at Larissa. Instead, Robyn tapped a fingernail against the frame. "You think I need to cover the whole door?"

Apparently that was how you didn't think about it. You focused on something small, something unimportant. You pretended it was the most important thing in the world.

Larissa remembered that. She had once lived her entire life like that.

"If you think the spray will get into the kitchen itself, yeah, you better cover the door."

Robyn nodded and grabbed a square plastic package. She ripped it open with a violence that surprised Larissa, and pulled out even more plastic—the clear, see-through kind—and proceeded to unfold it.

Larissa went back to the drop cloths as Oscar and Alan entered, carrying the machine—the sprayer, Petrovich had called it. Darren followed, holding the drip pans stacked to his nose.

Petrovich remained in the hall, small containers of spackle around him, as he spoke on a cell phone.

Larissa was having trouble catching her breath. She recognized the feeling. When she had flown into West Paducah, Kentucky, all those years ago and gone to Heath High with her mike and her camera crew, she had had the same response. Then she'd thought she was having a heart attack. Her producer had called 9-1-1, and an ambulance had whisked her to the ER.

She'd had a normal EKG, but the harried ER doctor had given her a sympathetic smile. *It's a panic attack. We've had a lot of those in the past twenty-four hours.*

She repeated those words to herself now, and reminded herself to breathe. She had expected at least one panic attack here, but she had thought she would be alone. She had pictured herself in a classroom or facing a half-painted wall, sweating and struggling to catch her breath.

She hadn't expected to be in the cafeteria, so close to the others.

Exactly where the main part of the massacre had happened.

"You okay?" Alan took the drop cloth from her hands and folded it nervously over his own arm. "You're gray."

"I'm fine, physically," she said.

"We're all fine, physically," Darren said, that anger still in his voice. "We're *lucky.*"

"Darren, don't start," Oscar said with a sigh.

Darren set the drip pans down. "I'll start if I want to. Miss Celebrity Girl Reporter is here either to get a story or to assuage a guilty conscience or both. I'm trying to repair my school."

"Don't," Alan said. "Don't compare pain."

Petrovich was still on the phone, but he had turned toward the group. He was watching the interaction.

Larissa swallowed hard. Her chest hurt and her breath still came in gasps. She bit her lower lip, knowing that real pain sometimes stopped the attacks.

"We all love this place." Robyn had just pried the top off one of the drums and held the wooden stir stick in her left hand like a weapon.

"Paint isn't going to fix this," Darren said. "Celebrity Girl Reporters writing angst-filled follow-ups are only going to keep this story alive so that our kids will have to deal with it day after day. I think Larissa should leave."

"I'm not writing anything," Larissa managed, but her face flushed all the same. She had three messages on her voice mail from unit producers—two at CNN and one at FOX, wanting her to do an exclusive, from the point of view of a former member of the club. They hadn't said that, but she'd heard the confusion in their voices: Why had you gone back there, was the subtext, instead of staying here where you could ruminate on it all?

"She doesn't know what we've been through," Darren was saying. "She doesn't belong anymore. She should go and leave us alone. She has no idea what it was like here. She—"

"She knows." Petrovich had come into the room. He folded his cell phone shut and slipped it into his pocket. "She probably knows better than all of us."

Everyone looked at her. Her flushed deepened, and the panic attack got worse. How did he know? No one knew, not even the reporters she'd worked with. No one had any idea at all.

"Oh, yeah?" Darren asked. "Because she covered Columbine?"

"I didn't cover Columbine," she whispered. It was West Paducah, and it had nearly destroyed her.

"Because she went through something similar," Petrovich said, "when she was a little girl."

"No," she said, sounding breathless even to her own ears. "I didn't go through anything similar."

It hadn't happened to her. It had happened *around* her, just like this one had.

"Sure you did," Petrovich said. "You were there. I remember staring at your face."

two

the next thing she knew, she was on the tile floor, her head cushioned by a drop cloth, and Robyn's warm hand clutching her clammy one. Alan put another folded drop cloth beneath Larissa's feet, and Oscar paced behind him. Darren leaned against the ruined wall, arms crossed.

When Petrovich saw that her eyes were open, he crouched beside her. "I'm sorry," he said.

Larissa shook her head, felt a slight ache at the back of her skull and raised her other hand toward it. Robyn grabbed a dry paper towel and wiped off her face.

"What happened?" Larissa asked.

"You fainted," Robyn said.

"I'd never seen anyone do that before." Oscar stuck his hands in his pocket.

"My wife fainted all the time when she was pregnant. You're not pregnant, are you?" Alan asked with real concern.

"No." Larissa felt a flush build in her cheeks again. She'd never fainted before, either. She'd come close, though, with the panic attacks and the rapid breathing, but her producers had always forced her into the van so that she could put her head between her knees and breathe.

The dizzy spells, the panic attacks, the angry lashing—so reminiscent of what Darren had been doing just this morning—had ended her on-air reporting career, and had led her to print, which should have been more satisfying, but wasn't.

"I'm sorry," Larissa said, trying to sit up.

Petrovich put one hand on her shoulder, forcing her back. "I'm the one who needs to apologize. I shouldn't have brought up New Lake National."

Larissa blinked at him. New Lake National Bank. Her father's bank. No one had mentioned that in a very, very long time.

"It's all right," she said, and pushed his hand away. "Now let me up, please."

They all studied her with concern, even Darren. Petrovich had obviously told them about the shootings. But he had been wrong. She hadn't been there. She had walked to the bus stop that morning, her hand in her father's, and after the bus took her away, she hadn't seen him again.

Robyn and Petrovich braced Larissa as she got to her feet. She felt weak and exhausted, but she wasn't going to let them know.

"You really don't remember?" Petrovich asked softly.

Larissa's eyes filled with tears, but she blinked them away. "We have work to do. The students are counting on us."

He squeezed her shoulder, and then nodded. "You're right," he said. "Let's get on it."

"You sure you're going to be fine?" Oscar asked.

"Get her some water," Robyn said, "and let her sit awhile. Then she'll be fine."

Alan smiled at Robyn. "You fainted, too, during your pregnancies. I remember that. You took a spectacular dive near the stairs about ten years ago. Who was that—Mike Something, the short basketball player who wanted to play center—wasn't he the one who caught you?"

"And kept me from breaking my nose." Robyn smiled. Then her smile faded and she looked at Oscar. "Let Larissa alone. Fainting is embarrassing enough without getting fussed over, so long as she's all right. You are, aren't you?"

She asked that last question of Larissa.

Larissa nodded, felt that ache in the back of her skull, and recognized it for what it was. No high school basketball player had caught her. She had fallen and hit her head against the tile.

"Good. Get her a chair, Darren," Robyn said.

Darren started for the kitchen.

"No," Larissa said. "I really am fine."

"I'm making you sit for a minute," Robyn said. "You're going to see if the dizziness comes back. We should probably expect things like this all week, when the students return. They'll have trouble."

"I'm not that delicate," Larissa said, although she felt delicate. She had never fainted before and yet, oddly, it didn't frighten her.

Not as much as that intent look on Petrovich's face when he'd told her he remembered staring at her. He knew all about her. And since she'd changed her name and never mentioned the bank shootings publicly—or even privately, except to her therapists—there were only two possible ways he had known.

He stalked her, did research no one else had done, and was trying to frighten her.

Or, more likely, he had been in New Lake when the shootings occurred.

Manatowa wasn't that far from New Lake. She'd thought of that often when she decided to accept the job here. She'd worried about the proximity, then decided that it didn't matter.

She had vowed never to return to New Lake, and so far, she had kept that vow.

Darren brought a chair to her. The wooden seat was shiny. The crime scene cleaners had done something to it, which meant that it had had blood on it.

Larissa's stomach turned. She forced herself to swallow hard and then sit down. She wasn't going to complain. Nor was she going home.

She had come here to clean up her school, and goddammit, she was going to do it.

But she did remember. Her sixteen-year-old sister Nadia had bounced out the front door without eating breakfast, just so she could flag down

Chip Karsters and catch a ride to school. Her brother Ric (short for the name he hated: Ulrich) poured himself a second bowl of Lucky Charms and spilled the cereal all over the counter.

Her mother had shaken her head at him while she got the dishrag from its perch on the faucet and wiped the little marshmallow bits into the palm of her hand, tossing them away in the garbage under the sink. Larissa finished her own bowl of cereal and snuck the banana that her mother had placed beside her plate back into the fruit bowl at the center of the table.

Her father had seen that as he came in from the hall, his briefcase in his hand. Instead of scolding her, he had winked, grabbed the banana himself, and stuffed it in the pocket of his suit coat.

At that moment, her mother had turned. "*Ach*, Conrad," she had said, removing the banana. "Let me pack you a proper lunch."

"I don't have time this morning, *leibschen*," he'd said, and kissed her head. "I've got to walk Larissa to her stop, and then get to work. We have a morning meeting."

"You don't eat right," her mother had said.

"I eat well." He'd patted his rounding stomach and kissed her on the top of her blond head.

Then he turned to Larissa. "You ready, *mein Tochter*?"

And even though she hadn't finished most of her bowl, even though the precious marshmallow stars still floated on top of the sugary milk, she'd grinned at him.

"Of course, Daddy," she'd said as she stood up. "Let's go."

She still didn't know what else Ric had done that morning. She thought about it again as she painted primer along the edge of the cafeteria kitchen's door frame, some white spatter landing on the side of her hand. She'd only put on the latex gloves that Robyn had bought for her first few swipes with the brush. The gloves were one-size fit all, but they didn't fit her. They were hot and uncomfortable, and they reminded her too much of what she was doing.

Larissa had always liked painting. She used to say it brought out her Zen side. She could paint and not think and, at the end of it all, be calmer than she had been when she began.

Which was probably why she had volunteered for this job, instead of several others that had come up at that self-same school board meeting, the one she had missed. Painting gave her a sense of control, even now, when she was still shaking from her faint.

Behind her, Petrovich and another man were putting plywood over the spiderwebbed windows. Darren used a small brush to fuss over the thin bits of drywall between the exterior doors. Oscar had taken the spackle and was repairing the holes in the floor with it, while Alan hovered not too far from Larissa in case she fainted again.

Robyn had gone to the principal's office with one drum of primer. The walls were better there—at least according to Petrovich—but they still needed paint. Leif had shot Vice Principal Walter Haigen as he came to the door of the office, trying to see what the noise was—the noise Leif had caused by shooting dozens of holes into the X-ray machine.

Larissa was feeling better, but still not entirely like herself. She blamed that not on the faint, but on the fact that she was in the cafeteria. But the feeling was another she recognized, from those days when she'd had a series of high-paid therapists in an attempt to save her life's work.

Sometimes the feeling came up when they asked her an oh-so-casual question: *How did Ric get to school that morning?*

She remembered everything else—Nadia bouncing out the front door, yelling her trademark *bye-bye-bye* as the door banged behind her; her father and the wink and the spilled Lucky Charms; even the film of sugar on top of the whole milk Larissa had poured over her cereal—but not Ric, not after he had sat at the table with his second bowl. Not even in the days following, through the parade of police and social workers and benumbed, frightened grandparents, did she remember anything Ric had done.

Ric didn't factor into her consciousness again until he clutched her so hard that she had trouble catching her breath, and said to a social worker in a voice she'd never heard before: *You can't separate us. It's not our fault.*

It's not our fault. That was why their grandparents had insisted on the name-change.

Because it wasn't their fault.

Grandfather had said, *You're not Muellers anymore. We're legally changing your last name to Johanssen. That way you won't get the questions.*

Or the looks, Ric had added.

Grandfather's gaze had skittered away, and no one else said a word. No one even protested, as if changing children's names when they were sixteen, thirteen, and ten was a normal, everyday thing to do.

For the rest of their lives, they pretended to be normal.

Sometimes, it even worked.

three

*t*he group broke for lunch around noon. Robyn came back from the principal's office, spattered with white primer and looking exhausted, as if touching those walls had taken something out of her.

No one had conversed much in the cafeteria, although a lot of work had gotten done. It was amazing how much people could do when they were avoiding a conversation.

Petrovich had sent his friend to pick up pizzas and when the man returned, the crew turned over a single table, took chairs from the kitchen, and set up in the middle of the large room. They had placed the rectangular table in its normal position—short ends facing the doors and the long wall—without thinking, but when Darren noticed, he asked them to turn it.

Petrovich and his friend looked confused, but Darren's question startled everyone else. They stared at the single table—yet another reminder of why they were here—and then Robyn sat down.

Robyn, who apparently was a lot better at pretending nothing had happened than everyone else was.

Larissa hadn't known her friend had such a trait. Robyn had always been her common-sense guide, the only person Larissa had known early in her years in Manatowa who was completely normal.

But, it seemed, even Robyn had her limits.

"We need to get used to this," Oscar said, then headed for the table. But he didn't sit down right away. Instead, he opened the pizza boxes. Steam rose off each pie, and Larissa's mouth watered.

One pepperoni, one all-meat, one with everything, one vegetarian, and for Larissa especially, one taco. Only Robyn and Alan knew how much she loved taco pizza and how rarely she indulged. She tried to smile her thanks to Robyn, but she was busy with napkins and paper plates.

Instead, Larissa caught Alan's eye and mouthed *Thank you*. He gave her a half-smile in return. No one felt like they could smile completely here, and that had to change, too. If things were going to return to something resembling normal—that word again, "normal"—then smiles would have to be allowed, as well as fights and critical comments and loving enjoyment of a favorite food.

Larissa took a real fork and a paper plate, then served herself two pieces of taco pizza. She decided she could eat as much as she wanted today—and that wasn't normal. Normally she regulated her food intake so that she retained her slim figure, a habit from her on-camera days.

Petrovich heaped his paper plate with two slices of all meat, two pepperoni, and one slice with everything. Apparently he had gotten a Pepsi out of the vending machine earlier. He set the can down beside her, as if he were staking his territory.

For a moment, she felt like she was in high school again.

"This is going to be harder than I thought." Alan picked the pepperoni off his slice. "How're we going to be there for the kids when we're having so much trouble ourselves?"

"That's what the shrinks are for." Darren had taken three slices of vegetarian. He sat as far from Larissa as he could.

"We can't leave the kids to the shrinks," Oscar said. He hadn't taken any food at all.

"That's not what I meant." Darren grabbed a fork from the pile. "The shrinks are for us, too. I think we should use them."

"I don't need to talk to anyone." Robyn had as many slices on her plate as Petrovich had on his. No wonder she had maintained all that baby weight. Or maybe she was just overeating today the way Larissa was.

"We all need to talk to someone." Alan sat beside Oscar.

"I don't." Robyn ripped the crust off one of the pieces of pizza on her plate. She ate the crust first, then started to rip the slice like she had ripped the crust. No fork for her.

It was as if she didn't care about niceties, which wasn't like Robyn at all.

"It's better to talk," Larissa said.

"Oh, really?" Robyn actually snapped at her. "How would you know?"

Larissa flushed and flattened the lettuce on top of the largest slice.

"Leave her alone," Alan said.

"No, seriously." Robyn dropped the torn-up slice onto her plate, and turned her chair toward Larissa. "I want to know. How does talking help? I mean, how many shrinks have you gone through over the years?"

Larissa's flush grew so intense that her whole face burned. She had trusted Robyn with that information. Larissa had never expected Robyn to break that confidence.

Robyn leaned toward her. "I thought it was just because you couldn't handle such a high-profile job, but it wasn't, was it? It was because of this thing Pete's been talking about. Going to shrinks really helped you, didn't it?"

Robyn usually didn't use sarcasm either, but she seemed to wield it well this afternoon. Larissa couldn't look at her.

"Robyn, knock it off," Alan said.

"I mean, she quit great jobs, can't have a relationship, refuses to have children—"

"Robyn!" Several voices chorused this time, and finally Robyn shut up.

The one bite of taco pizza that Larissa had managed stuck in her throat. She swallowed once and couldn't dislodge it. She swallowed again, and felt air go down. She hoped she wouldn't get the hiccups like she sometimes did when she was upset.

"That was unfair," Alan said. "Larissa's had a tough morning—"

"We've all had a tough morning," Robyn said. "*Some of us* had a tough week."

Larissa sighed. She pushed her plate away. She scooted her chair back and then stood. She couldn't stay here. She couldn't be the focus of everyone's anger just because she had not been at the school the day Leif Soderstrom decided to destroy everything.

"I'm sorry," she said. "I didn't mean to start something. I—"

"Sit down," Alan said, waving a hand. "You didn't start a damn thing. I mentioned how hard this was going to be, and you just made an observation. One, I think, you had every right to make. In fact, you probably have more right than the rest of us, not just because of this bank thing Pete mentioned, but the fact you've been to a lot of crisis spots. You know what to do. You—"

"No, I don't know what to do," Larissa said. "I've never known. As a reporter, I went to crisis locations, interviewed people like you and got the hell out. I had no idea how they went back to class or managed to go home after their child was murdered or rebuilt in the same place that a hurricane flattened. I have no idea how people pick up their lives. Robyn's right about that. I'm no expert."

She pushed her chair in. During Larissa's speech, Robyn had finished the slice she had torn up and had started shredding another.

Robyn wouldn't look at Larissa, either.

Larissa squeezed the top of the chair, then let go.

Petrovich grabbed her wrist. His fingers were strong. "No one's doing well. And no one has the right to lord their experiences over anyone else."

He wasn't speaking to her. He was talking to them.

Robyn kept her head bowed. Petrovich's friend was staring at the group as if they'd lost their minds. Darren still held his plate filled with slices. Oscar's were already gone. Alan stopped eating mid-bite and set his slice down.

Petrovich kept his hand on Larissa's wrist.

"Larissa went through hell as a kid," he said. "So did I. That's why I'm here. Because people helped us rebuild thirty years ago, and because this is my community, too."

"My daughter can't sleep," said Petrovich's friend.

Larissa looked at him in surprise.

He was balding and thick with muscle. He had a tattoo along his neck that disappeared into his shirt, and several others running down his arm.

Larissa wouldn't have expected him to have a daughter.

"She wasn't even in school," he said. "She had that flu. She's been crying for days, and she won't sleep, and I'm afraid it'll be pneumonia."

"Who's your daughter?" Alan asked.

"Marcy Hoagland," the man said. "I'm Tom."

He nodded at Larissa, since she was clearly the one who didn't know him.

Marcy Hoagland was a wisp of a girl. She looked like she belonged with the elves in *The Lord of the Rings*—long blond hair and narrow eyebrows and delicate features. She was always tired because she juggled school with figure skating—getting up every morning to practice two hours before classes began, and leaving early to practice three more hours before she went home and did her schoolwork.

Larissa had spoken to Marcy's mother during parent/teacher conferences, but Marcy's mother—a wisp thickened by middle age—had believed that the skating was the most important thing in Marcy's life.

She can always go back to school, Mrs. Hoagland had said. *She can only skate like this for a decade or so.*

Larissa would never have thought that the delicate and precise Mrs. Hoagland had a husband who looked like he could bench press the table with everyone on it.

"Have you taken her to anyone?" Darren asked Hoagland.

"Again with the shrinks," Robyn muttered, but Hoagland ignored her.

"Yeah." Hoagland's voice was quiet. "She's seeing my wife's—well, you know."

He seemed embarrassed by the admission. In this, the Midwest hadn't changed from Larissa's childhood. Needing help was a weakness. Going to doctors or therapists or anyone in a helping profession wasn't admired. It was frowned upon. It was an admission that the family was broken.

The family was supposed to take care of all problems. The family, which of course had two parents at home, children, and all the extended relatives.

The very thing that Larissa lacked.

"The therapist," Hoagland said, "he says she'll be like that for a while. Her emotions'll be everywhere. It's grief and shock and just fucking horrible."

His voice broke. He bowed his head, then shoved the heel of one hand into his right eye.

"Sorry," he said. "Sorry."

Larissa couldn't look at him. She tried to slip her wrist out of Petrovich's grasp, but he momentarily tightened his grip.

"No one's going to be normal for a while," Petrovich said. He still hadn't looked at her. "It's wrong to expect it."

He sounded so sure of himself. But if they could be sure of anything, it was that the world—their world—had changed.

"Then why are we even painting this place?" Robyn asked.

"Because," Oscar said, and then didn't finish. Instead, he grabbed more pizza, and dropped it on his plate as if he were disgusted with himself.

"We're painting," Alan said, "because everything is different now. The walls may as well be, too."

"We know that everything is different." Robyn pushed her plate away.

As she watched that single gesture, Larissa realized that she had never seen Robyn angry before. Frustrated, yes, but never truly angry. Robyn had always been the voice of reason, even when her children broke something or screamed at her. Robyn remained calm.

Robyn was always calm.

Except now.

"If we want to acknowledge that everything is different," Robyn snapped, "why the hell are we covering it up?"

It took Larissa a moment to realize that Robyn meant the damage that Leif had caused. Apparently, she saw the painting as a cover-up, not as a needed repair.

"We're not covering anything up," Petrovich said gently. "When you break your arm, you set the break and then deal with the consequences."

"This isn't a broken arm," Robyn said.

"No," Darren said quietly, "it's much worse."

His words had the effect of a shout for silence. No one spoke for the longest time. No one even moved.

Then Petrovich let go of Larissa's wrist. He brought his hand down.

He had kept her in the cafeteria long enough for her to realize that everyone was coming apart, just in different ways. She didn't need to leave. She could stay, if she could put up with the sharp words and the occasional blame.

She would have to anyway, particularly if she wanted to survive the next week. Theoretically, adults had more control than students. Theoretically, this lunch was mild considering all the things that faced her.

She had prided herself on being tough. Even when it became clear that she needed to change professions or go slowly crazy, she had gone about it stoically, telling herself it wasn't a loss but an opportunity. And she had believed that, clung to it in fact, all through graduate school when she was not only the oldest person in her classes but also the most famous—even more famous than the professors.

She had been just as tough when she learned the job she had applied for, the one in Minneapolis, no longer existed, but the wife of one of the men who had interviewed her had told someone in Manatowa. The job itself was a dream teaching position—a school that knew how to use grants and government funds to improve, not just run to catch up—but it was in small-town Minnesota, a place she had once vowed never to return to.

She had returned, and she had survived, even thrived.

She would survive this, too.

Larissa pulled her chair out and sat, sliding her plate with the cold pieces of pizza toward her. Then she picked up her fork.

No one's going to be normal for a while, Petrovich had said. What a refreshing change from the pretending her grandparents had done—the hiding and the lying and the looking the other way, all in the name of *normal*.

No one's going to be normal for a while.

If ever.

But they would be able to continue, and that was what was important. Moving forward.

She wanted to say that, but she didn't dare. She hadn't gone through this shooting. She was living the aftermath, not the event itself.

And that mattered to everyone in the room, whether they admitted it or not.

Oscar took another piece of pizza. Somehow his seconds had disappeared. Then Darren took another piece even though he still had some on his plate.

Robyn didn't look at any of them.

Alan grabbed his plate and tossed it into a nearby garbage can. Then he grabbed a drip pan and picked up a paintbrush from the line that Robyn had made on the floor earlier that morning.

Petrovich got up, followed by Oscar, and Hoagland, who walked back to the shattered glass. Only Darren, Robyn, and Larissa remained at the table.

"I owe you an apology," Darren said to Larissa.

She shook her head. "You don't."

"I do. I'm not angry at you. Three of the kids who died, they were on my team."

It took her a moment to realize he meant his debate team. They had taken the state title last year, although to most of the school that had been a joke. The students would rather have had a state athletic title than the multiple titles it had gotten in forensics, debate, and competitive drama.

Darren had been responsible for two of the three programs. He'd given nights and weekends year-round.

"I know," Larissa said. "They were in my classes. Leif, too."

"Can we not say his name?" Robyn glared at Larissa. "Please?"

But the please didn't sound like a request. It was an order.

"Isn't it bad enough that he destroyed everything? Do we have to acknowledge him, too?" She was shaking.

Everyone in the cafeteria turned toward her.

"Yes," Oscar said. "You have to get used to it, Robyn. The kids'll want to talk about him."

"Not in my classroom," she said.

"In all our classrooms," Alan said.

"You don't have real classes," Robyn snapped.

Alan stared at Robyn for a long moment. He was holding a dripping paintbrush over the nearest drop cloth. His expression was hard—the expression he used for students fighting in the halls.

"Go home, Robyn," he said.

Robyn turned toward him, her mouth open in shock. No one talked to her like that. No one had to, because Robyn was always the calm one.

She closed her mouth, then looked at everyone, meeting all their gazes as if she were taking a poll.

"I volunteered," she said.

She sounded bewildered, like a kid who had been hit from behind.

"We all did." Alan set the dripping paintbrush in the drip pan, then wiped his hands on his pants.

"You didn't tell Larissa to go home, and she fainted," Robyn said.

Larissa bit her lower lip. They'd given her the opportunity to leave, but they hadn't asked her to. She'd almost gone on her own to avoid being disruptive, but Petrovich had held her in place.

"Larissa doesn't need to go home," Alan said.

"Neither do I," Robyn said.

"Yes," Alan said. "You do."

"Because I yelled?" Robyn asked. "Darren's been yelling all morning."

Alan's hands were shaking. He hadn't moved away from that drop cloth.

"Yelling's fine," he said. "We're all angry. We have to deal with it somehow."

"Then what's your problem?" Robyn asked.

Alan sighed and looked at the others. No one stepped up. They all seemed to be waiting—as Larissa was—to hear what he had to say next.

"You can't deny what happened here," he said.

"I'm not," Robyn said. "I'm working here, aren't I?"

"But you said your kids can't talk about it," Oscar said, then looked at Alan for approval.

Alan nodded.

"The kids have to talk," Oscar said. "You can't shut them up."

"They will not talk about anything but their studies in my classroom," Robyn said with a fierceness that was frightening.

"Everyone will talk about it," Alan said. "You can't stop them."

Robyn's lower lip was trembling now. She shot a frightened glance at Larissa, and Larissa suddenly understood. Robyn had third period lunch, too.

Alan was about to say something else, but Larissa raised a hand to silence him. She made sure that hand wasn't in Robyn's view.

Larissa leaned toward her friend.

"Where were you?" Larissa asked gently.

"What do you mean?" Oscar asked, but Robyn didn't have to. Robyn knew that Larissa meant during the shooting.

Larissa knew this because Robyn's eyes had filled with tears.

"Were you in the cafeteria?" Larissa asked in the same soft voice.

Robyn shook her head.

"On your way, then?" Larissa asked.

Robyn shook her head again.

"You're usually here when I am," Larissa said. She had taken on her reporter's role—the observer, the calm one who asked questions, not for therapeutic reasons, but to gain information.

Information, she used to say, was the key to survival.

By the time her students asked her what that meant, Larissa no longer knew.

But it was a valuable skill to have, this ability to ask pointed questions, to focus a discussion. Suddenly everyone was watching Robyn, not thinking about their own pain.

"Were you here?" Larissa asked again.

Robyn started to shake her head and then stopped. "I don't know," she said. "I honestly don't know. I just…ended up…outside."

Traumatic memory loss. Larissa had run into it a lot over the years. People often forgot where they were, so they didn't have to remember what they saw.

"I was in class," Darren said as if to encourage Robyn's memory.

It was no longer about Robyn. This was the conversation they'd all wanted to have.

"I was in the men's room," Alan said, then raised his eyebrows as if playing for a laugh. But no one laughed.

"I have a staple gun," Oscar said. "I'm not supposed to because the kids could misuse it. But I loaded it and held it near the door until they gave us the all clear. I suppose someone'll take it away now."

I was in a hotel room, Larissa thought. *Or maybe in a bar, drinking with my sister's friends on my sister's tab.*

Petrovich was watching her, as if he could read her thoughts. He didn't say where he was, and neither did Hoagland.

The three of them didn't have to. They weren't in the school, and no matter how hard they argued that they were all affected, they weren't all affected in the same way.

Three of them had not had to flee for their lives. Three of them hadn't listened as a teenage boy with too many guns killed students.

Three of them had been in no danger at all.

"I'm not sure I want to be here anymore," Robyn said in a watery voice.

"You don't have to be," Petrovich said, but for once he missed the point. Robyn wasn't talking about that afternoon's work.

She was talking about never wanting to come back at all.

"I know." Alan walked over to her and put his arm around her. "Let me call your husband."

Robyn shook her head. "I can drive home."

"Let me at least walk you to your car," he said.

"Okay." She didn't look at anyone else. She let him guide her out the main doors, past the plywood repairs and into the corridor where, theoretically, her coat was stashed.

"She doesn't have to come back," Darren said to Larissa. "They told us we can take a leave if we need to."

Larissa nodded. She'd gotten that phone call. She wasn't going to take a leave.

"Someone might want to remind her of that," Larissa said. "I don't think she'd like hearing it from me."

"I'll talk to her husband," Oscar said. "I bowl with him."

Darren's gaze met Larissa's and, for the first time that day, he smiled just a little. She recognized the smile. It was his sarcastic *what a surprise* smile, one of the few things about him that she really and truly liked.

She smiled, too, but looked down to hide it.

"We have another crew coming in about three hours," Petrovich said. "I'd like to have the primer done by then. Think we can finish?"

"Not the trim," Oscar said.

"I like trim," Larissa said. "I'll do it."

"We can finish." Darren got up from the table. He collected the remaining paper plates, but put them near the pizza. "I'm going to leave this for snacks."

"Good idea," Petrovich said. He had returned to the windows, making sure none of the rest had hidden cracks.

Larissa suspected the school would find signs of trauma for weeks to come.

She went to the row of brushes that Robyn had laid out, pausing over them. Poor Robyn. She was probably quite confused right now.

Larissa wasn't—at least, not about this. She knew how personally anguished she was, how difficult the next few weeks would be, and how—eventually—the emotions from this would all recede and become just a part of her life.

But she had surprised herself with that faint, and the fluttery feeling she still had when she looked at Petrovich. That intensity in his eyes when he said that he remembered staring at her—why couldn't she remember him?

Rather than focus on the part of her childhood she couldn't accurately remember, she crouched and picked up one of the tapered brushes. She had finished the trim outside the kitchen before lunch. There was only the trim along the floor and the ceiling.

Darren had taken care of the fussy job between the exterior doors.

One of those doors opened, letting in a blast of cold air. Larissa turned in time to see Hoagland letting Alan back in. He was rubbing his arms. He had gone outside without his coat.

"How is she?" Hoagland asked.

"Not good," Alan said. "I'm beginning to wonder if I shouldn't call the teachers union so that we can all have a meeting tomorrow."

"What kind of meeting?" Oscar asked. He was fiddling with the sprayer. He'd used it on part of the wall just before lunch.

"We have to find out who is stable enough to handle the kids, and we need to know if there're going to be enough subs willing to come here." Alan stopped rubbing his arms and blew on his hands to warm them.

He had been one of the union reps at Manatowa High since Larissa had joined the staff. He was one of the few who would do the job. Most people wanted the union benefits, but not all the hassle of dealing with both the union and the school board.

"Maybe we should just let Monday happen," Darren said.

Alan frowned at him.

"We can't control it," Oscar said. "It's going to be messy no matter what. A lot of people who say they can deal won't be able to."

"And a lot who think they can't deal will be able to." The flush on Darren's cheeks betrayed him. Clearly he had signed on today so that he could test himself before the students got here.

Larissa wasn't that much of a planner. She had simply been acting out of her own guilt.

"The days after are harder, aren't they?" Alan looked at Larissa. He expected her to answer him. He expected her to know.

But Petrovich saved her. "The day the event—whatever it is—happens, you're just reacting. In the aftermath, you get to chose how to live with the new reality."

"You know," Alan said, "you do sound like you've had a lot of therapy."

"It all starts with twelve steps." Petrovich gave him a rueful smile and left the windows. "Anyone want to help me check the corridor?"

"I will," Oscar said. "Then if there isn't anything, we can finish the principal's office."

But Alan hadn't stopped looking at Larissa. He extended his hands in a *what are we going to do?* gesture.

"I'm worried because I can't control this," he said.

"I know," she said softly. "Believe me. I know."

four

he second group of volunteers arrived promptly at four. Larissa's group had just finished the primer coat, and Petrovich had been worrying aloud if they should start on the first paint coat when his replacement—a woman Larissa had hired to paint the exterior of her own house—walked in. She reassured him that his group could leave, and seemed amazed at all the work they had gotten done.

The cafeteria no longer looked as imposing as it had. Drop cloths covered the floor. Brushes rested on drip pans and stir sticks sat on plastic near the paint drums. The pizza boxes, with just a few slices remaining, still littered the table, as did Pepsi cans, empty water bottles, and the early morning Starbucks cups. Even the fluorescent lights, which they'd had to turn as the afternoon progressed, changed the ambience.

Usually Larissa found fluorescents cold, but they seemed to warm the cafeteria, making it seem safer than it had been just the week before.

The new volunteers walked in, still bundled in their coats, and looked around like people who had been away for decades.

Larissa recognized almost everyone: both track coaches (the girls' and the boys'), two science instructors (one biology and one physics), and both special ed teachers. The only surviving assistant principal, Ken

Durbin, followed, his skin a sallow gray. He was carrying his coat over his arm, and he looked absolutely terrified.

Larissa's group did little more than exchange pleasantries. Everyone remembered how it felt to walk in here the first time, and no one wanted to get in the way of the new group's reaction.

Petrovich talked to his replacement as he described the work left to do. Then he thanked his own group and told them to leave.

Larissa was surprised to find that she didn't want to. She was bone-tired—her arm muscles ached from the unfamiliar use, her shoes pinched, and the back of her head still throbbed—but she felt like she could work forever. The Zen of painting had happened after lunch, and that calm silence, the repetitive movements, and the sharp scent of the primer had soothed her.

Still, she rinsed off her brush in the industrial kitchen's stainless steel utility sink, and then washed her hands, scrubbing hard to remove the flecks of paint that had somehow gotten through the gloves. The paper towels above the sink scratched her skin, but she didn't care.

She returned the brush to its spot in Robyn's lineup just as the newcomers were choosing their own brushes. Then she waved her goodbyes and headed to the corridor to get her coat.

The corridor itself stopped her. It looked bigger and brighter than it ever had. It smelled of fresh paint, and the drop cloths covered the floor here as well. Apparently Oscar and Petrovich had worked hard to finish this part of the wall too—not the part in the ring, but the extension from the principal's office, that wide part of the corridor that Leif had run through with his assault weapons slung over his back.

He would have been too young to think of himself as Rambo. One of her faults as a teacher was she didn't know modern references. Had he thought of himself as some comic-book hero, avenging a wrong? Or a comic-book villain, also avenging a wrong?

Had he hoped that all this would end with the police shooting him? Had he planned to die on that cafeteria floor like everyone else?

In the end, he'd shot himself, alone in another corridor, with the police outside and terrified classmates only a few yards away, taking all the answers to all those questions with him.

Now, of course, the media was prying into his past, trying to figure out what "set him off." His parents seemed bewildered and lost—how did someone feel when they learned they had raised a monster?

Then she flashed on her grandparents' faces—not her grandparents Johanssen, but her grandparents Mueller. They too had come after the shootings, and they had sat on the Johanssen couch, looking greatly diminished.

Larissa's grandmother Mueller—known as Grossmutter, while her grandmother Johanssen was called Grandmother—had caved in on herself, her eyes black and lost in the lined wreck that was suddenly her face. Grossvater had kept his arm around her, pulling her close. From that moment on, his face locked into an expression of nothingness—no laughter, no tears, no anger. It was as if he had purged himself of emotion, and Larissa hadn't remembered he had ever had any until she had seen some of the photographs her grandmother Johanssen had hidden in the attic.

Grossmutter and Grossvater—one caved in and one expressionless—that was how people looked when they had created a monster.

We are not certain we would be gut for die children, Grossmutter said that day. *We do not know what went wrong.*

Larissa had taken her grandmother's words as rejection for years, until a therapist had reminded her that the killings had taken place in the late 1970s.

No one had therapy then, the therapist said. *At least, not middle-class people in the Midwest.*

That therapist had been a New Yorker. She had said Midwest as if it were as remote as Siberia. Maybe to her it had been.

But she had been right. No one had helped her grandparents Mueller with the destruction of their family. They shrank inside themselves until they died, one after the other, in their tiny, lonely house on the outskirts of New Lake.

Larissa hadn't even mourned them. She had just gone on.

"Looks good, doesn't it?"

Larissa started, then turned. While she had been lost in her memories, Petrovich had come up beside her. He had finished his conversation with the new team and had already put on his own coat.

"Fresh," she said, hoping her voice sounded calm. "I don't remember this corridor ever looking so fresh."

He turned away from the paint. "You heading out?"

She nodded. "I just need my coat."

He walked her to the front. Her coat was still crumpled beside the door. The principal's office door was open, which looked odd. That door was never open, not even during school hours.

Lights were on inside, and drop cloths covered the carpet, the furniture, and the computers.

"May I ask you a personal question?" he said.

Larissa crouched as she reached for her coat. She mentally braced herself.

Everyone asked why she quit her high-profile job to teach high school in rural Minnesota. She had a pat answer for it, but she wasn't sure she wanted to use that answer with Petrovich. He had been honest with her all day.

She owed him the same.

She grabbed her coat, folded it over her left arm, and stood. "Ask away."

A frown created a deep line between his eyes. "You really don't remember me?"

She used to get this a lot. People she'd interviewed years before would ask her that question, or later, when she was a regular face on CNN, people who had asked for her autograph more than once expected her to remember as well.

"I'm sorry," she said, falling back on the old answer. "I don't."

His frown deepened for a moment, then he took a deep breath, and slid her coat out of her arms. He held it open for her, a courtesy a man had not done for her in years.

She slipped into it. It was too warm for the corridor.

"It's amazing how the memory works," he said as she turned toward him. "You saved my life and you don't even remember."

Her breath caught. An instant headache built in the back of her skull, radiating off the place where she had hit her head. But the blow hadn't caused the headache. The headache came from talking about New Lake.

She used to get headaches all the time when she went to her therapy sessions.

"I did what?" she asked, unable to stop the question.

"You saved my life." His cheeks were flushed. He was clearly embarrassed now. "You grabbed me and pulled me under that desk. Then you crawled in front of me. You said he'd never shoot you, and you were right."

"What?" she asked again.

"He was swinging the gun around and he bent under the desk and saw you…." Petrovich let the words trail off. "You really don't remember any of this."

"In the bank?" she asked.

"Yeah," he said. "I was there with my father."

And his eyes filled with tears. He swiped at them.

"Sorry," he said. "I only just started talking about that part."

"What part?" She was too hot and the headache had grown strong and she felt so confused that she was almost dizzy.

"Watching my father die," he said. "He was Peter Petrovich, too. I thought maybe you knew."

"My grandparents didn't let us see the coverage." Her voice sounded wooden as it covered very clear memories: Nadia stealing the neighbor's newspaper, Ric pounding his fist on the brand-new console TV with its silent screen, the transistor her grandfather kept pressed to his ear so no one else could hear it.

"Wow," Petrovich said quietly. "And here I am, blundering into all of this. I'm bothering you again, aren't I?"

She gave him a weak smile. "It's been a tough day."

He nodded. "I made it worse."

"No," she said. "It's bound to bring up old stuff."

His eyes were red, just like his cheeks.

She put a hand on his arm. "Memories aren't always reliable," she said gently. "You've got me confused with someone else."

"No, I don't," he said. "I was a year behind you in school. I remember when you came back, with a new name and a new haircut. You didn't talk to anyone."

She was so hot. "I know."

"I wanted to thank you, but I couldn't get close."

"You don't have to," she said. "I wasn't there."

"What?" It was his turn to sound surprised.

"I wasn't at the bank," she said. "I was on the bus to school."

"No, you weren't," he said.

"I remember it vividly," she said.

"You couldn't have been on the way to school," he said. "There were no buses that day. It was a Saturday. Saturday, January twenty-fifth, at one in the afternoon."

"Small-town banks aren't open on Saturdays," she said automatically, and as the words left her mouth, she knew they were wrong.

Small-town banks had been open on Saturdays when she was a child. Some were open until noon, some until two. Most banks were locally or regionally owned, and the hours were set by the managers, not by some corporate flack who didn't understand the community in which the bank resided.

It was in the 1980s when banks reduced their levels of service, relying on ATMs to do the work that weekend tellers used to do.

Petrovich was watching her, that frown line between his eyes so deep that it looked like his concern for her had permanently furrowed it. From the cafeteria, the sound of country music floated down the hall. Someone had brought a radio.

"It couldn't have been a Saturday," she said, very quietly. "I went to school."

He sighed deeply. He clearly knew he was in a dangerous area. "I have clippings."

Clippings that she was forbidden to see. Clippings that she had never researched on her own, not even when she had the chance that day in the University of Minnesota–Minneapolis library when she had researched Watergate from primary materials for an undergraduate paper.

She put a hand to her forehead. She had thought of looking that day, and she hadn't.

She remembered thinking of it, though. It hadn't been a random thought. It had been an important decision. She had even talked about it with a shrink later on.

What made you stop? The shrink asked.

I had a paper to finish. I was already behind.

Surely it wouldn't have taken long.

Larissa had shaken her head and hadn't spoken her answer. But she had remembered the light feeling, the giddiness and the fear just the idea of looking at those papers had brought.

"Why would you keep clippings?" she asked.

Petrovich reached toward her, and then stopped, letting his hand fall. "My mother did. There was a lawsuit, you know."

"Against whom?" Larissa asked. "We were destitute."

"The bank. For inadequate security."

"It wasn't the security that was the problem," Larissa said, and wondered where that came from. It wasn't her observation. She had to have heard it before.

"Still," Petrovich said. "The bank settled with all the families."

Except hers, of course. They couldn't settle anything with hers.

The headache had grown worse. "I need to go home."

"Can you drive?" he asked. "You're looking pale."

"I'll be fine." Home wasn't that far. She could make it.

"Is there someone there for you? Because I really shook you up. I didn't mean to—"

"You're going to have to stop apologizing around me." She made herself smile. "You didn't do anything wrong."

"But I didn't know—"

"That's right," she said. "You didn't know."

She reached into her pockets and removed her gloves. They were wool-lined leather and fit perfectly, left over from her reporting days. Then she took her car keys out of her purse.

Petrovich watched her. Apparently he had little to say when he wasn't apologizing.

She pushed open the glass doors leading into the airlock and the blast of cooler air hit her like water. Her heart was pounding hard and she still felt dizzy.

She turned.

Petrovich was watching her, the concern still lining his face.

She made herself nod at him, so she wouldn't seem so curt.

He nodded back.

Then she shoved open the outside door, stepping into the February cold. She wouldn't see those clippings. What was in the past belonged in the past. Her grandmother had always said that.

But what her grandmother hadn't told her was that the past sometimes reared up and clamped a vise on the brain. It shocked you and made you faint and forced you to leave a job that you loved. It gave you panic attacks and heart palpitations and tears when you least expected them.

It hurt, just like the present did.

And sometimes, it hurt even more.

five

arissa's house was in a cul-de-sac in a quiet neighborhood about a mile from the school. In the spring and fall, she walked to work. But she was glad she hadn't walked today, even though her headache made her a driving hazard. She wasn't sure she could have made it the entire mile—ten minutes versus five, from the moment she got into the car to the moment she pulled onto her street.

No reporters had gathered here. She had found their footprints in the snow when she had gotten home; the unmistakable tracks of high-end boots that camera operators always wore, pressed deeply into the snow because of the camera's weight; the cord trails, looking like a snake had come through, and the marks of high heels crossing her yard.

She didn't know then, and wasn't sure now, if they had come to her house because they had known that Larissa Johanssen, a former member of their tribe, lived there, or if they had come because they went to every teacher's address. When her next-door neighbor had told them she was out of town, they had not come back.

However, she kept expecting them to. Someone would send a producer or a flunky to her home to convince her to comment on air. And once she did that, her hard-won privacy would be gone forever.

She pulled into her driveway, feeling her shoulders relax. She loved this house. It was the first house she'd ever owned. She had owned an apartment in New York. That place had cost eight times the price of this house, and only had 865 square feet.

This house had more than 3,000, something she would have derided as a McMansion in her New York days, even though it wasn't anywhere near the McMansions built in St. Paul or Minneapolis or even a growing city like Rochester.

Hers was the modern equivalent of a track house—designed on the same lines as her neighbors, the differences only minor. The previous owner had painted her house a robin's-egg blue that she'd hated until the first winter when she had seen how cheerful it looked against the snow.

The entry and living room had a cathedral ceiling, and two fireplaces—real ones—to combat the cold of a Minnesota winter. The house had central air, an eat-in kitchen, and a spectacular bedroom. There was even a home theater in the basement, something she had thought she would change but, like the robin's-egg blue, she had learned to love.

She had vowed not to make any changes at all that first year—she wasn't sure how long she'd stay in Manatowa—and when she realized she could spend the rest of her life here, she had already become someone she didn't completely recognize: A woman who lived alone, who had a den, a study, a home theater, and three bedrooms in her oversized house.

The only change she had made was to turn one of the bedrooms into an exercise room. Even that felt decadent, but she hadn't regretted it when the temperature dipped below freezing.

This place had become her haven, her fortress, her private palace. And she was more relieved than she wanted to admit that it wasn't under siege.

She had pressed the garage-door opener on her visor as she turned onto the block, and the door was already up. She drove in, then pressed the button again, and listened as the door rattled closed.

All these trappings of suburban life—a large car, an oversized house, and a garage-door opener—would have made her sneer in her reporter days. Now she appreciated every bit of it. She understood why the majority of Americans lived like she did now, rather than like she had before.

She turned off the ignition, then rested her chin on the steering wheel. Her head wasn't as bad, but she still felt vaguely ill.

Then she took a deep breath, and reminded herself that she had planned for a difficult day. She had fresh lasagna from a nearby restaurant in her refrigerator, a chilled bottle of her favorite wine, and several romantic comedies on DVD, so that she could forget the day and think only pleasant thoughts.

But she had expected to be clearing the recent shootings out of her brain, not the shootings from thirty years before.

Clippings, Petrovich had said. He had clippings. From a Saturday. And she had been there. Saving his life.

She rubbed her forehead with her gloved right hand. The cool leather startled her and made her lean back. She let herself out of the car.

The garage smelled faintly of gasoline and exhaust. Even though there were shelves lining the room, she had nothing on them. The workbench near the stairs went unused. She wasn't handy, not the way the previous owner had been, and the double-car garage looked too big with the single car parked close to the door, and nothing else inside except a lawn mower, a snow blower her lawn guy had talked her into buying, and an expensive bicycle she'd only ridden twice.

She climbed the two stairs to the house, unlocked the door, and stepped into the kitchen. Her kitchen. A place of miracles that her mother, dead these thirty years, could never have imagined.

Copper pots gleamed above an island. The floor had an Incan pattern that mimicked the pots and the dark wood and picked up highlights from the granite countertops. Her entire nuclear family could have fit around the island, but she also had a kitchen table that, when she added the leaves, seated ten.

All for her.

The kitchen wouldn't have felt as close as it had that morning, when her sister blew through it to catch a ride with Chip or her brother spilled the cereal or her father had winked at her....

Then she pushed the door to the garage closed and leaned on it.

What was that memory? It was a before-school memory, not a Saturday-morning memory. On Saturdays, her family had gone its separate ways. The big family breakfast happened on Sunday mornings, before church, or on special occasions like a birthday.

On Saturdays, she got up and poured her own cereal. She was allowed to eat it in front of the television in the living room as long as she used a TV tray and didn't spill on the carpet. Her sister—already a teenager—slept in, and her brother disappeared with his friends shortly after Larissa got up.

If the shootings had happened on a Saturday, why didn't she have Saturday-morning memories? Why didn't she remember her dad taking her to the bank, holding her hand like he always did, and leaving her with one of the employees near the front? Why did she have a memory from a school day, when her parents died on a Saturday, a Saturday she didn't remember?

Finger by finger, she pulled off her gloves. Then she put them in the pocket of her coat and pulled the coat off. The headache bit into her skull with new ferocity.

If she stepped out of herself, out of the shocked woman who had fainted when someone confronted her about her past, out of the stubborn patient who never really allowed any therapist to get all the way into the event, she could figure out why she had been wrong about that day.

She had told Petrovich—accused him, actually—of the same problem. Traumatic memory loss.

How many people had she interviewed over the years who could remember the days before the accident just fine but the day of the accident was gone? How many survivors of horrible crimes remembered the events just after the crime but nothing before it?

How many witnesses had she seen eviscerated at trial because they couldn't remember the most minute details of a day that had gone horribly wrong?

She tucked her coat over her arm, kicked off her shoes, and opened the closet on the far wall. She hung her coat up and started to close the door, then stopped. Her hands fluttered to the top shelf. A hatbox, half-hidden by scarves and winter caps, nestled against the back wall.

She'd kept that hatbox through seven moves and a dozen purgings of her possessions. She'd kept it and never opened it, not even on the day her grandmother placed it in her hands.

Because she had known what it was.

Now she grabbed the footstool she kept in the back of the closet and stepped on it, reaching toward that top shelf. Her hands brushed the box, and she was surprised at how thin and papery it felt.

In her memory, it felt indestructible, something so precious that it could survive anything.

Your mother was so proud of this, her grandmother had said.

A hat? Larissa asked, even though she remembered. She remembered when her father had brought it home. She'd been maybe seven, and she was supposed to be asleep. But her parents' laughter woke her up.

Her father had been promoted and he had bought her mother the hat she'd been coveting from the local department store.

The box still displayed the store's logo: *Le Grande Shoppe*, the letters so flowery that they were almost unreadable. They'd faded against the blue and white background, looking more gray than black.

Still, she could see them as if they were new, just like she could see that hat on her mother's head, looking ridiculous with her fluffy cotton bathrobe.

Larissa clutched the box. If she opened it and the hat was ruined, she would be heartbroken. In the past, that thought—and the tears that suddenly lined her eyes—would be enough to make her put the box back.

But now, when she had painted a school cafeteria where some of her students had died at the hands of another student, on a day when she had learned that she had been in that bank (and she still wasn't sure she believed it), a day when she learned that clippings existed that contradicted everything she remembered, she needed to see if this memory was accurate as well.

The hat had been a cloche with a feather—a Robin Hood hat, she'd called it when she'd been formally introduced to it the next day. Only the hat wasn't green. It was purple with a dyed-to-match feather that brushed against the side and rose just slightly above the top.

It had accented her mother's dark hair and made her eyes sparkle. The purple had brought up the color of her cheeks and made her look young.

Larissa blinked hard, waiting until the threat of tears passed, and then grabbed the edge of the box lid. She folded her fingernails underneath so they wouldn't scratch that thin paper, and she made sure she didn't pull too hard, so that she wouldn't accidentally rip it.

The lid came off as if the box had been opened just the day before. The sharp scent of mothballs made her sneeze.

The hat looked fine—a bit smaller than she remembered, but just as new and pretty as it had been that night, more than thirty years before.

With a shaking hand, she touched the edge of the hat, surprised to find felt. It hadn't been very expensive at all. It had just been made to look expensive.

But her mother hadn't been able to afford it on her own, and her father had bought it as a special gift, something precious, something so dear that it had caused a celebration of laughter that long-ago night.

Larissa pulled the hat from the box. Then she stopped off the stool, carefully set the box on that stool, and turned the hat over in her hands. The label inside had no signs of wear, no sweat marks like the labels inside Larissa's baseball caps. The feather hadn't clumped and even though the odor of mothballs clung to it, it looked as modern as a hat she'd seen in Macy's in Minneapolis on her way to Hawaii.

Very 1970s, very now.

She put it on her own head and realized her headache was gone. The sharp smell of mothballs had cleared her sinuses the way that smelling salts did.

Slowly she pushed the closet door wider so she could see the full-length mirror she'd hung inside.

Her mother's face stared back at her. The same blue eyes, the same narrow chin, the slightly crooked nose that marred an otherwise classic

Norwegian look. The hat picked up silver highlights in her own blond hair and gave her a jaunty air.

Although she didn't feel jaunty. She'd had no idea until now how much she resembled her mother. If she'd been pressed only a few hours ago, she would have said that she really didn't remember what her mother had looked like.

She took the hat off and ran her fingers around the narrow brim.

"I took care of it, Mommy," she whispered. She had been so afraid that she hadn't. And really, it hadn't been her care that had preserved the hat. It had been those smelly mothballs and the fact that she'd kept it up high, away from sunlight, away from anything that would have ruined the box and the hat itself.

Carefully, she placed it back in its box, replaced the lid, and got back on the stool. Then she moved the scarves and hats aside, and tucked the box back in its corner.

She didn't have much from her first decade. A few pictures she'd stolen from her grandmother's house, some books they'd let her recover when she was finally allowed into her childhood home, a stuffed dog she kept in her own closet upstairs, and the hat.

Nadia had had some record albums her parents had loved as well as a quilt their mother had made. Nadia once confessed she lost the albums in a divorce and the quilt got ripped and worn from overuse so she threw it away.

Ric had probably gotten something when Grandmother had finally divided those few leftover possessions, but when he died, his studio apartment had nothing personal. Just his clothes and some scratchings on various notebooks. He didn't even have furniture other than a mattress in the middle of the floor.

Larissa got off the stool and looked at herself in the mirror again. She no longer reminded herself of her mother. Her forehead was too broad, her eyes too far apart. Her chin didn't even seem quite as narrow.

This was the face she'd seen on countless reports, narrating hours'—probably years'—worth of video, the face that was preserved on DVD and video upstairs as well as on a private website backup just in case she decided to return to the world of television news.

One of her shrinks had made her do that, preserve her past like that, even though she hadn't wanted to. And like that hat, she hadn't even thought of revisiting those images until now.

Instead, she closed the closet door. The silver she had seen in her hair when she'd worn the hat wasn't silver at all but paint from the day's work. She needed a shower and then some dinner. Enough reflecting on the past. She needed to rest and pamper herself. She'd learned that much, at least, from all her years of therapy. She'd learned how to take care of stress before the stress got worse.

She crossed the kitchen into the back hallway, the one that led to the double-flight of stairs. On the end table she'd placed near the kitchen door rested her cell phone in its recharger. She had deliberately not taken it that morning.

Purely as a matter of reflex, she picked up the phone, and noted twelve new voice mail messages since she left home. She sighed. She'd been getting more and more messages as her former colleagues realized where she had ended up.

Rather than obsess about the messages while she was in the shower, she played them back as she went up the stairs. Most were, as she expected, requests for interviews from old friends and acquaintances. Her former editor at *The Times* had some sensitivity: He said, *Listen, Larissa, I know you're probably not ready to write about this, but think about it, maybe as a long personal piece for the Sunday magazine. You'll bring a unique perspective…*

She skipped the rest of the message as she stepped onto the upper floor. The master bedroom was here with its private suite—one room for a couch and chairs, another for the bed, and yet another for the bathroom that was nearly as large as her New York apartment had been. The bathroom had a Jacuzzi tub built into a windowed alcove. She could darken those windows and watch a television installed above the tub instead, if she so chose.

And she might choose that later. Now she needed to get out of the paint-splattered clothes and wash her hair.

She was halfway through the messages when a voice she hadn't heard in nearly two years startled her.

The voice was female and thick with a Brooklyn accent. *Larissa, honey, I've waited days to hear from you, then I realized you're probably devastated. Call me.*

Her agent, Tomasina Liu. Tomasina had been both a confidante and a business partner when Larissa had been in New York. She had brokered five lucrative book deals, ones that had allowed Larissa to finance that expensive and tiny apartment.

Larissa really didn't have to work for a living anymore, particularly when she was living somewhere as inexpensive as small-town Minnesota, but she couldn't imagine another forty-plus years of idleness. And she hadn't wanted to write. She had wanted to do something with her life.

Three messages later, Tomasina called again. *Okay, I know you're hurting, darling, and you're not going to call me to whine because you don't whine. You also know that I'm going to remind you that you have a skill, and this is hot news. Now, before you delete, hear me out. Douglas Brinkley, the historian, sold a book days after Katrina hit New Orleans and it hit* The Times *list. Everyone loved it because his love of the city came through. I know you won't want to profit from a tragedy, but here's my idea: Give the money to the families of the victims. It won't replace what they've lost, but it'll help. Or donate it to the community. You know best. But you're also best suited to write about this. You don't want Jane Sloane to write one of those insta-books on your home, do you, because you know it'll be tacky and horrible and put everyone, even the survivors, in the worst possible light. So think on it, call me any time, but do call me before Monday, okay? Even if you just want to yell at me.*

Larissa smiled instead. She was glad she had known Tomasina for years because she would have thought the call crass otherwise. Tomasina had waited nearly a week before making this presentation, even though she probably thought time was of the essence. For Tomasina, this was about as delicate as she got.

She'd also probably been worried. A lot of Larissa's friends had, and earlier in the week, she'd sent an e-mail to her entire list letting them know she had been out of town and out of harm's way.

She'd hoped that would silence them, but it hadn't. People were curious about the sensational—hell, she used to make her living covering the sensational—and she knew that. She just wasn't used to being on the receiving end.

The last message crackled.

Larie? It's Nadia. Call me soonest on my cell. We just surfaced and turned on the TV for the first time in a week, and my God, are you all right? I mean, Jesus. What the hell's wrong with Minnesota? I told you not to go back there. I have a house—well, David has a house—in London. Just go there for a few weeks. Quit the stupid job and get out. If I don't hear from you by tomorrow, I'm coming there. And no complaining. This was what we should've done for Ric.

Larissa sank into a chair, still clutching her phone, the screen asking her if she wanted to delete this message. Leave it to Nadia to revive all the guilt Larissa felt about Ric.

It was Ric's death—Ric's *suicide* (*come on now, Larissa,* one of her shrinks used to say. *Euphemisms get us nowhere. Call a suicide a suicide*)—it was Ric's suicide that had started her panic attacks, and put the first dent in the armor she had worn for more than two decades.

Ric's inability to cope with his own past had wedged open a hole into her past, and it had broken out—or tried to—and made it impossible for her to distance herself from the events she was covering. That last year on the air, she'd run a finger across her neck a dozen times, asking the cameraman to cut just before she'd burst into tears, ruining her makeup and making the producer in the control room ask her if she was all right.

When she realized that she could no longer handle on-air—that print reporters could freak out in the safety of their own cars—she applied at *The New York Times* (and the bastards had made her submit writing samples). They'd hired her, and had been very pleased with her work. She'd liked being in New York, but the panic attacks got worse. And finally, after years of therapy, she realized they wouldn't get better (*unless you get to the core issues that are causing them*, her last therapist had said) and so she resigned.

Her editor hadn't accepted her resignation. Technically she was on leave without pay. But that leave had lasted almost six years now, and she knew she was never going back.

She wasn't even tempted to write that piece for the Sunday *Times* magazine supplement. She wasn't going to call her editor back. But she would have to call Tomasina and say no to that idea. Only she wasn't going to do it tonight.

She wasn't going to do anything except that shower, have dinner, and watch some movies.

Except she did need to call her sister.

She didn't use the callback number Nadia had left. Instead, she called Nadia's old number, the one she said wouldn't work in Barbados or the Virgin Islands or wherever the private island her new husband had rented for the month was. Nadia's old phone didn't call out from there, although she had assured Larissa she'd get her messages.

Larissa trusted that now.

"Hey, Nad," she said, when the voice mail picked up. She made sure her own voice sounded light and carefree. "I'm glad you're having fun. You shouldn't have the TV on at all, you know. This is the honeymoon of a lifetime. I do appreciate the worry, but I was still in Hawaii when the attack happened. I'm fine. Honestly. I just spent the day with a bunch of co-workers and I have a lot of company. So have fun and forget about me. I promise, I'm not Ric. I'll be here when you get back."

She worried about the reference to Ric after she hung up, and then decided that it didn't matter. Nadia had brought him up first.

Nad would worry, but not enough to call again. She'd keep the message to let herself off the hook if something did happen, and she'd remind herself that Larissa had told her to stay away.

Not that anything would happen.

Larissa had missed the worst—this time.

Apparently she hadn't thirty years ago, but she still wasn't entirely convinced of that. She'd ask Nadia what she remembered when they saw each other again.

They'd never spoken of that day—at least not that Larissa remembered—and now wasn't the time to do so.

She would be fine. After a shower, some wonderful delicious lasagna, and a long night's sleep.

In the morning, she would decide what to do about the clippings.

In the morning, she would decide how much of the past she could afford to let into her present.

In the morning, she would remember just how strong she was.

six

*i*n the morning, she woke up thinking about writing. Not her own, but her students'.

Larissa stretched in her queen-sized bed, squinting at the near darkness. Her digital alarm told her it was ten in the morning, but the outside light filtering through her curtains told her it was before dawn. She got up, grabbed a robe, and pushed the curtains back only to see more fog.

The weather was as depressed as Manatowa was.

The town had already gone through a dozen funerals. She had missed the Muslim and Jewish ceremonies because she was still traveling, and had gone to a funeral earlier in the week. The others she had skipped per Principal Meiers' orders.

Helen didn't want anyone to feel obligated to attend all the funerals. She wanted teachers to go to the funerals for the students who meant something to them, and no more.

Larissa had only known a handful of the students who were killed, and one of them was Leif. She hadn't gone to his funeral.

No one had, except his parents and the media.

She sighed and pulled on slippers. Then she went to the kitchen to make her breakfast. The smell of freshly brewed coffee floated up the stairs.

At least she had remembered to set up her automatic coffee maker the night before.

The kitchen looked gray and grim in the half light. She flicked on the overheads and the brightness immediately lifted her mood. She got out a bagel, some fruit salad she had made the night before, and some cream cheese, but she didn't get the papers off the porch like she normally would have.

She wanted to think—and she didn't want to be distracted by the Sunday *New York Times* and the Minnesota papers.

She had a contractual obligation to put out an issue of the student newspaper each Friday that school was in session. On top of that, she had to compile one video news report to be shown on Monday during homeroom. It was a short, fifteen-minute newscast, but it had become a school tradition.

Obviously she wouldn't put out a newscast this Monday, but she would have to do one the following Monday.

And before that, her students had to put together an edition of the paper.

Larissa poured herself a cup of coffee, then added milk and some fake sugar. If this were thirty years ago, she would have had no doubt about what to do. She would have ignored the big event and done some fluff stories. Or at most, she would have done obituaries for the students who had been killed, tastefully leaving out the manner of their death.

In those days, no one would have wanted students to closely examine the events that transpired the week before.

She wasn't sure she wanted them to examine those events now.

Her bagel popped out of the toaster. She gripped the edge with her thumb and forefinger, careful not to burn herself, and put the bagel on her plate. Then she spread a lavish amount of cream cheese over the top, and refused to think about the calories.

Her students were already traumatized. If she made them write about the events, instead of moving forward, would she traumatize them more?

Real reporters had already learned how to separate themselves from the trauma. The reason she had quit, ultimately, was that the wall of separation she had built had crumbled. She couldn't be effective anymore.

She and her colleagues used to argue about whether or not they had developed that separation wall before they had become reporters or after. A surprising number of real reporters had come from traumatic backgrounds—abused or abandoned children; growing up in a war zone; or survivors of some personal event like a rape or a terrible physical assault.

A handful hadn't had that background or never admitted it. They claimed they learned on the job.

But could these students learn? Should she even make them try?

She alternated bites of the bagel with some spoonfuls of fruit salad and sips of her coffee. She used to sit like this in her favorite deli, figuring out how to write a particularly complicated piece or planning her strategy for the research and interviews she had to do before writing.

She hadn't done this kind of thinking since she'd become a teacher. She did most of her lesson plans at her desk in her classroom, and saved her at-home time for relaxation.

Tomasina would say that this sitting and thinking at home was a good sign.

Larissa set down her spoon.

She was not going to write a tell-all book. Or even a true-crime story about this shooting, which would appear at least a year after the event, and would traumatize this community all over again.

Apparently she had become a true community member, and she didn't want to screw it up. Or maybe, she had actually gotten close to people, closer than she imagined. She didn't have the distance necessary to write a book about this event.

She didn't have distance at all.

Which brought her back to her students. Writing did help get feelings onto the page. What she would do for her classes—all of them—would be free-writing sessions. Journal writing for her creative writing students, and general impressions for her journalism classes. Her English classes would also do free-writing.

That didn't solve the issue of the newspaper or the newscast. She needed to talk with Helen Meiers before she went any further with those.

Larissa's education classes hadn't prepared her for something like this. Neither had the one ethics class she'd been forced to take for her master's degree.

She was on her own.

seven

*L*arissa's cell phone rang as she backed her car out of the garage on Monday morning. She stopped, wondering if they had finally decided to delay classes for a few more days. Instead of a local number, she saw Tomasina's name on her screen.

Larissa hit *Ignore* and continued to back up.

The persistent fog had thickened overnight. The weather forecasters said that a storm front, with some wind, was moving in by mid-week, but the fog would remain until then. Everyone was warned to drive safely, since freezing fog created icy streets.

She hadn't really noticed. Everyone drove cautiously because visibility was low. Headlights would loom out of the fog only seconds before the car appeared.

The fog made her feel as if she'd been cocooned. It muted sound and it dimmed any light. Her neighborhood had been reduced to a handful of houses, sliding into view and then getting swallowed up behind her.

She had the radio off—she didn't want to listen to cheery music or blather this morning—and so she was surprised when she reached the school's block. Media trucks hogged the parking lanes. Reporters, huddled in politically correct woolen coats, did live remotes, their leather-gloved right hands clutching mics and their left hands holding notes below camera level.

Her stomach twisted. The media was banned from school grounds, but that didn't stop them from standing just outside the grounds with Manatowa High School in the background, and filming all the survivors as they hurried past.

If she had known, she would have taken side roads to the back parking lot. Instead, she kept her head down, hoping no one would see her. She drove as carefully as she could with her face averted and the deepness of the fog, her heart pounding. She didn't want an old colleague to recognize her and then try to follow her home.

Lights nearly blinded her. Voices shouted around her. She looked up, saw two cameras pointed at the driver's side window, and several more trained her way, their lights so bright she could hardly see.

She was tempted to gun the car, but that would cause her car to slip on the ice and maybe run down old friends. She felt like she was being attacked by paparazzi, not journalists, and she finally understood why so many people had trouble telling the difference.

The voices coalesced into her name. Some people used first names and others used her last. Someone pounded on the passenger window and she jumped.

Focus on driving, she mentally repeated to herself. *Focus on driving, focus on driving.*

Finally she turned off the street onto the long road that was actually a driveway and part of school property. Her shoulders ached from tension and her fingers clutched the steering wheel so hard that her nails were embedded in the tips of her gloves.

She turned into the first driveway, and circled the school, parking in back instead of in her regular spot. Then she put her forehead on the wheel and made herself take several deep breaths.

It had felt as if she had been assaulted. She'd always been told that threading through a group of reporters was terrifying—sometimes it had been terrifying being in one—but she had always wondered whether the targets were overreacting. They were all in the news; they all knew that a frontal media assault was part of the territory. Sometimes she saw neophytes run the gauntlet—often because of some tragedy or heroic act, and she did feel sympathy for them—but for most, she figured they had asked for it (in some cases demanded it) and they should have expected the tactics.

She should have expected the tactic. The first day of school after a shooting was always news.

She took another deep breath, shut off the ignition, and smiled a little at herself. Her car had become a refuge, just like the station's van had always been a refuge when she was reporting. She was reluctant to get out, but she knew she had to.

It took more strength than she expected to pull the door handle, push open the door, and step onto the ice-covered snow. The parking lot had been plowed, but the wait had caused a thin layer of something her grandmother used to call *schmutz* to build underneath.

She grabbed her briefcase and her purse, then locked the car and headed into the building. Hardly anyone had parked back here. She was alone, although she heard shouting up front as the reporters recognized someone else who arrived.

She certainly hoped it wasn't one of the student survivors. A few of them had made the mistake of talking to the press that day, and now they were all instant celebrities, Heroes of Manatowa High School, their actions either misunderstood or blown out of proportion.

When she'd been watching the coverage in Hawaii, she'd winced whenever she'd seen her students on the screen. They had had no idea that day that they were signing up for a certain amount of notoriety. And whenever this story came up—and it would when the next kid went postal and decided to shoot up his school—all of them would receive calls for comments on the actions of those future survivors.

Her boots slipped on the ice. She pulled open the double doors that opened on the gymnasium side of the building. The small metal detector on this side had a new sign—*Anyone carrying backpacks, purses, or briefcases must enter through the front door.*

The guard, standing beside the detector, was a police officer. He was tall and thin, with a careworn face. Larissa didn't know his name, but she recognized him.

"Guess I have to go around front," she said, holding up her briefcase.

He shook his head. "You're a teacher. That rule's for non-staff. But I have to check your stuff."

There was a small table behind him. He took her briefcase, flicked it open, and methodically searched it. Then he opened her purse, finding the nooks and crannies that airport security never found, along with some gum wrappers and a pen bleeding ink that should have been tossed a long time ago.

"You're clear," he said.

"Thanks."

He nodded, but didn't say anything else. Instead he stood at attention, rather like an honor guard at an official ceremony.

She hurried down the hall past the doors to the gym. Inside, she heard echoes of a basketball on the court, and adult voices talking about keeping things off the expensive court floor.

Some students were pulling books from their lockers. Manatowa had bucked the trend from few years ago of pulling lockers out of the school, in the mistaken assumption that nothing like that could happen here. Or maybe it was a confidence brought by the metal detectors and the security guards.

She hadn't minded the search. In the past, she might have, or she might have felt embarrassed that he was seeing her purse's disorganization. But she was relieved he was here, just like she was appalled at the presence of reporters.

The inside of the school felt safer than it had on Saturday just because of him.

A few students nodded a greeting at her as they passed, but no one talked. Everyone seemed somber and a little frightened.

She was walking against the tide, heading down the nearest wheel-spoke corridor to the ring. When she reached it, she circled around until she found the main entrance corridor.

A lot of students were standing near a new metal detector and X-ray machine. The line bunched in the airlock and then ran outside. Both sets of airlock doors were closed, however, so that no cold air could get in and no warm air could get out.

Minnesotans were ever-practical.

The problem seemed to be that the X-ray machine was jammed. Someone—apparently the installer—was trying to loosen the top.

She ducked into the principal's office, which smelled of fresh paint. It looked better than it had on Saturday. The plants—a thriving ficus that was as tall as she was, and some kind of tree that looked a little too thin—had returned to their places near the door. The chairs, with their padded seats and wooden backs, no longer had plastic covering them.

All three secretaries sat at their desks, but for once the desktops were neat except for the giant calendars that acted as blotters and the computers with their screen savers running.

Two of the secretaries were on the phone. One—the youngest by nearly two decades—wore an earpiece and looked like a corporate receptionist. The other—a heavyset woman with graying hair—held a landline to her ear and played with the cord.

Both women were wearing business suits for the first time since Larissa started at Manatowa High. The older secretary had a small, almost unnoticeable cross pinned to lapel. The other secretary toyed with an obviously new remembrance bracelet on her left wrist.

"Help you, Ms. Johanssen?" Doris Kiernig, the third secretary, asked. She too wore a suit, a tasteful gray that contrasted with her colleagues' black. A black mourning band circled her left arm. The gray accented her silver-blond hair—a natural color in these parts for older women. No one, especially these no-nonsense women—would think of coloring her hair.

"I know you guys are probably swamped," Larissa said, automatically summoning her Midwestern politeness, "but I need to see Principal Meiers today if at all possible."

Doris sighed. "Everyone needs to see her today. Can it wait?"

Larissa shook her head. "If I'm going to produce a newspaper by Friday and have a newscast next Monday, I need to talk with her today. I'm not sure what I can legally and ethically ask the students to report regarding the attack."

Doris winced at the mention of the shooting. The younger secretary shoved her bracelet farther up her arm, and bowed her head. The other secretary stopped playing with the cord and looked at Larissa.

"There won't be anything today, right?" Doris asked. "We didn't schedule time for it."

"That's right," Larissa said. Her stomach twisted. Poor Helen Meiers. She would have to make her morning homeroom announcement after everything that had happened this past week.

"Let me see." Doris had opened a calendar program on her computer. The principal's day schedule was the only thing on there, and it looked horribly full. "I can squeeze you in after the assembly. There will be about fifteen minutes leeway for students to get to homeroom. Will that work?"

"We're having an assembly before homeroom?" Larissa asked. "I missed the announcement."

"Because we haven't made it yet. We're waiting for first bell. I've got some hall monitors putting up signs. So, can you meet her at the assembly and talk on the way back here?"

Larissa frowned. She had hoped to talk in the office, but the in-transit discussion would have to do.

"Yes," she said. "Thanks."

"I'll let her know you need to see her," Doris said, "and what it's about."

"That's fine," Larissa said.

Doris nodded, pulled the keyboard forward and made a notation. Then she wrote something on a yellow Post-It and stuck it on a piece of paper already bathed in Post-Its.

Larissa smiled at her, then ducked out of the office. The hallway was getting crowded. The tech or whomever he was had fixed the X-ray machine and the line near the door had almost disappeared.

Still, the halls were eerily quiet. Students walked with their heads down. A number of the girls clutched their books to their chests like shields. A large group of boys, many of whom used to taunt Leif, leaned against the arch heading into the ring. No one stood near the cafeteria doors. No one had even written on the plywood. If the glass had broken because of someone's carelessness instead of during a shooting, that plywood would have been covered in graffiti by now.

Larissa nodded at several students, said hello to others, and hurried down the hall to her room. She wanted to get there before the announcement for the assembly.

The journalism room was on the other side of the ring, across from the cafeteria. The wheel spoke was diagonal from the one that led to the gym, but the journalism room was built into the link between the spoke and the ring, making a larger space.

None of her first-period students waited outside the door. Someone had already taped a sign on it announcing the assembly that would take the place of first-period classes. She unlocked the door and slipped inside, locking the door behind her.

The room's familiarity soothed her. A long white board ran along the wall to her right. A blackboard used to cover the space behind her desk, but she had covered it with pictures of important or famous faces. Windows on the far wall showed a not-so-interesting view of the space between the spokes and part of the ring itself.

As she looked, she realized she could see the plywood through a double set of windows. Any students who had been here during third period, doing research or lab work, could have watched the events unfold through the cafeteria doors.

She shivered. She usually never looked that way. Normally, she focused her attention on the back part of the room. She had her own window, which was dark at the moment. It opened into the first of two rooms she'd created. The first was a journalism lab, with five computers (three donated and two she purchased) that her newspaper and media staff could use. The second, impossible to see through the darkness, was the studio. The studio took the place of her office, and it wasn't much bigger than a closet. But smaller equipment and some creative engineering design by Alan Deela gave her just enough soundproof privacy to create a downloadable newscast that aired every Monday morning.

The actual broadcast facilities were in a room behind the principal's office. The principal usually used it during homeroom to make pertinent announcements. It only broadcast locally—meaning the signal usually did not reach far outside the high school, although of late, they'd been simulcasting it on the Web as well.

She was glad there would be no newscast this morning. The real media would pick it up and abuse it in their stories of the so-called return to normality at Manatowa High School. By next Monday, if nothing else horrible happened, the media would be long gone, and Manatowa would return to its private practices—although she would argue against a webcast for several months, maybe to the end of the school year.

She unlocked the journalism lab, turned on the light, and felt relief when she saw that no computer had been left on during the long absence. She then went all the way back and unlocked the studio. She put her purse inside, and locked the door again. She shut down the journalism lab as well, not willing to let students in there just yet.

She put her briefcase on the desk, opened it, and set graded papers on her desktop. On a normal morning, she'd make sure she had everything, but she wasn't even sure she would return papers today. Instead, she put them in a desk drawer, set the briefcase behind her chair, stuck her keys in her pocket, and headed out.

The door to the main part of the room she left open and unlocked, with the lights on, just in case some of her homeroom wanted to sit out the assembly in private. First bell sounded as she went into the ring, and students changed direction like sheep, all of them heading to their first-period classes.

Then the announcement squealed over the PA, and everyone froze. The individual looks of terror startled her. Every student turned toward the speakers, as if expecting something awful to happen.

Instead, Doris's voice crackled, announcing an assembly that would take the place of first period. Attendance was mandatory, but clearly no one had thought how they would enforce it. Usually assemblies happened during second period, just after homeroom, and the homeroom teachers led their students to the gym.

But clearly, Principal Meiers wanted to set the tone for the return to classes. She didn't want to saddle her teachers with it.

Larissa applauded the idea, but wasn't so sure about the execution. A handful of girls wiped at tear-filled eyes as they continued to listen to the announcement. A few boys looked down. They were clearly all relieved that nothing else terrible had happened.

That was when she remembered that Principal Meiers had gone on the PA to tell everyone who could to get out of the school. Assistant Principal Walter Haigen lay dead in front of the office door, and Helen had locked herself in the broadcast room to give her students instructions on how to escape.

Larissa had been in that broadcast room countless times. If the door to the principle's office was open, then someone standing in the corridor could see whomever was in the broadcast room.

And that person had her back to the door.

Haigen's body had blocked the office door open. The secretaries had barricaded themselves under their desks.

But Helen had bravely gone into that broadcast room, turned her back on the shooter, and told her students how to escape.

Larissa's stomach clenched. She had been in dangerous situations, but she had never deliberately turned her back on that danger. She wasn't sure if she could do so now.

She wasn't that altruistic.

Even before the announcement ended, students changed course. Now they flowed like a river toward the gymnasium. She joined them.

"Hey, Miz Johanssen."

Larissa turned. Joe Omart had come up beside her. He was shorter than she was and had that stick-thinness that boys who were growing too quickly sometimes had. Usually he wore a vest over a dress shirt, with a tie tucked underneath, along with a pair of dark pants. This morning, however, he wore a red-and-white-checked flannel shirt and some faded blue jeans. He also had new wire-rim glasses that made his face look smaller than before.

"Joe. It's good to see you." She had already decided that would be her greeting today. No *How are you*, no overly hearty warmth.

"You too." He wasn't carrying any books, which was also unusual for him. He was one of her best students, and a very enthusiastic reporter. Ever since he'd seen *Good Night and Good Luck*, the movie about broadcast pioneer Edward R. Murrow, Joe had worn bulky black glasses and that silly vest. He'd also asked repeatedly for time on the Monday broadcast to do commentary.

Larissa had told him he could do commentary when he learned how to have his own screen presence, not when he copied someone else's.

So far, that had worked. Learning a personal broadcast style was harder than learning how to speak on the air.

"I thought maybe you wouldn't come back." He didn't look at her as he said that.

She had never seen Joe so subdued.

"I love it here," she said. "Why wouldn't I come back?"

"A lot of teachers aren't," he said. "That'll be part of the announcement today."

She had known that teachers had a chance to opt out, maybe permanently, but she hadn't realized a lot of them had taken it. She had assumed most would be like her, Alan, Oscar, and Darren—battered, but not cowed. She figured only a few, like Robyn, would discover they were too traumatized to return.

"You know that for a fact?" she asked.

He gave her a sideways look, but it lacked its usual implied withering sarcasm. "I've been collecting information for days," he said. "I don't know what we're going to use for the broadcast and what we're not."

Larissa sighed. "I don't either, yet."

They walked the rest of the way in silence, just like most of the students around them. She was heartened that he was thinking of the broadcast, but worried at the same time. He'd been gathering information. She hoped he'd also been doing some talking of his own.

"The new glasses look good," she said as they reached the open gymnasium door.

Joe touched them as if he had to reassure himself that they were there.

"Leif stepped on the other pair," he said and headed toward the bleachers.

She froze for a moment in the door, letting the students flow around her. She had to remember that casual comments would draw responses like that.

She couldn't cringe from them. She had to treat them for what they were—both fact and revelation. Everyone had a story from that day. Everyone had a reaction.

And unlike the faculty, most of the students had to return. The only other high school in Manatowa was Cathedral, the Catholic high school. It limited its enrollment to Catholics only. She'd heard that a few wealthy parents sent their children to East Coast or European boarding schools this past week and a couple other parents planned to homeschool their children (at least until the school board tested them and found them wanting on curriculum). But most of the high-school-aged kids had nowhere else to go.

They were due back at Manatowa High School on Monday morning, and they came.

The gym was already filling up. Even though Manatowa had an auditorium, it was too small to handle the entire student body, so large events had to come to the gym.

Someone had placed the canvas floor cover over the basketball court, but it looked even more dangerous to her, with bits of canvas bunched along the edges. A podium with a mic stood near the bleachers. Behind it, booths were set up like they usually were during science fair. Each booth had a table and two chairs, along with dividers separating one booth from the next.

Some people she didn't recognize were lined up against the far door. They were adults and wore dress clothes. Most of the men and a few of the women wore business suits. None of them had the black armbands that so many students were wearing.

Larissa hadn't thought to put on something like that. She'd see what she could find in the teacher's lounge during her third-period break.

The gym echoed with the sounds of students climbing the bleachers, and there was conversation here—finally. Most of it was simply students calling each other's names as they found a place to sit near their friends.

Larissa took a seat down front where the rest of the teachers were. A few always climbed to the top so that they could observe whether or not the students were acting out. Walter Haigen used to do that, too. It had been one of his functions as assistant principal.

Helen Meiers was talking to Alan Deela. She was a short fireplug of a woman, whose power seemed to emanate from her square smallness. She wore a tailored charcoal suit with flats that only brought her to Alan's chest. He had to bend to hear her over the yelling and the pounding of feet on the metal bleacher steps.

The senior class president, Jessi Carter, and her boyfriend, Dave Frent, unfolded metal chairs behind the podium. Jessi, who was also a star basketball player, wore black and three-inch heels, even though flat-footed she was half a foot taller than her boyfriend.

The boys always joked that Dave got the better end of that deal, particularly when they were dancing, but to his credit, he never said anything even suggestive about his tall girlfriend. He seemed proud of her academic and athletic achievements, which surprised Larissa, since Dave couldn't match Jessi in either area. He was lead trumpet with the band, however, and there was talk of his attending Julliard in the fall, although to Larissa's knowledge, he hadn't even applied yet.

The second bell rang and a handful of students scurried in. The hall monitors watching the doors kept them propped open so that they wouldn't make noise as the assembly started and stragglers came in.

Oscar was one of the last group through the side door. He slipped into the empty spot beside Larissa.

"You okay?" he asked, and she knew he wasn't asking about the assembly or the strange day. He was asking about the faint. "No after-effects?"

"Nothing that a nice glass of wine and a hot bath didn't cure," she said.

He smiled, then leaned around her and waved at someone farther down on the bench.

She looked that direction and was startled to see Pete Petrovich several rows down. He half-smiled and waved at Larissa, then put his arm around a slender girl whose long brown hair was pulled into a ponytail behind her back.

Larissa had never learned the girl's name, but she recognized the face from passing her in the hallway. Larissa didn't teach any freshman classes, so she had a chance to get used to the faces before they showed up in her sophomore writing classes.

"I didn't realize that he had a daughter going to school here," Larissa said to Oscar.

"Daughter and son." Oscar peered at her. "I thought you knew P.J."

She knew a kid named P.J., but didn't have him in any classes either. He had startled her one afternoon two years ago when she'd seen him in the hall. He looked like someone she had met before, but she couldn't recall where.

She frowned. Had P.J. looked familiar because he resembled his father at the same age?

"What does P.J. stand for?" she asked.

"Pete Junior." Oscar grinned. "He never wanted to be called Skip or Chip or Junior or Pete for that matter. He forced them to call him P.J. from little on."

"And the daughter?" Larissa asked.

"Diane, named for his late wife."

She got a sense that Oscar had added that about Petrovich's wife for her sake.

"I thought you knew him," Oscar said.

"He says we went to school together," Larissa said. "But I don't remember much from those years."

Oscar nodded. "Wonder how many kids here'll blank out this year."

The squeal of a microphone prevented her answer. Helen had gotten behind the podium. She had to stand on a stepstool, which was just barely visible from Larissa's position to the right of the podium. The stepstool always made Helen look out of proportion. A woman that square couldn't be that tall.

She adjusted the microphone and tapped it, which made Alan, who sat behind her, wince—and probably drove the sound system guy in the booth above the gymnasium nuts.

"Welcome back to Manatowa High."

Helen's voice silenced all noise in the gymnasium. Even the students still climbing the bleachers stopped and sat down.

"I know for all of us it's been one of the worst weeks of our lives, but I for one am glad to be back and to see so many familiar faces."

If Larissa thought she was going to have a rough time greeting her students, she hadn't realized that Helen would have a rougher time. She had to balance the sadness with a sense of moving forward.

"I know many of you came with your parents today," Helen said. "I want you all to know that parents are welcome in any classroom for as long as necessary. We want to make the transition back to routine as easy as possible."

Larissa looked around. As she did, she realized a number of her students had adults sitting beside them. A few sat as far from the parent as possible, but others leaned against their parent as if they were still very little children.

"We have a lot of announcements and a lot of business to get through," Helen was saying, "but first, I want to talk about last Tuesday."

A rustle echoed through the gym. Larissa had tensed. So, it seemed, had everyone else.

"None of us knew when we arrived here last Tuesday that we would become national headlines. We have lost sixteen of our students. They were friends and family, and we will miss every last one of them. We also lost several staff members, including Assistant Principal Walter Haigen, who died trying to stop Leif Soderstrom from getting into the school."

Murmurs started.

"Yes," Helen said loudly, silencing the murmurs. "I said Leif's name. Because we have to talk about him. We have to acknowledge what he did and learn how to live with it. It will be part of our lives from a long time."

More murmurs. Helen held up a hand to silence them.

"But I don't want to dwell on Leif Soderstrom."

"Good!" a boy shouted from the back.

"I want to talk about our missing friends. The people who were injured and need our visits and prayers. And the people who died."

She shifted a piece of paper, then put her hands on it and stared at the crowd.

"I'm going to talk about them, too. We can't deal with this by failing to remember. We must honor the dead, remember their daily lives—not just the acts of heroism as the media has done—and we must cry for them. We must mourn. At the end of the assembly, we will hand out a list of when and where the remaining funerals will be held. There will also be a memorial service next Saturday night at eight. I urge you all to attend."

Larissa made a mental note. More funerals. Sometimes it felt like this would never end.

"I want to talk about the people we've lost," Helen repeated. She picked up that piece of paper. "I didn't know them all very well, but I asked family and friends for a few words. I'm going to share them here."

"Oh, Jesus," Oscar muttered.

Larissa agreed. She had expected to cry today, but she hadn't expected to be forced into it during first period. Although she understood what Helen was doing. She was opening the doors that might have remained closed, making sure conversations were possible.

The people lining the side wall had to be counselors. A few of them were nodding as Helen spoke.

As Helen went down the list, each name was greeted with some sobs and cries of recognition. A few received "Yo"s from the back, as male friends tried to acknowledge their pain.

A couple of parents helped some students out the side doors. Other students folded themselves forward, listening with their hands over their faces.

Oscar teared up almost immediately.

Larissa didn't. She listened dry-eyed to the recited names, not even having to use the old reporter's trick of biting the inside of her cheek to keep the tears at bay.

She had known these students, admired several of them, and had high hopes for a few more. Some she only recognized in passing.

Helen went through the list alphabetically, placing the adults with the teenagers so that no one seemed more special than anyone else.

It was the strangest recitation Larissa had ever heard in a high school gymnasium. She'd sat in here four times now, watching her students walk from folding chairs in the middle of the floor to a makeshift stage at the end of the room to get their diplomas. She'd been here countless times to cheer on the sports teams. She'd attended dozens of assemblies, a few dances, and more concerts than she wanted to think about.

But she had never listened to a principal's voice break as she worked her way through a list of murdered people.

"Please," Helen said as she finished. "Let's have a moment of silence for everyone we have lost."

More rustling as heads bowed. A sob—choked, as if the person tried to repress it—resounded, and another. Then actual silence.

Larissa bowed her head. But she couldn't picture the students who were gone. All she saw were the photographs that had been in the newspapers these last few days—not the students as they lived, but as they had been before a formal photographer on class photo day: goofing or too serious or looking away at the wrong moment.

She wished she could remember them laughing or walking down the hall. But she couldn't. She accepted the students as part of her world and unless they were in her classroom, they were little more than chang-ing fixtures—a set that altered day to day.

She regretted that, but knew it wouldn't change. There were simply too many people in Manatowa High. She would never know all of them, no matter how hard she tried.

Then a bit of feedback as Helen touched the microphone and her voice, soft and gentle, said, "Thank you."

Heads lifted. People moved. Something thudded behind Larissa—a dropped book or purse.

"Today," Helen said, "will not be a normal day. I'm not sure if we'll ever have normal days again—not as we used to know them. We'll have different days and we'll come to accept that as normal. But for now, we live in a new reality. To help us cope, dozens of counselors have come from all over the area. We have set up booths behind me so that you can talk to a counselor one-on-one. These booths will be in the gym for two days—which means no practice and no gym classes during that period. If you have practice or classes scheduled, come here to check in. Your coach or teacher will tell you want to do next."

The rustling grew. The students needed to move. So did Larissa. The bleacher seat dug into her thighs. She stretched her legs and shifted, but couldn't get comfortable.

"Please talk with the counselors, even if it's just to say hello. Don't be ashamed to ask for guidance or help or a sympathetic ear. My office door will be open all week. I will have extended hours. I'll be here before school and after school, so come see me if you have concerns. Or talk to the counselors. Some of you will need more time than others. That's fine. Your teachers will give it to you. Please, people, make sure that you allow your friends space to grieve. We're all going to be on edge for a while. That's the new normal. Let's forgive each other a little easier and be more understanding than usual. My office door will be open...."

Larissa looked around, moving her head only slightly, another old reporter trick. Some students were wiped at their faces with the back of their hands. A few girls were using tissues. Some boys leaned their heads to the side, using their hands to cup their faces and their thumbs to wipe their eyes.

"…please pick up the funeral schedules on your way out the door. We'll have more copies in homerooms today and tomorrow. You're going to have about a half an hour before the first bell for homeroom. Use that time to set up counseling appointments. We have some volunteers here today who'll be at the tables behind me to set those up. You can also come in here any time and make an appointment. Please use this. Don't suffer through this grief alone."

Helen gripped the side of the podium almost as if she needed it to hold her up. Maybe she did. She was assuming the role of the strongest person in the room.

Larissa wondered if she had used a counselor or even consulted with any before today's assembly. Because this was all so new, she had no idea if Helen had.

Nothing would surprise her, especially today.

"Thank you for coming," Helen said. "Thank you all for being so brave last week. We are a school, but more importantly, we are a family. And we will get through this—together."

She moved away from the podium, effectively ending the assembly. With a small gesture, she indicated that the teachers up front should stand.

Oscar and Larissa stood together. Larissa's legs were wobbly and she suddenly wasn't as certain as she'd been this morning. If anything, the assembly had shaken her more than she realized—and put some doubt into place. She wasn't trained as a counselor. She couldn't handle distraught students. Part of her had wanted this day to be normal, just like everyone else did.

The clangs and bangs and voices rose as the students started to leave. The gym was filled with conversation. Some students—mainly those with parents beside them—headed toward the appointment tables.

"I understand you had a question." Helen stood in front of her. Larissa looked down at her, always startled that such a forceful woman could be short enough to make Larissa feel as tall as Jessi Carter.

"Yes, I do," Larissa said. "Although after your speech this morning, I think I know your answer."

The students mingled around them, some talking, some getting into lines, as Larissa explained her concerns about the newspaper and the short newscast.

"My training fails me here," Larissa said. "In the real world of journalism, we would be obliged to cover the event even if someone else had already covered it. We would have to assume our readers needed our input. I don't think that's wise here, but I don't want to be complicit in a non-discussion of the event."

Helen nodded. She hadn't taken her gaze off Larissa's face, which was amazing, considering the chaos around them.

"I'm not even sure how much coverage we should do in the future," Larissa said. "I'm out of my depth here."

"If you didn't have to cover the event, as you called it, what would you do as a follow-up?" Helen asked.

"In the real world?"

"Yes," she said.

"We'd do stories on the aftermath. The first would of course be a tribute issue to the dead and an update on the injured. Then we'd cover any legal proceedings, the school's recovery, and individual survival stories." Larissa glanced around to see who was listening in. A few people stood nearby, but they appeared to be waiting and trying very hard to give Larissa and Helen privacy.

"The tribute issue of the paper would be a good idea," Helen said.

"I know. I was planning that," Larissa said. "But what about after?"

Helen frowned. "I see your concern. But we can't ignore it, and the paper is a good way to keep everything from fading away. I think any student who refuses to cover a particular story connected with the shooting should be allowed the refusal. I know that's not your normal policy. And clear anything off school grounds with me before you assign it."

"As it relates to the shooting," Larissa said.

"Naturally," Helen said. "If it's a play or an interview of a local businessman, do what you'd normally do."

Larissa nodded. It all made sense.

"Which leaves us with the newscast. I'm wondering if you want to suspend it for the rest of the year. It's a great learning tool, but I hesitate to simulcast on the web as long as we're in the national eye, and I'm not sure about the in-school broadcast either. Some of my former colleagues have equipment sophisticated enough to pick up anything we broadcast internally."

Helen nodded. Her attention had wandered toward the sign-up lines. More students were in it than Larissa had expected—and now not all of the students had their parents with them.

Petrovich stood in one of the lines, his arm still around his daughter. A boy nearly as tall as Petrovich, but lanky and awkward, hovered near him.

"I hesitate to get rid of something that makes this school unique," Helen said. "How long do you think the national press will harass us?"

"It's hard to say," Larissa said. "If nothing happens in the news, you'll have them for a month. If something else happens, you'll lose all but the most junior reporters. If a lot of something elses happen, they'll stop bothering us sooner rather than later."

"How about suspending the broadcast for another week? We'll reassess next Monday. Is there something your broadcast students can do in the meantime?"

Larissa bit her lower lip. "I got an idea during your speech. I haven't given it much thought, so I'm not wedded to it—"

"Quickly, Larissa. I have several others I need to talk with."

Larissa nodded, amazed at how quickly she had slipped back into her Midwestern tendency to overexplain rather than offend. She never used to do that when she pitched a story in New York or Atlanta.

"I'd like them to make a tribute video for the ceremony on Saturday."

Helen turned back to her, eyes bright. For a moment, Larissa thought she saw tears. Then they faded.

"Perfect," Helen said. "How much time do you need in the ceremony?"

Larissa shrugged. "Can I let you know later in the week?"

"Certainly." Helen reached out and touched her arm. "Thank you."

"For what?" Larissa asked.

"Coming back," Helen said. "You of all people have somewhere else you can go. The fact that you've returned means a lot more to any of us than I can say."

Larissa's cheeks heated. She nodded, but didn't answer. She wondered if Helen knew about the requests still filling Larissa's voice mail, requests for interviews and articles and appearances.

Helen wasn't dumb. She had probably figured it out. Her own voice mail was probably filled with similar messages.

"I love it here," Larissa said for the second time that day. And, for the first time, she realized that it was true.

he rest of the day went by quickly. Larissa's students were subdued for the most part, and grateful to write instead of talk. She tried to ignore the empty seats in three of her classes, but her gaze kept going back to them, as did the gazes of the other students.

Her newspaper staff liked the idea of the tribute issue. She had no trouble making assignments. The trouble came with the after-school meeting of her broadcast staff.

Broadcast staff usually met during the last fifteen minutes of first period. Her only class on the interaction of various media—called, of all things, Media Relations—met during first period, and a handful of those students had earned their way into her broadcast news slot.

Some of the newspaper reporters occasionally did a live feed or reiterated something they had learned while doing a print piece. But mostly, she kept the two staffs separate.

She had chosen the time for Media Relations so that the broadcast staff could put the finishing touches on the short newscast every Monday—and sometimes even get a chance to practice before recording the final version.

She never let them finish the newscast on Friday. She wanted them to get used to the pressure of producing a finished product on short notice, and sometimes she gave them a last-minute story to interpolate into the newscast.

Today, however, she'd managed to get the word out that she needed the staff for a short afterschool meeting. She had also asked the newspaper staff to join the broadcast staff. Usually she tried to restrict the amount of material she had for broadcast.

For this special broadcast, she felt that too much couldn't hurt.

It took fifteen minutes from final bell for her students to gather in the journalism room, which was remarkably speedy. Sometimes it took students as much as a half an hour to cross the ring and arrive in her classroom for an afterschool event. She knew a number of them drove off-campus to get a Big Mac or a latte before returning for the afternoon, and she usually didn't begrudge them that.

She worked them hard in the hours she had them, and she didn't mind if they took care of themselves beforehand. Sometimes she saw herself as the anti-coach. Instead of docking them for being late, she simply made a mental note of the time and kept them that much longer. A few students noticed, but not many. Her volunteer reporters were enthusiastic and ambitious. Getting into a good college from a rural Minnesota school was difficult enough; these students wanted to improve the odds any way they could.

Joe Omart sat in the front row, a stack of books beside his desk. He had extended his short legs and slumped, not a usual position for him. He seemed tired.

Beside him, Tofee Grice was typing something on his laptop. Tofee, whose real name was Christofer, even had skin the color of toffee. When he grew into that face, he would be one of the most handsome men she had ever seen. Right now, though, his cheeks still had a childish roundness and he hadn't yet hit his growth spurt. He put up with a lot of teasing from the other students, and mostly he took it. So she had been surprised at the brashness he brought to his reporting. That, plus a natural writing talent and sense of story, made him one of the stand-outs on this year's newspaper staff.

The broadcast staff sat in the back and were unusually quiet. Class president Jessi Carter leaned her head against the back wall, her eyes closed. Normally, she couldn't have made an afterschool meeting during basketball season, which cut into her airtime. But she had come today.

Her boyfriend, Dave Frent, sat beside her, his head buried in his arms on top of his desk. Hannah Maxwell sat beside him. She was checking her makeup in a compact mirror. Tubes of lip gloss and eyeliner lined up on her desktop.

Larissa had brought Hannah to the team not because of her intellect or reporting skills but because she had a natural presence in front of the cameras and she was the best cold reader of the entire group. When some of the good reporters on the newspaper staff complained, Larissa had smiled at them.

You wanted to learn broadcast, she had said in her most reasonable tone. *One important fact about broadcast is that you must look good in the way that society defines* good. *Yes, you need some abilities, but they're abilities that work well with the camera. Anyone can write copy behind the scenes. It takes someone easy to look at to read it.*

From that point on, the newspaper staff called Hannah and her usual co-anchor, Drew Ashanti, the Vapid Mouthpieces. In the way of most teenage nicknames, these were both cruel and apt. But the *vapid mouthpiece* label could be applied to most anchors, particularly on the local level, and Larissa hadn't protested the moniker.

Now, in light of Leif's actions, she wondered if she should have.

Drew Ashanti was the only person in the room who was watching her. He was a stunningly beautiful boy of such mixed ethnicity that she couldn't begin to guess his background. He had dark, almond-shaped eyes, high cheekbones, and a romantic-movie-hero jawline. In the past year, he'd developed large shoulders and gained enough height so that he towered over Larissa. He was blessed with a deep anchor's voice that made even poorly written copy sound good.

His right hand was in a cast. He'd grabbed Leif by the ankle in the cafeteria, trying to pull him down. Instead, Leif had shot him in the wrist and palm, and then advanced deeper into the cafeteria, shooting as he went. Friends had dragged Drew into a makeshift fortress they'd made of overturned tables and chairs, and another of Larissa's reporters, Kaitlyn Brandt, had tied her shirt around the wounds, slowing the bleeding. Some believed she might even have saved his life.

Kaitlyn sat by herself in the center of the room. She was a tiny girl, not even four feet tall. Half a dozen birth defects twisted her spine and kept her from reaching her full growth. She wasn't pretty—her nose was too small and her mouth too big—but she had an effervescence that made up for a lot. Except today. Today she seemed so subdued that she almost disappeared.

The other students had already taken out their notepads, just like Larissa had trained them to do. Half of the newspaper reporters were writing, probably beginning the assignment they'd received earlier in the day.

Larissa walked to the door, closed it, and thanked them all for coming.

That got their attention. Pens poised above paper, like reporters of old, they stared at her. Even Dave Frent lifted his head from his desk and turned his chair slightly so that he could see her.

"First," she said, "we're not doing the weekly broadcast next Monday. We might not do a broadcast for the rest of the month."

The moans from the back row were loud. Joe and Tofee grinned at each other. They were the ones who had come up with the Vapid Mouthpieces nickname, partly out of jealousy. Joe had always believed he should be on the air, with his greater reporting skills and his Edward R. Murrow mannerisms, not the pretty people in the back row.

"We already have material," Jessi said. "Drew actually has video footage of his shooting and rescue on his phone, and we've edited it. We worked all weekend. We wanted to show you."

"And," Dave said, "we have some good stuff from other kids of the evacuation and what it was like to wait outside when the shooting was still going on inside."

Larissa felt a start of surprise. Some of the cell phone footage had shown up on the networks, and there were rumors that some more graphic footage had been on YouTube, but had been removed at the request of parents and the school.

She hadn't expected her students to have the presence of mind to take footage for the broadcast.

"Not to mention there's this great photo that Mandi Edwards took of our own Kaitlyn saving Drew's life," said Hannah.

Mandi Edwards was the best photographer Larissa had ever had on the newspaper staff. She sat one row ahead of Kaitlyn. Mandi was a heavyset girl with bad skin who wore mismatched clothes, mostly because she didn't seem to care what she wore. She cared about her cameras, though, and she had half a dozen of her own, from film cameras to digital. She let the other students use the two school cameras. Hers were higher end and much more sophisticated.

She toyed with the lens cap of the camera she wore around her neck and did not look up, even when her name was mentioned.

"And my dad golfs with the news director of Channel 2 in Duluth," Hannah said. "He's already said he'd give us some of their helicopter footage for the report."

Larissa felt breathless. She hadn't expected this reaction. She had expected the students to be relieved that they didn't have to report on the shootings.

"Excellent work," she said. "I didn't expect you to have so much done. I'm going to have to think about what we can do with it. I'm sure there's something."

Although she wasn't. She was vamping, trying not to dampen her students' enthusiasm, but at the same time, trying not to encourage them to continue on this line of thinking.

"But Principal Meiers has already made her position clear. She feels that we need to move forward, and that everyone has seen enough footage of the shootings. She wants us to focus on the aftermath, not on the shootings themselves."

"Even in the paper?" Drew asked, his deep voice carrying across the room.

"Especially the paper." Larissa leaned against her own desk. "Here's the problem. Everyone in the school knows what happened. The local media has covered it, and the national media won't let it alone. By the time we get to do a broadcast, what we have won't be news anymore. And our mandate is to focus on the news."

More moans from the back. But none of the newspaper reporters said anything. Several of them studied their hands. They hadn't even protested when Larissa mentioned this at their earlier meeting. Their silence, more than anything, convinced her that she and Principal Meiers had made the right decision.

"What do we do with all this footage?" Jessi asked. "We saved it for our broadcast."

She was almost whining, something Jessi rarely did.

"My dad wants to sell it to *Inside Edition* or something," Hannah said. "He says we'll make a fortune."

"Not necessarily," Larissa said, "and you won't like how they edit it. And they will edit it. Remember the various coverages we studied last fall on something as simple as the presidential debates—something we could all see as they happened, and yet the editing made the coverage subtly biased. That'll happen with anything you sell to *Inside Edition*."

"Or CNN," Kaitlyn muttered.

"Or CNN," Larissa agreed. She was a bit surprised that the protest had come from Kaitlyn. Kaitlyn was usually sensitive to other people's feelings, including her teacher's, and she didn't usually let anyone say anything even remotely negative (no matter how deserving) of CNN.

"We own it," Hannah said defiantly.

"Yes, you do," Larissa said, "and whatever you decide to do will be your family's decision. I would hope, however, that you sit on the footage until we can figure out how best to use it here."

"You just said we aren't going to do anything on the news." Dave sounded plaintive.

Joe shifted in his seat. The newspaper staff hated it when the broadcast staff referred to their program as "the news."

"That's right. But you all didn't let me finish," Larissa said. "A lot of things have changed."

"No kidding," Drew said. He rested his cast on top of his books. He was left-handed, so the injury to the right didn't hurt his writing ability or his drawing ability. He was one of the school's star track team members, but he didn't need his hand for that, either.

Still, Larissa hadn't thought to ask the prognosis for his hand, and she didn't dare do so right now.

"As I said," Larissa raised her voice just a little, "we aren't going to have a broadcast this week, and probably not for the next two. But we will have to work harder than ever."

Everyone looked at her. Even the students who hadn't raised their heads since they came into the room met her gaze.

"We're going to produce a documentary." Larissa used the word on purpose. "It's going to be professional quality, and it's going to be a tribute to everyone we've lost, student and faculty. It's going to air at the memorial service."

"On Saturday?" squeaked Ryan Cogsworth. His voice was changing—late, considering he was a senior—and she never knew what pitch she'd hear from him. That was the only reason he was strictly newspaper. He was a handsome blond who photographed well, and he had the best reading style of anyone in class—when his voice worked properly.

"Yes," Larissa said. "This Saturday. Which is why the entire newspaper staff is here. They're already working on a tribute issue. They will work in tandem with the rest of you. I want the broadcast staff to find any and all video they can of the people we've lost. We're going to do a montage of each individual and of the entire group, if we can."

"Only positive stuff, right?" Mandi asked softly. She was still playing with the lens cap.

"That's right," Larissa said. "It's a tribute. No one at the memorial will want to relive the events of last Tuesday. They will want to remember their friends and loved ones in the best possible way. We're going to help with that."

"We have an agenda, then," Joe said, as if an agenda were bad.

"A necessary bias," Larissa said. "Are we ready to start planning?"

"Can we do a documentary of the shootings, too?" Hannah asked.

Larissa leaned on her desk and crossed her arms. She hated saying *no* more than once. Repeatedly saying *no* was one of the few things she hated about teaching high school.

Before Larissa had a chance to repeat her arguments, Hannah bulldozed forward. "Honestly, Miz Johanssen, we have enough stuff for an entire Ken Burns special."

"And I have already interviewed enough people to fill a book," Joe said.

Larissa frowned at him. His words echoed. But she couldn't dwell on them—not yet.

Half the students in the room weren't saying anything. Most were looking at their hands. Larissa could sense their discomfort with the entire topic.

"All right," Larissa said slowly, "let's talk about this for a minute."

"Good," Hannah said, "because I was thinking we could start with, like, the other shootings from other schools, kind of as background and—"

"No," Larissa said. "I didn't mean talk about the details. I meant let's talk about the wisdom of doing the project at all."

"You already said it," Dave said, glancing at Hannah as if he didn't want to steal her argument, but knew he could debate better. "You said that big stories get covered whether the people in them want them covered or not."

She had said that, in class, dozens of times.

"This story is being covered," Larissa said.

"And one day, we'll be surfing and we'll see some dumb documentary with news footage on the History Channel," Dave said.

Larissa frowned. Tomasina's voice suddenly reverberated in her head: *You don't want Jane Sloane to write one of those insta-books on your home, do you, because you know it'll be tacky and horrible and put everyone, even the survivors, in the worst possible light.*

"I'd like to hear from some of the students who haven't spoken about this topic," Larissa said. "Tofee?"

Tofee looked up, clearly surprised she had called on him. He shook his head slightly as if he wanted her to call on someone else. But she continued to look at him.

He shot a worried glance at Joe, then squared his thin shoulders. "Isn't this—I don't know—exploitation or something?"

"Which?" Joe said. "Some happy feely obituary documentary, or covering the real news event from the point of view of those involved?"

Tofee swallowed. The entire group of students stared at the two down front. Larissa couldn't remember ever seeing those two boys disagree.

"The documentary that Hannah wants to make," Tofee said.

"They made movies about 9/11 almost right away. They made a movie about that plane that went down in Pennsylvania, like, the next year." Hannah's voice was rising. She had clearly expected these arguments.

"If you want to work in Hollywood, then go," Mandi snapped.

Larissa raised her eyebrows. Mandi never snapped at anyone. Usually she remained quiet.

"I don't want fighting," Larissa said. "I want a discussion. Clearly this idea is making some people uncomfortable. Let's hear why."

"Because they hate video because they're not pretty enough to be on it," Hannah whispered loudly to Drew. He grinned.

Clear revenge for the *vapid mouthpieces* nicknames.

"No," Tofee said before Larissa could admonish Hannah. "Because I actually care about those people who died. I don't want to hurt anyone worse. And making this—God, how come you're such a fucking ghoul?"

Hannah raised her hands as if he'd hit her.

"All right," Larissa said. "That's enough from both of you."

Hannah kept glaring at Tofee. Tofee shoved his chair sideways so that he couldn't see Joe. Joe was staring at Tofee as if Tofee had turned into someone else.

"I'm going to take the documentary off the table for now," Larissa said.

"Man!" Dave said and leaned back so hard his chair slammed into the wall. "Un-fucking-fair."

"And if there's one more curse word in this classroom, everyone who swore will be removed from the staff, is that clear?" Larissa's own voice rose. She made herself take a deep breath. She almost never had trouble with her student staff.

The kids stopped looking at each other. Some slipped down in their chairs as if they were trying to avoid meeting her gaze. Others bowed their heads. Hannah grabbed her compact mirror and checked her makeup as if she were completely unconcerned.

"The fact that this is such a volatile issue in this room makes it impossible to work on right now," Larissa said. "If we can't agree, then imagine how the other students and their parents will feel?"

"I don't think an obituary documentary is a real tribute," Joe said.

"What do you want to do?" Kaitlyn asked. "Make some kind of weird commentary?"

This was getting to personal, and despite Larissa's attempts at keeping the students calm, nothing seemed to work. Even Kaitlyn, the normal peacemaker, had stopped being nice.

"No," Joe said. "But we're not just some statistic here. A lot of kids were really courageous, and a lot of stories got missed by the mainstream media because they only asked the kids who got named or pushed themselves in front of the cameras. I mean, jeez, Kaitlyn, did anyone talk to you? You probably saved Drew's life."

Kaitlyn swallowed hard, and Larissa realized she was probably close to tears.

"I said no to interviews," she said softly.

"Jesu—." Drew cut himself off before he swore. "I made sure I told everyone what you did. God, Kaitlyn, you were brilliant in there."

Kaitlyn looked down. She hunched her shoulders forward.

"It's okay," Larissa said. "You don't have to participate in the media frenzy. None of us do—"

"I didn't talk to anyone because they'd film me!" Kaitlyn looked up. Tears streaked her face. "They'd say, 'Handicapped student Kaitlyn Brandt ripped off her shirt to save star athlete Drew Ashanti.' They'd make me sound like a special needs kid who happened to strip in front of the entire class. That's why."

Larissa felt the color fade from her own face. All of the students looked at Kaitlyn now, all except Tofee, who was glaring at Larissa.

"See?" he said. "Exploitation."

"No," Joe said. "That's them. None of us would treat you that way, Kait. You know it. We all think you're damn amazing."

Jessi took some Kleenex from her purse and handed the entire pocket pack to Kaitlyn. "It's okay," she said so softly that Larissa almost didn't hear her. "I lost it in math today."

"I'm not losing it." Kaitlyn took the pocket pack anyway. "They already pity us. Haven't you listened to the damn news? We're some backwoods school, definitely not Columbine where rich kids go, but a place in the good old Midwest where good old families struggle on dying farms and send their kids to inferior schools. What would they think if they saw me? You're a hero, Drew. You tried to stop him and you got hurt doing it. You look like a hero. You're what they want, not me. Me, I'd be the crippled kid who was so pathetic the only way she could get noticed was to bandage the hero's hand."

"Kaitlyn," Larissa said, not knowing how she'd follow up.

"It's true," Mandi said. "They showed footage of the most broken-up kids outside, not even the ones who saw anything."

"Everyone's traumatized," Ryan said. "Whether they saw it or not. C'mon, Mand, we all lost friends."

"No kidding," Dave said.

"And a tribute is good enough," Kaitlyn said. "They deserve a tribute."

"What about the rest of us?" Joe asked. "Don't we deserve to tell the story our way?"

"Maybe," Larissa said as loudly as she could, partly to shut down the debate. "But not this week."

Moans again from some. But others crossed their arms and continued to look away.

"I'm going to think about all of your arguments. Hannah, hang onto your footage. Don't do anymore work with it right now, but put it on a disk for me. I want to look at it. I want to look at everything you all worked on this weekend."

"You won't sell it to CNN, will you?" Kaitlyn asked, and in her voice, Larissa heard a very real fear.

"No," Larissa said. "My old colleagues have been calling me, and I haven't answered. I'm part of the community here. I'm not going to mouth off just to get some air time. But Joe's right. The best way to control a story is to tell it yourself. I taught all of you that. I want to think about it now."

"I don't want to be part of a stupid documentary!" Kaitlyn said.

"You don't have to be," Larissa said. "And we may never tell this part of the story. Ever. Right now emotions are too high. Let's work on the obituaries. That's going to be hard enough."

"It's not news," Joe said. Hannah was nodding. Two weeks ago, Larissa would never have thought that the both of them would be on the same side of any argument.

"It is news," Larissa said. "It's important news. Maybe the most important news of all."

"Yeah, right." Hannah snapped her compact closed.

"*The New York Times* won a Pulitzer prize for the obituaries it ran after 9/11," Larissa said. "It took weeks, but the staff tracked down the family of every person who died in the World Trade Center and wrote a compassionate, realistic view of that person. We didn't just hear about a handful. Every newspaper in the country ran those obituaries. Everyone who chose to got to know the people who died that day just because they showed up to work."

Joe pushed his new glasses up his nose. Hannah bit her bottom lip. Drew rubbed his hand over his cast.

"Well, we lost friends last week just because they came to school. We do them a disservice if we say that the obituaries themselves aren't news. They're the center of the story. Not Leif. Leif can't be the star of this drama like Dylan Klebold and Eric Harris were at Columbine. Y'all know their names, right? Do you know the names of anyone who died that day? Or the people who tried to stop those guys?"

Dave's cheeks were red. Jessi had closed her eyes, but her lashes were dotted with tears. Kaitlyn had her arms wrapped around her misshapen torso, the Kleenex pack clutched in her right hand.

"Can we get the obituaries in national newspapers?" Ryan asked.

"Maybe," Larissa said. "But probably not. We're a little late getting started. But there's a good chance if we do an excellent job on the documentary we'll get some airplay—and that'll be the same kind of thing."

"I'm not sure I can do it." Mandi put her lens cap on the desk, then took the camera from around her neck. Her hands were shaking.

"You don't have to if you don't want to," Larissa said. "None of this is mandatory. Principle Meiers and I agreed that anyone can back out at any time."

Silence filled the room. Everyone looked at Larissa, as if expecting her to quiz them on whether or not they wanted their assignments.

But she wasn't going to. If someone wanted to back down, he could. But she wouldn't make it easy.

She almost smiled at herself. She wasn't the anti-coach. She was the anti-Grandma, hoping her students would face what had happened to them, instead of forget it the way her grandmother had urged her to.

"What are the assignments, exactly?" Ryan asked, his voice breaking painfully. He cleared his throat, then asked the question again, and his voice cracked in the exact same spot.

Larissa took a deep breath. Then she went to her desk where she had written down the names of everyone who died. She grabbed the slip of paper.

"I want teams working on each name. You'll all have more than one name, I'm afraid, and that's if everybody participates. I don't want any of you to write about your friends."

"Why not?" Jessi leaned forward.

"Normally," Larissa said as gently as she could, "obituaries are written by people who don't know the deceased. You get interesting and valid perspectives that way. We don't have that luxury. We all had at least a nodding acquaintance with those who died. But not everyone knew everyone else well. So I want to get as close to real reporting as I can. You'll be surprised what the families and friends will tell you if they think you do not have an agenda."

"I thought we had one. I thought we had to be nice," Joe said, looking down. He still seemed disappointed about the other documentary.

"Yes, you do. That's another reason to go this route. Not everyone who died was a saint. We won't say that, but it'll be easier if some of us who write the pieces never know the dark side of our subject."

"I don't know how to do this," Dave said.

"I have the 9/11 obituaries," Larissa said.

"You kept them?" Jessi asked, as if Larissa had done something horrible.

"I downloaded them yesterday," Larissa said. "I'll leave them in the room for everyone to look at."

"We can just download them ourselves," Joe said.

"You can, but it'll be expensive. You have to pay to access *The Times'* archive."

Even though Larissa didn't. For the first time, she traded on her status as an employee on leave to download that material. She had a hunch that would bring another phone call from her former editors there.

"Okay," Hannah said. "How do we do this? Do we pick teams?"

"The teams will pick themselves." Larissa braced her sheet of paper against a yellow legal pad, then grabbed a pen. "I'm going to read a name. I want to know who was close to that person, if any of you were. Just raise your hand."

"What if we don't want to do this at all?" Mandi asked.

"Then you're free to go," Larissa said.

Mandi put the lens cap on her camera. She grabbed her coat.

"How're we going to do this without Mandi?" Kaitlyn asked, her voice still thick with tears. "She's our photographer. She knows the best shots to use."

"I'm not video," Mandi said, even though she had often been behind the camera or helping Larissa with the editing.

"Maybe she could edit," Ryan said. "She could, you know, help with the visuals."

Mandi froze with her coat half on and half off.

"If she doesn't want to participate," Larissa repeated, "she doesn't have to."

But Mandi didn't move. After a moment, she sighed and shrugged the coat off.

"I don't want to write any of it," she said. "But I'll edit."

"Then you'll have to see all of it," Joe said.

"Yeah," Mandi said. "But I don't have to think about it."

"You will, though," Drew said.

Mandi shook her head. "Images aren't real. They're pixels. I can handle pixels."

Larissa wasn't so sure. "Don't let them pressure you. Make the choice that's best for you."

Mandi bit her lower lip so hard that Larissa could see a drop of blood welling. "I can quit any time, right?"

"Yes," Larissa said.

But Dave spoke over her. "It might be hard if you're leaving on Friday. None of us have your skills."

"Any time," Mandi repeated, never taking her gaze off Larissa.

"Any time. Including Saturday afternoon, if you have to."

Mandi nodded. "Then I'm staying."

There was a small round of applause, led by Drew, who banged his good hand against his desktop.

"It's going to be hard for all of us," Tofee said.

"I guess." Mandi sat down.

And feeling the undercurrents of stress float through the room, Larissa silently agreed. It would be a hard week for all of them.

She only hoped they would all make it to Saturday with their sanity intact.

nine

hile the students read some of the 9/11 obituaries and planned how they would research theirs, Larissa wrote a note to the parents. She wanted each parent to know that the students didn't have to do this work, and if the parent worried that the student might be harmed by it, the parent could pull the student from the task.

She left a line for the parents to sign and was tempted to have the parents call her as well. But she had to trust her students a little bit. If things got too overwhelming, she would pull them from the job, whether they liked it or not.

The meeting broke up around five. Some of the teams remained, talking and worrying. She wanted them to get photographs from the families and maybe a video record. That would be hard in the few short days they had. But everyone seemed ready to try.

And, as she expected, none of the teams were predictable. Usually the broadcast students worked together and the print students worked together. Here there was a mix—and to her surprise, it was often one popular student with one not-so-popular student.

She doubted Jessi Carter had ever said more than a few sentences to Ryan Cogsworth, and yet they teamed up on a student neither of them remembered seeing, probably because he wasn't in college prep. His class list was minimal, and Larissa suspected his attendance probably had been as well.

All of the pairs worked that way. And the more enthusiastic students, like Joe and Dave, took two names instead of just one.

Larissa waited until five-thirty before asking the last of the students to leave. Then she shut off the lights and locked all the doors in her room. For a moment, she leaned against her desk, feeling an exhaustion that seemed to come with the February twilight.

She had had a plan to deal with the stress on Saturday, but she hadn't planned for today—an amazing oversight, if she actually considered it. Because, while Saturday was her first day in the school since the shootings, today was her first day back, dealing with the complex emotions—not just hers, but everyone else's as well.

Now that her students were gone for the day, she wasn't sure how to deal with everything she'd felt, the empty desks, and the questions this last group had brought up.

The very things Dave had spit back at her, the things he'd said about controlling the story.

The things that Tomasina had implied in her phone message.

You don't want Jane Sloane to write one of those insta-books on your home, do you, because you know it'll be tacky and horrible and put everyone, even the survivors, in the worst possible light.

Where did truth end and exploitation begin? She honestly didn't know the answer to that. It had seemed clear-cut when she'd been on-air. Exploitation was excessive coverage of non-newsworthy events. Covering student reactions to a school shooting—even seeing how those students coped in the few days following the shooting—was news.

Continuing to cover those students, their loves and their grades and their day-to-day existence, long after the shootings were over, was exploitation.

Most celebrity coverage was exploitation.

People in the news would have to expect a momentary (and sometimes permanent) loss of privacy. But when that news story went beyond the actual need to know and into other matters that didn't relate to the story itself, then exploitation had begun.

She would have said, back then, that she never exploited. That she vigilantly guarded against exploitation.

But after this week, seeing how it had felt just to drive into school this morning, dealing with the phone messages and the requests for interviews, she wondered if her old reporter's definitions were wrong.

She used to come in, get the "truth," and leave. Then she would move to the next story, not as an impartial observer, as she had once thought, but as an outsider.

In last week's chaos, who would have told her that Kaitlyn Brandt was one of the best students in the school? That Kaitlyn had more friends than even the most popular students, and those friends came from all spectrums?

No one would have thought to ask the questions, and no one would have volunteered the information. Traumatized students were dealing with their own reactions, as were terrified teachers. The administration was busy handling the death of one of its own, as well as how to function in the future.

No one would have thought to guard the kids against the story of the day—the rush-in, rush-out, shorthand form of journalism that reduced everyone to a simple one-sentence description and a thirty-second sound bite.

Larissa grabbed her briefcase and put the assignment lists in it. She hadn't passed out the papers. She wondered when she would. If she would.

The world had divided itself into a Before and an After, and she felt like she had in the days after 9/11, like she wasn't going to be able to cross the divide—at least not all the way.

That year, she had started her master's degree. She didn't think of herself as a journalist the day the towers fell, but she had remembered how it felt to live in New York. She could picture the neighborhoods; she knew the names of all the buildings around World Trade.

She had cried for three days as she watched the coverage.

She hadn't cried at all when she watched the coverage from Manatowa High.

Her hands paused over the briefcase for a moment. The difference was pretty simple. On 9/11, she had cried because she could. She wasn't covering the story. Tears were a luxury, one she could indulge in for the first time during a national crisis in her adult lifetime.

But the shootings here weren't a national crisis—although they were part of a national epidemic. They were a local story. A personal story.

At heart, they weren't a story at all.

The shootings had happened to her, even though she hadn't been physically in the building. The shootings would forever change her life.

She snapped the briefcase closed and locked it reflexively. All reporters knew that the major events they covered were life changing to the victims and survivors. Sometimes that was even part of the story.

But not often.

Or maybe not often enough.

Maybe that was where truth ended and exploitation began, when the reporter forgot she was dealing with a human being, someone who would have to go home and make dinner, someone would have to deal with three empty chairs on the first day back, someone who would never sleep soundly again.

Dave had brought up the right argument, but had twisted it the wrong way. Ryan was closer to the heart of it all.

When did a story become exploitation?

At what point did the need-to-know function as little more than a salacious interest in one's neighbor?

When did the need-to-know help others cope in a similar situation? Stories of survival often led to changes in the ways institutions handled a future crisis.

The only way stories had any impact was for them to focus on the human lives involved, as clearly and as honestly as possible.

Given the short time frame.

And the single-sentence description of a life.

In thirty-second sound bites.

Kaitlyn Brandt had made a decision: she couldn't cope with being portrayed as pathetic. She had fought her entire life against that label. She fought against it every single time a stranger met her, and in some ways she had overcompensated to the point of genius.

But she had been right. She never would have gotten fair play, just like Drew hadn't. He was perfectly cast as the square-jawed hero who had tried to step in.

But he had failed.

Did he feel guilt about that? About failing to live up to the portrayal? The image?

She ran a hand along the edge of her desk. She was shaking. She didn't know when the shaking had started.

Because maybe she had just reached the heart of her own past?

The clippings.

The thought made her shaking worse.

Her grandmother had protected her for a reason. It had had its basis in love. In no way could the reporters have seen her father as she had seen him—the man who held her hand when he walked her to the school bus stop, the man who had made her mother smile when he bought a cheap hat, the man who had winked at her over breakfast in the last week of his life.

Larissa swallowed, then wiped her palms on her shirt. She was hot and tired and stressed. She had a long week ahead. Tomorrow, after school, another funeral. Then work with the students. The work would only increase as the week progressed. She would probably have to do some of the editing on Saturday, and she would have to oversee not just the production of the documentary, but every word of the newspaper as well.

She had to remain steady. It was the only way to survive the week.

And the memories of the past weren't helping.

But she couldn't silence them.

She wished her grandmother was still here, so that they could talk about those weeks after her father had killed a dozen people in the bank, and then turned the gun on himself.

But her grandparents—all of them—were dead. Like Ric was dead. And she couldn't trust Nadia's memories of anything.

Larissa remembered so little, and yet the memories were back there, hovering, as if they were waiting to break through the wall she'd hidden them behind so many years ago.

They couldn't break through this week.

They didn't dare.

She had to stay strong.

If not for herself, then for the kids.

And in that small phrase, she heard her grandmother's voice.

Her grandmother, who had lost a daughter that day and gained three traumatized children.

Her grandmother, who used to sweep Larissa in her arms, even when Larissa grew too tall to sit in her grandmother's lap.

Her grandmother, who had died with tears in her eyes, apologizing for something she had never done.

Larissa pulled the briefcase off the desk, then walked to the door, pausing only to shut off the light.

Places didn't protect you from the past.

Places held the past.

The murders would remain here as a whispered story, long after this group of students and teachers were gone.

Was the story of her father's breakdown still whispered in New Lake National Bank? Did people cross the street to avoid the building? Or had they all forgotten, viewing it as one of those many tragedies that happened in places like this, out of control because people were out of control?

She now lived only fifty miles from New Lake, but she hadn't gone back there. Not once in all the years she'd taught at Manatowa High.

She couldn't go back now, either. She had too much to do.

But, for the first time, she wasn't grateful for the excuse to stay away. For the first time, she wanted to go to New Lake.

She wanted to examine the old tragedy so that she didn't have to focus on the new one.

Her old shrinks would have had a field day with this.

She was glad she wouldn't have to confess to them.

She was glad that she would be spending this evening alone.

ten

he first funeral that Larissa felt she had to attend was at 2 p.m. on Tuesday afternoon. She had to leave in the middle of her sophomore English literature class, and she had a hunch she wouldn't be back until final bell.

She had to go back, of course. She had to be there for her afterschool journalism students. But she also knew she wouldn't feel like going back.

The funeral was at Christ the Redeemer Church, which was two blocks down from City Hall. Christ the Redeemer had been built when City Hall was built, sometime around 1900, and it shared the same granite structure, making the church seem much more foreboding than Midwestern churches usually were.

For the first time since she got back from Hawaii, Larissa had worn a dress. It was black and fell to mid-calf. If she were being stylish or sensible, she would have worn knee-high boots, but she wanted to look solemn, and that called for nylons and simple black pumps.

She had pulled her long blond hair back and worn no makeup. Her students knew just from her clothing where she was going to go that afternoon. Some of those students were wearing black as well.

She had left her 1:30 class reading *Huckleberry Finn*. She had bought sixty copies with her sophomore classes in mind, knowing that parents would object to the language—the N-word as it was now called—and would, as usual, miss Twain's message about the necessity of tolerance.

At first she'd thought she'd skip the Twain unit, but on Sunday she had reconsidered. Twain was the perfect antidote at the moment. His language was almost too difficult for the average non-college-prep high school student, but his stories were good, and his humor appealed to teenagers who hadn't absorbed all the lessons of political correctness.

His world was far enough away from the realities of Manatowa High that reading him might feel like an escape, but close enough (alcoholic parents were common this far north) to give the book a universal appeal.

She had a note on her door for her 2 p.m. class. The note was the school-sanctioned one that the administration had passed out for teachers who planned to attend at least one funeral.

No one got docked this week for missing class. Not students, not teachers, not anyone.

The drive to Christ the Redeemer was easy. The fog remained, but it wasn't as thick as it had been earlier in the week. Now it resembled the normal heavy grayness that came with cloudy winter days.

But the lack of snow for the past week had allowed the road crews to plow as close to the pavement as they could get. Sand covered most of the ice, and driving wasn't as treacherous as it had been the day before.

She had never been inside Christ the Redeemer. She knew there was a parking lot on the City Hall side of the block, and she parked there. She pulled her black scarf around her nose and chin, then clutched her coat closed—not to keep herself warm, but in the vain hope that the reporters lingering outside wouldn't recognize her.

These reporters were ghouls. She had no other word for them. The individual funerals were stories she would never have covered—although, if she were honest, she would probably have gone to the large memorial service that was going to be held on Saturday.

But these services were private and unbelievably sad. Every local place of worship and every funeral home established a no-media zone around the exterior. Someone knew that the cameras would want footage of crying family members and good old Midwest reserve wouldn't allow for that.

Still, trucks with television station logos parked along the wide street, and several had small satellite dishes on top, signaling not just local coverage, but some national as well.

Larissa kept her head down, and hurried across the street, her inappropriate shoes sliding on the ice against the curb. Orange cones blocked the church-side of the street from television crews, and she had to identify herself to a traffic cop when he stopped her, asking how she had known the deceased.

"I'm her English teacher," Larissa said, and was surprised to hear her voice—her once-golden voice—crack.

He waved her on, and she kept her head down until she reached the stairs. They were a never-ending gauntlet of marble and poorly cleared ice. She clutched the metal railing, her leather gloves sliding on the ice-coated surface and walked up as if she had suddenly aged forty years.

An elderly gentleman in a well-worn black suit held the double doors open for her. She stamped her shoes on the rugs in the entry, startled at the hot air blowing at her from both sides.

Every building in Manatowa had some form of double entry to keep the hot air in and the cold air out, but this was one of the few that actually had heaters in its entry on this side of the interior doors.

She let her scarf fall away from her face, pulled her coat open, and then nodded at the elderly man as he opened the interior door for her.

Another elderly man stood in the entry, next to several huge floral arrangements and a photograph of Summer Hubly. It was blown up like a studio portrait, but it wasn't. It was a photograph of Summer sitting on a dock, lake water sparkling behind her, catching and matching the light in her amazing blue eyes.

Larissa felt her breath catch. The reality of the deaths was coming to her slowly—the empty desks, the names on the funeral sheet, this photograph.

Until she'd seen it, she could pretend that Summer was on an extended vacation with her family or out sick with the flu. But somehow, the lilies and the roses and the carnations brushing against Summer's beautiful, lost face, made Larissa realize she would never see the girl again.

Summer had been a promise—a sophomore girl who laughed a little too loudly and didn't always pay attention in class. More than once, Larissa had confiscated her cell phone, and only last November had called her to the journalism room for a private meeting because Summer had plagiarized her fall paper.

Larissa, believing that Summer was simply lazy, had given her a fresh assignment with the threat that the administration and her parents would find out if she downloaded her essay again. The assignment had not had anything to do with the short stories they'd been reading. Instead, Larissa had asked Summer to write one thousand words about the most beautiful place in her world.

Summer had written about that dock.

She had received an A, Larissa's silence, and the beginnings of an understanding. She hadn't plagiarized again, and she worked extra hard, asking just before Larissa left if she could sit in on the Media Relations class instead of going to her study hall.

The last thing Larissa had done before leaving for Hawaii was put in a transfer slip, so that Summer would receive study hall credit for auditing the media class.

A third elderly man pulled open the large oak doors leading into the sanctuary. The men looked official. They were probably deacons or some form of church elder. Larissa wasn't entirely sure of the various hierarchies in the different church denominations, and she wasn't about to ask.

Instead, she stepped inside and stopped, stunned at the size of the sanctuary itself.

It was almost as large as the school's auditorium, and each pew was filled with well-dressed people in black. Half the school was here. She recognized students and teachers, as well as poor Helen, who didn't dare miss a single funeral.

An entire stage faced her, with steps leading up to the pulpit, and a raised loft behind. An elaborate organ filled the space between the pulpit and what seemed to be a secondary pulpit. The wall behind the loft was covered in pipes.

Suddenly she remembered seeing an article about this place: it had the finest church organ in the northern part of the state, imported from Europe and assembled here at great expense.

On the carpeted rise just below the two pulpits was a beautiful brown casket, gleaming in the artificial light. The casket's lid was closed.

That detail alone made Larissa close her own eyes for just a moment, willing back the shock. She hadn't learned—she hadn't wanted to learn—how exactly her students had died, where the shots were fired and how many rounds they had received.

Summer, beautiful Summer, had been so damaged that her parents and the funeral home had clearly decided that closing the casket was the best decision.

"Lari," someone whispered.

Larissa went cold. She opened her eyes but didn't turn in the direction of the voice.

No one called her Lari anymore. In fact, the only people who had ever called her Lari were journalism colleagues who pretended they knew her better than they did. She always used it as a private test of assholeness. If she had had some success, and someone she had met only a few times (or had never met) called her Lari, she knew that person was overly ambitious and truly didn't care about her feelings.

Her real friends called her Larissa. Her family sometimes called her L'issa, although rarely after they had moved in with their grandparents. Nadia occasionally called her Larri, rolling the "r"s because she knew it annoyed her.

"Lari." The whisper came again.

She turned and saw a middle-aged woman who was too thin and too overdressed for a funeral. The woman wore thick makeup and had a glittery prettiness that some female news anchors coveted.

Larissa struggled for the woman's name, but couldn't remember it. They had met, but they had never worked together.

The woman patted the pew beside her. "Over here."

She held what looked like a cell phone in her left hand. But Larissa recognized it. It was a tiny video camera, one with poor resolution for video but high resolution for candid shots.

Larissa walked in that direction, catching the attention of a handful of students who had sat near the back. She didn't look at them.

Instead, she leaned into the pew, put one hand on the padded cushion, and smiled sadly as if she and the reporter were sharing a touching moment.

Then Larissa snatched the video camera out of the woman's hand.

"Hey!" the woman said a little too loudly.

Larissa removed the memory card and the battery. Then she handed the camera back.

"It's a funeral," she said. "In a church. Have some decency."

"Me?" the woman squeaked. "You just stole my memory card."

Larissa felt her cheeks heat. She hoped she had never acted so badly when she was reporting. She dropped the memory card and stepped on it. The crunch of plastic against marble was one of the best sounds she'd heard all day.

"Oh, sorry," she said quietly. She crouched, picked up the remains of the memory card, and handed it to the woman.

Then she scanned the back pews, looking for another ghoul. She thought she saw a cell phone or two slide into a pocket, but nothing more—certainly no famous faces or old colleagues.

The woman was still sputtering. She felt her pockets for another memory card, apparently not realizing that Larissa had removed the battery as well. This time, Larissa repressed a smile of satisfaction. The woman would figure out the battery was gone only after the funeral started.

Larissa went up three more rows and sat next to Drew Ashanti. He had gotten Summer as his assignment. He hadn't met her, even though she had dropped in on the Media Relations class more than once.

Summer had been the toughest one to assign. She had somehow touched the lives of everyone on the staff.

Drew had a notebook out, along with a pen. As Larissa sat beside him, she took the notebook and closed it. Then she slid the pen through the metal ring binder at the top.

"Funerals are private," she said. "You can make notes after, but you can't use any of the stories without permission. And this is not the place to ask for permission."

"I knew that much," he said. "I just wanted to note names, so I knew who to talk to."

"They'll probably be in the program," she said. "Otherwise, ask. People will remember."

He nodded, then slipped the notebook in the backpack at his feet. Up front, the organist played Mendelssohn. Odd that Mendelssohn was appropriate for both funerals and weddings.

Larissa glanced forward and saw the organist in his seat, his black robe making him look like something from *Phantom of the Opera*.

She closed her eyes and calmed herself. The encounter with that woman had stressed her. She was here to think about Summer, about all the people lost.

About the faces she would never see again.

Her father's face loomed in front of her. Startled, she opened her eyes.

"You okay, Miz Johanssen?" Drew asked.

Apparently she had made an involuntary sound.

"Yeah," she said, even though she wasn't sure it was true. "I'm fine."

eleven

*t*he service took exactly one hour. The minister invited everyone to have coffee and conversation in the basement dining area, but Larissa couldn't stomach that. The funeral had been hard enough.

She left the church in small group of people, none of whom she knew. Drew was going to go to the reception to listen to stories, although Larissa had cautioned him again not to speak to anyone for his obituary. He could save that for the following day.

A wind had come up. At first she thought it was blowing the fog around, then she realized that a minor snow squall had settled over the town. Snow, as fine as mist, pelted her forehead and her cheeks above her scarf.

Her phone rang. She had turned it off for the service, then turned it on as she left, just in case there was a problem in her class. She fished the phone out of her purse and glanced at the display. Tomasina.

She hit *Ignore* and the ringing stopped.

The police officer was gone from the curb, but the cones weren't. As she stepped into the street, the phone rang again. She was looked at the display and saw Tomasina's name. Again, she hit *Ignore*.

The road had become slick with the new snow cover, and her inappropriate shoes slid. She kept her hand around the phone, nearly losing her balance, arms waving. Then she looked over her shoulder—an old reflexive habit—and found at least one camera on her.

Several others were turned toward the other mourners.

"Fucking ghouls," she muttered to herself, deciding at that moment that she hated parts of her old profession. Maybe she should have gone to the reception with Drew to make sure he didn't accidentally slide into ghouldom. When she got back, she would advise all of her students to be cautious in the funerals—if they went at all.

Her phone rang a third time. She stepped onto the sidewalk and looked at the display. Once again, Tomasina.

This time, Larissa flipped the phone open and snapped, "What?"

"You're avoiding me," Tomasina said.

"Yeah, Tommi. I just came from a funeral." Larissa stepped under the overhanging doorway of the First National Bank building.

"I know," Tomasina said. "I can see you."

Larissa leaned forward, saw the camera still trained on her, and turned her back. "What channel is that?"

"What channel isn't it?" Tomasina said. "I've got you split-screened on three different cable networks."

"Vultures," Larissa said.

"Well, they're not the only ones."

Larissa felt herself go rigid. "What do you mean?"

"The cameras that aren't watching you are following Jane Sloane."

Larissa let out a small sigh. That was who the familiar woman had been, the one who had called her Lari.

It had been years since she'd seen Jane Sloane, and she hadn't recognized her. Sloane had lost fifty pounds and had learned how to use makeup—at least makeup for the camera. Larissa remembered seeing her on *Larry King Live*, and remembered thinking that Sloane had become a full-fledged celebrity talker—the kind who spoke with compassion about whatever event had happened, and yet somehow still managed to sound a little too interested in the details.

"Well, that explains it," Larissa said.

"Explains what?"

"Whose memory card I smashed in the church." Larissa leaned against the cold stone. "She'd been trying to surreptitiously film the funeral."

"You smashed her memory card?" Tomasina sounded amused.

"And stole the battery from her camera. She'll have to do this funeral from memory."

Tomasina cackled. "I miss you, kiddo."

Larissa would have smiled if she'd had the energy, but she felt wrung out. Her face itched from the snow pellets that had hit it, and from the dried tears. She had finally cried, just a little, but enough to make her feel the weight of all the pent-up emotion.

Tomasina was still talking. "...with Jane Sloane there, and God knows who else is going to come. You know it was inevitable. First there was Columbine—"

"It wasn't the first," Larissa said.

"Whatever." Tomasina couldn't be budged from her speech. "Then the stranger-killings, like that poor Amish school, and now with this and Virginia Tech, we're back to student murderers again. It's a trend, and all the true crime writers with too much time on their hands are going to destroy your little community."

Larissa glanced at the camera trucks. They were still parked across from the church. Several cameras were filming the church steps now, but some still focused on her.

"While you were refusing to call me back," Tomasina was saying, "Sloane got a one-point-two million dollar advance for the Manatowa story. She promises to deliver the book so that it can come out on the anniversary of the shootings. She's also saying she'll make this a national book—I'm thinking she'll talk to the same old experts on these kinds of tragedies and try to give it some relevance. I think—"

"Please, Tommi," Larissa said. "This is personal for me."

Tomasina stopped, and for a minute, Larissa thought she was done. Then she took a deep breath and Larissa cringed.

"I know, hon," Tomasina said. "I do. That's why I'm hounding you, honestly. You saw what she's going to do. She's not going to treat these people with compassion, and she's going to keep every dime of their story. You have the ability to write a better book—a book with heart, a book that shows your community—and you can donate the money back to whatever fund you want."

"Tommi—"

"Just listen." Tomasina practically screeched in her ear. "I might never get a chance to pitch this at you again. You can bring down Sloane and her ilk. You've already done a lot of the work. You *know* these people. You can deliver a book by, say, June, and we can have it out in October, if I make the right deal, and that'll take all the teeth out of Sloane's book."

"It'll only make her more aggressive." Larissa was freezing. The sharp-edged snow was circling in the growing wind. "She'll hurt people more."

"Not if she doesn't know when you're going to deliver."

"That won't work," Larissa said. "The publisher would have to promote."

Then she stopped herself. It sounded like she was actually considering this idiocy. If she wrote that book, no matter what happened to the profits, she would have to move out of Manatowa.

Then she frowned. Unless she wasn't alone. Unless the entire community helped her write the book.

"We can withhold that information until August," Tomasina was saying. "They'll still get time to promote, and it'll be too quick for Sloane to finish hers and for the publisher to get it out. Remember, she thinks of herself as some kind of artist. She said just last week that she won't 'churn out a project,' as if she's writing Shakespeare instead of true crime."

"Tommi—"

"Please, Larissa, let me finish. I—"

"No." Larissa wiped her gloved hand against her face. The snow had melted, leaving her skin wet. She was cold. "I'm still being filmed."

"I can see that. It's bizarre talking to you half a continent away and seeing you—"

"And I have no idea what kind of mics they're using. I will talk with you. I have an idea. But I have to run it through some people first."

"Time is of the essence in this, Larissa. You know that."

"I also know that in your business, time is measured geologically."

"Not for newsworthy books," Tomasina said. "If the market gets too crowded—and believe me, it will by next week—then no one will want yours, no matter how involved you are."

"Oh, I think they might," Larissa said. "And I think I have a way to control all the information as well."

Tomasina whistled. Larissa moved the phone away from her ear for just a moment, then put it back when she guessed the whistle was done.

"Can't you share a little?" Tomasina asked.

"No," Larissa said. "Not now. Behind the scenes you can line up a few people, but let them know that they'll have to donate to a Manatowa fund, too. It can't just be my money that goes. And that goes for some of your fees as well."

"Always planned to, kiddo."

Larissa didn't doubt it. Tomasina knew marketing and she knew how to take advantage of any situation that arose, but she had a good heart.

Tomasina wouldn't have proposed this idea at all if she had thought Larissa would write one of those exploitative true crime books, the kind that focused on the murderer instead of the victims.

The kind that Jane Sloane specialized in.

Jane Sloane would write a book about "understanding the criminal mind." She'd dissect everything she could find in Leif's life, and she'd find experts to say he had been crazy from the beginning, that everyone who had known him was culpable in his actions.

She specialized in those kinds of books, and in saying that her Manatowa book would be national, she was guaranteeing that she'd focus on Leif. If she focused on the community, the book would be too regional.

Larissa promised to call Tomasina within the next few days. Then she snapped her phone closed.

It started to ring almost immediately. The area code on the display was Atlanta. Probably a CNN cell.

She shut the phone off and put it in her purse. Then she stepped out of the miniscule shelter provided by the doorway.

Two reporters waited at the end of the block. Several others were crossing the street to join them.

She was trapped. She had to get to her car, and she couldn't do so without going directly toward them.

She straightened her shoulders. Everyone else in Manatowa had had to deal with the media gauntlet. Apparently it was her turn to do so now.

She had to walk slowly because of her inappropriate shoes. Her feet were blocks of ice and her calves ached from the sharp pellets of snow that had shot straight through her nylons. She'd been aware of being cold when she spoke to Tomasina, but she hadn't realized how cold she had been. She was shivering.

As she got closer to the slowly growing crowd of reporters, she tugged her scarf over her nose, as if she were a bank robber in an old western. It wasn't so much a bid not to be recognized as it was a somewhat vain hope that without much of her face, no one would put her on the air.

Still, she could see cameras trained in her direction, mics clutched in the hands of eager reporters, all of whom had removed their hats and mittens and heavy coats in an attempt to look more attractive.

She didn't recognize anyone. That, at least, was a blessing.

As she reached the crowd—which had now grown to about a dozen people—she put her head down.

"Larissa!"

"How did you know the deceased?"

She pushed her way in, saw only a sea of microphones before her, and felt people clutching at her coat.

"Tell us about Leif Soderstrom. I heard he was one of your students!"

She had to move cautiously because of her stupid shoes. They were sliding in roadside slush.

"How come you won't talk to the media?"

She used her elbows as weapons as well as the heels of her pumps. She made sure she stepped on booted feet, shoved reporters out of the way, "accidentally" knocked into cameras.

"Why did you leave the business and move here?"

It felt like she had walked into the center of the snow squall. The distance from here to City Hall seemed interminable.

"Did you lose any family members in the tragedy?"

But she had to get there. These assholes would follow her all the way to her car. She didn't want them to see the make and model, even though she was sure some of them already knew it.

"How come everyone missed the warning signs?"

"Doesn't Manatowa High have metal detectors?"

"Tell us about the funeral."

She almost stopped at that last comment. She almost turned and berated these young things—these unknown and (she hoped) unknowable reporters—about the very etiquette she had mentioned to Drew.

But she didn't. She bit back her comments. Even the most reasonable thing she could say—*For godssake, the people of this town are in mourning. Leave them alone*—would get play for the next hour or two, until someone else blundered and spoke to these idiots.

And because the press had somehow decided that she was a newsworthy figure (she was one of them, no matter how peripherally), the comment might get play for days—a former reporter who had disappeared under mysterious circumstances (never mind that she had given notice and actual reasons for quitting) lecturing newer or better or more savvy members of her old profession. *See how distraught everyone in Manatowa is? Even a reporter like Larissa Johanssen has lost her composure.*

She finally made it to City Hall. She went inside instead of going to the parking lot. She'd been in the building a few times, mostly for school board meetings, and she knew exactly where to go.

She got past building security by telling them she had been at the funeral and she was being chased by reporters. The guards at the door could see that much was true. They would help her. Everyone in town was sick of the media.

Then she slipped off her shoes—they were wet with melting snow and even more slippery than they had been outside—and ran across the marble floor.

She had thought her nylon-covered feet were already so cold that they couldn't get colder, but she was wrong. At least the stockings enabled her to move quickly.

She went around the corner and reached the elevator banks, which dated from the 1930s and had elaborate scrollwork, as well as lighted Art Deco numbers above the doors. One elevator was on the ground floor. She pushed the call button, glancing over her shoulder.

Shouting echoed from the entry. Reporters protesting, and guards insisting, and people crying her name.

The doors pinged open. She reached around them and punched one of the upper floors, but she didn't get on. Instead, she ran for the stairs, not putting on her shoes until she reached Parking Level 2.

As she crossed the concrete, her shoes clicking, she thought she had lost the reporters. Then she saw someone standing beside her car.

She cursed silently, but kept walking, hoping that whoever he was, he wouldn't call his friends to complete the story.

The garage was dark and nearly empty, and for the first time in years, she felt nervous as she walked forward. There was no guarantee that the man waiting for her was a reporter, but this was Manatowa, and except for Leif, the town had had no real crime—stranger-on-stranger crime—since the weather turned cold.

Still, she had to work hard not to appear frightened.

When she got a few yards from her car, the man stood up.

"Lissy."

Only one person ever called her that, and he used to do it to annoy her.

Gavin Quinn. She hadn't seen him since he started his hot-spots-of-the-world reporting tour.

"Shouldn't you be in the Middle East?" she asked.

He ran a hand through his hair. It was still thick and black, a perfect accent to his bony, intellectual face.

"They took me out of the field," he said.

"This isn't the field?"

"Shit, this isn't even reporting," he said.

"I agree." She grabbed her keys out of her purse. "Who sent you? Who figured you could get me to talk?"

"No one," he said. "They're all babies. No one remembers illicit affairs from twelve years ago."

"Has it been that long?" she asked. It didn't feel like it had been that long. Although, as she got close enough to touch him, she realized that his skin was weather-beaten and covered with lines that hadn't been there before.

And he was too thin. Scary thin. The kind of thin a reporter who only ran on coffee, cigarettes, and booze cultivated.

"I'm here," he said, "because this is what they consider pasture."

"Mm-hm." She let her skepticism fill her voice.

He held out his hands. "No hidden cameras, no microphones. Just me and you, babe. I figure you could use a drink after all that."

"I could," she said, "but I can't stay."

"School's out," he said. "My watch tells me classes ended fifteen minutes ago."

He knew she was teaching, then. Probably the entire nation knew she was teaching now. She hadn't watched enough of the recent coverage to know what the talking heads were nattering about. Apparently some of them had been nattering about her.

"I have some things to do," she said and walked around to the driver's side.

"Don't blow me off," he said. "I come as a friend."

"I used to use that trick, too," she said as she unlocked her car door.

"I mean it." He ran his hand through that thick hair again. "You know why they pulled me off?"

"No. What'd you do, file a story without running it through the U.S. Military first?"

"Oooh," he said. "Sarcasm."

She nodded. "I've been watching how well embedding works. You guys are all compromised."

"Yeah," he said. "But that's not why I got sidelined."

"I truly do have something to do," she said.

"I got sidelined," he said as if she hadn't spoken, "because I had a meltdown. Off camera, but serious enough to scare the entire production team."

"Talk to me when you've had several," she said.

"I am."

She looked at him over the roof of her car. There were shadows under his eyes, and the lines around his mouth weren't laugh lines. They made his face seem very sad.

"Time to get out of the biz," she said.

"And teach high school?"

"Hell, no," she said. "Write a book. Become a talking head. Stay in the studio. Look what it did for Wolf Blitzer."

"It turned him into a bad reporter."

"But a marketable commodity." She pulled her door open. "I'm sorry, Gavin. I do have to go."

"Can I see you privately? Maybe dinner tonight? Maybe later in the week?"

She leaned against the car. Did he truly believe now would be a good time to solicit her help? Was he that self-involved?

And what did she really owe him, for old times' sake? Their affair hadn't been illicit, like he had said, but it had been ill-advised. They were working on the same stories, and they compromised a bit too much—sharing information that they shouldn't have, considering that they had worked for rival networks.

"It's not much to ask, Lissy," he said.

But it was. He had left her without notice, heading to Bosnia. He'd ended their affair by e-mail, two days after he had witnessed her first breakdown.

"This week," she said, "I have another memorial service, and classes to teach. Right now, I have to go back and pretend I'm okay for the twenty or so students who are working on an afterschool project. I don't get time to myself. And even if I wanted to risk a dinner with you—a dinner that's probably going to be about my reaction to the shootings, a dinner that could very well show up in print somewhere without my name but with my words attributed to an unnamed source—I don't have the emotional stamina. I'm sorry you broke, Gavin. I'm sure whoever sent you here has a first-class health insurance policy. Use it to hire the best shrink in Manhattan. That'll help you more than I can."

Spoken aloud, the words sounded crueler than they had in her head. And she wasn't sure she had spoken them because she didn't have the mental energy to help him or because he had left her when her breakdowns began.

"L'iss," he said and reached for her.

She shook her head, and got into the car. She slammed the door so hard that the entire chassis shook.

He stepped away. As the automatic lights came on, she could see his hands, spread open, revealing that he had no small camera, no small microphone, and no notebook.

Or maybe he was just pleading with her, showing her that he could be open.

"I'm sorry," she whispered.

Then she put the car into gear and swung around him as she drove out of the parking garage.

Not every reporter broke. Some, overwhelmed with the relentless displays of destroyed humanity, moved to another kind of reporting, usually moving "up" to covering Congress or the White House beat. Some became producers and stayed out of the field.

Others got so cold that a starving child, begging for help, couldn't move them.

A few got surprised by the remnants of their own humanity. She'd heard it most often during Katrina. How many big-name reporters had she heard express shock that such poverty existed in America?

You expect it in the Third World, said one well-known anchor. *But not here.*

As if people in the Third World were expendable.

As if they didn't matter at all, but Americans did.

125

Gavin had said he would never be like that. He had vowed his heart would never close. His stories had always had a human center. No matter where he went, he looked for the impact of the event he covered on the poor and the downtrodden, the ones other reporters often ignored.

His work was good too—two Peabodies, an Emmy for reporting, and one Pulitzer for a print series he did for the *LA Times* when the big networks wouldn't let him run the story with video.

Maybe she had been too harsh with him. Maybe she should have given him some time.

Maybe he had left her when she had broken down because he didn't want to look at his future, because he didn't want to know where the open-heart version of reporting led.

But she kept driving to the school.

She hadn't lied to him. She had no room for him or his problems this week, even if she believed he wouldn't use her remarks in a future story.

She had her students—her remaining students—and she had the new problem of Jane Sloane.

And she had the clippings, itching at the back of her brain.

She didn't need one more thing. And, as she pulled into the teacher's parking lot at Manatowa High, she resolutely put Gavin Quinn out of her mind.

twelve

arissa arrived back in her classroom to find Mandi alone in the computer area. She had given Mandi the key so the girl would have extra
time to work if she needed it. Mandi was editing footage together and
wiping away tears.

Larissa had planned to grab the pair of jeans she kept in her drawer
and change into them. Instead, she went into the computer area without
removing her coat, banging the door loudly as she entered so that she
wouldn't startle Mandi too badly.

Mandi bent her head and rubbed her thumb and forefinger under
her eyes, so that Larissa wouldn't see that she'd been crying. It was the action of someone who had made that movement countless times before,
and the very smoothness of it broke Larissa's heart.

She walked behind Mandi and peered at the screen. A toddler sat on
the back of a horse on a dirt road that ran through a field of corn. His
parents stood on either side of the horse, holding the little farmer in place.

Larissa couldn't tell who he was just by the photo of the parents.
They weren't young, but they had a Norwegian solidity that was common to the area. The father had a buzz cut that suggested he might have
been in the First Gulf War, and the mother had settled into her baby
weight. Both had red faces from the heat or possible sunburns, and both
looked so proud of that child they could burst.

"Who's that?" Larissa asked softly.

"Alvin Kjos," Mandi said, pronouncing the name correctly—Keyos—which Larissa hadn't done when she'd first had him as a student.

He had grown from a chubby cherub in bib overalls into a slight boy who rarely spoke in class. She'd always had the sense that he was brighter than his work suggested. He'd gotten straight Cs without, so far as she could tell, opening a single book.

"Were you friends?" Larissa asked gently.

"No." Mandi's voice sounded thick. "I didn't know him at all."

Larissa knew better than to ask why Mandi had been crying. Mandi hadn't wanted her to see the tears, and Larissa wouldn't comment on them until Mandi did.

"But look at that," Mandi said. "They didn't know. None of them. That afternoon when they put him on that horse. They had no idea he'd be dead in fifteen years."

Shot. Murdered in his own school.

The unspoken words hung between them. Larissa didn't know how to comfort Mandi, or if comfort was what Mandi even wanted.

"I'm amazed you got this so quickly," Larissa said.

Mandi didn't seem to mind the change of subject. "The parents brought in a pile when they heard about the obituaries. Not just the Kjoses, but some of the other parents as well. I had to make them label the pictures."

She turned now, looking up at Larissa.

"They were grateful," she said, as if the parents' reaction surprised her.

"I know," Larissa said. What else could they be? Angry, she supposed, at one of the students who lived. But so far, her reporters had been spared that. She supposed someone would suffer it. She hoped it was someone with enough spine to survive it.

She put her hand on Mandi's shoulder. Through the thin sweatshirt that Mandi wore, she could feel Mandi's bra strap cutting a grove into her skin.

"If you want to take a break, get some lunch or something, I'll scan some of the pictures in," Larissa said.

"Kaitlyn's bringing me a burger," Mandi said. "But thanks."

Larissa squeezed Mandi's shoulder, then let go. "I'm going to change, then."

Mandi nodded, already cropping the shot so that part of the field disappeared, leaving only the smiling child, his parents, and the horse, glowing under a perfect ray of long-lost sunshine.

Larissa grabbed her jeans, her extra tennis shoes, and a pair of thick winter socks she'd brought at the first snow, then headed toward the ladies' room.

She was alone there. She checked the mirror as she came in. Her cheeks were ice-cube red, and she hoped that was temporary—that she hadn't been in the storm too long. Her hair hung limply around her face, and the shadows under her eyes made her look as tired as she felt.

She went into a stall, removed her pumps and stared at them. The heels and soles were coated in dried salt water. She'd have to clean them before the big memorial service. Then she removed her skirt and the nylons, and slipped the socks over her frozen feet.

The material against her skin warmed her, and that set off a spasm of shaking.

Teaching school was supposed to be easier than reporting. She had planned on emotional involvement, but she had thought it would be affection for some students, exasperation for others, a struggle for the handful who had promise or who needed extra help to achieve their dreams.

She hadn't expected this.

And oddly, she couldn't retreat to the place she had once lived, inside an icy shell that had kept everyone else at bay, even when she had been cracking apart.

She waited until the shaking stopped, then she went back to the classroom. Through the glass partition, she could see Kaitlyn and Mandi sharing burgers on a table far from the computers. Two chocolate shakes dripped onto folded bags and four jumbo-size french fries littered the rest of the eating area.

The girls were deep in discussion—they didn't even see her—and she slipped out again, not wanting to disturb them. Mandi had needed someone to talk to, and better that she talk to one of her close friends than a teacher whom she probably thought wouldn't understand.

Larissa hurried down the hall. Her feet were thawing, giving her the strange sensation of half-chill/half-fabric as they moved inside her shoes. She didn't see any other students. One of the janitors—a man whose name she didn't know (and that made her feel guilty, just like the dead security guard made her feel guilty; how could she go through day after day waving at people and not bothering to learn their names?)—was mopping the floor outside the biology lab. He looked up, visibly shaken, as she passed.

Right now, she preferred the school empty. It seemed safer. It wasn't that she feared her students—she didn't—and she didn't think she was in any kind of physical danger. But she could feel the repressed emotions, the terror that lurked behind each glance, the sadness in each unfinished smile. She felt as if she were standing near a creaking dam, waiting for the cracks to blossom into full-fledged leaks before it burst open and emotion drowned them all.

The light was still on in the principal's office, but that didn't mean Helen had returned yet from the funeral. Larissa peeked through the door, and saw Doris Kiernig at her desk, sorting through a stack of letters.

"Is Helen in?" Larissa asked.

"Just got back." Doris glanced at the window between the offices and clearly noted the closed blinds. "I'm not sure she wants to see anyone."

Larissa nodded. She understood that. Part of her wanted to go back to her nice safe house and not emerge until June.

Doris used the phone as an intercom to let Helen know Larissa was there. Then Doris nodded, and Larissa stepped past the desk.

The door wasn't closed tightly. Helen was sitting behind her desk, pulling off her winter boots. A pair of tennis shoes waited. Her own dress shoes stood beneath an umbrella stand near the rod that controlled the blinds.

"They get harder," Helen said.

For a moment, Larissa thought she meant the boots. Then she realized that Helen was talking about the funerals.

"I had convinced myself that they'd be easier by the end of the week, that I'd be used to them." Helen managed to get the left boot off. Her nylon stockings had a run on the side. She stuck a finger through it and moved it away from her toes.

"I'm not sure you can get used to death," Larissa said.

"Some people do." Helen struggled with the other boot. It didn't seem to want to come off. "Coroners. Doctors, I'll wager. Soldiers. Policemen."

Larissa didn't say anything. The soldiers she had covered for various post-duty stories she had done over the years always seemed traumatized by death. Some of them had been stoic about it, but many of them had cried when she mentioned a lost friend.

She had never quite gotten used to that—particularly from the men. She was old enough to expect men to hide their emotions. When they didn't, she was always startled.

Helen got the boot off and tossed it beneath the umbrella rack. The boot hit the wall before landing next to her dress shoes, leaving a moist black welt beneath the window.

"I'll be glad when this week is over," she said.

Larissa nodded. She would be glad, too.

"You have a problem, right?" Helen said. She slipped on her tennis shoes without untying them.

"I have something I need to run by you," Larissa said.

"I gave you free run of the journalism once we figured out what they should do for the memorial service. I'm sure whatever you decide is fine." Helen rubbed her eyes. "Sometimes I wish I was a college dean, not a high school principal. It would be nice to keep some whiskey in here."

"It's not about the stories," Larissa said. "I knew that several kids were badly injured. I know that a few might need extensive care. I'm going to assume that their families don't have the coverage, right?"

Helen closed her eyes. "The school's not liable, either. I checked. We did everything possible to prevent something like this from happening. We can't plan for the kid to assassinate the guard."

"I know." Larissa kept her voice low. She wished she could wait to bring this to Helen, but she couldn't, not with Jane Sloane in town. "I'm not talking about liability."

Helen rubbed her eyes, then opened them. "Okay," she said with a sigh. "Let's not talk about mental health issues. Let's just talk physical healing. Kishi Ikeda will probably never walk again. Pippa Ohlin will need more plastic surgery than Michael Jackson. And Drew Ashanti will need four or five surgeries just to have minimal use of his hand again."

Drew hadn't said anything to Larissa about that. He hadn't mentioned the extent of his injuries and she hadn't asked.

"That's just three. The others are just as bad. Only a handful of the businesses in this town pay for their employees' health insurance. I'm expecting some kind of lawsuit, and maybe some help from the state, but these families are essentially shit out of luck."

Larissa had heard her students use that phrase, but never Helen Meiers. Helen was always proper, even when they were alone in her office.

"What if I can do something about that?" Larissa asked.

Helen sat up. "You know some wealthy Good Samaritan?"

Larissa did know some wealthy people, but none well enough to tap. She shook her head.

"My idea is unorthodox, and honestly, it's not even mine. It's my book agent's."

"They want you to write the definitive book about the Manatowa shootings." Helen closed her eyes. "I think you'd have to get approval from the school board, and even then I'm not sure how they'll feel about it, even if you give away half your money."

"You ever hear of Jane Sloane?" Larissa asked.

"I helped Pastor Erlander toss her out of the church this afternoon." Helen opened her eyes again. They were bloodshot. "I understand you destroyed her camera."

"I didn't destroy it. I just made sure she couldn't use it."

Helen nodded. "I would have thought, after that, that you'd want to stay far away from the tell-all book."

"I do," Larissa said. "And I don't want her to write it either."

"But...?" Helen said, deliberately dragging out the word.

"But I had an idea."

Helen sighed. "I don't want these kids exploited."

"I know," Larissa said. "But Jane Sloane's presence is a sign they will be, whether we want it or not. And I've read her crap. She's going to focus on Leif and all the crazy shooters who've come before him. She's going to make it seem, by the end of that book, and with every single interview she does, that it's our fault he shot up the school. That all of us missed the signs. That—"

"Maybe we did." Helen rubbed her eyes again. "Last year, four of our students committed suicide."

Larissa frowned. She wanted to continue, but she had to go with the rhythm that Helen established, not with her own. "I heard of two."

"Two others were recent graduates. I didn't know any of them."

Larissa had. She'd had the girl, Selena Jones, in her sophomore English class. There had been counselors on scene after that too.

"But I think at heart they're all the same. The suicides. Leif. He just turned his anger outward. And we should have seen it."

Larissa knew that platitudes wouldn't work here. Neither would reassurances. So she tried a fact.

"Lawyers and insurance companies have already given you a pass," Larissa said. "They said that you did everything you could. No one is going to successfully sue the school district. And, believe me, if the lawyers and insurance companies believe this couldn't have been foreseen, then it couldn't have been."

Helen gave her a tired smile. "I'm not talking about the cold numbers. I'm talking about the humanity."

"Two thousand students, Helen," Larissa said. "I teach about two hundred of them each year. So maybe I know six hundred kids in this school. Maybe. I recognize more by sight. But to know how they feel, deep down? I don't think I know that about any of them."

But she understood how Helen felt. Larissa had felt the same way when she learned Leif had been the shooter. Leif, who was going to be one of her projects when she came back.

She had waited too long.

But she wasn't sure he would have responded well. She wasn't sure if it hadn't been too late the moment he entered high school for the first time. Or when he'd gone to middle school. Or grade school.

No one could be sure of those things.

"Yeah," Helen said. "I'm just tired."

"I know," Larissa said. "And if I could wait on this proposal, I would. But I think this is important, and it's important to start now."

"Be quick," Helen said. "I'm going to get out of here tonight."

"I don't want to write a book about the shootings," Larissa said.

"Hallelujah," Helen said.

"I want the community to do it, and I'll edit. All proceeds would go to a fund for the victims and their families."

"What?" Helen stopped rubbing her eyes and looked directly at Larissa.

"I want people to tell their own story in their own words. The kids, the parents, you." She paused to gauge Helen's reaction.

Helen was frowning, but hadn't looked away.

"The book would cover the time period from before the shootings to life after. Anyone who wants to will be able to participate."

Helen took a deep breath. Then she stood, went to the small dorm fridge half hidden by a large fern and pulled out a bottle of water. She waved it at Larissa.

Larissa nodded.

Helen removed another and brought them both to the desk. As she handed Larissa hers, she said, "I've seen those books. They're always about the murderer."

"If they're written by outsiders, they are. Jane Sloane's book will be all about Leif, as will any other book by the so-called true crime writers."

"Isn't that what the public wants?"

Larissa tugged open the cap on her bottle of water. "I don't think so. The public likes tales of survival. And that's what this would be. The survivors would talk about their lives, their experiences, and how they make it through each day."

"But it will come down to Leif, you know." Helen sat heavily in her chair. "Right now, that's all the press wants to know about. How come we didn't see him disintegrating? What was wrong with his family?"

"I know," Larissa said. "Some of that is an attempt to make a story last. Some of that comes from unimaginative reporters. Most of it, though, is a couched question of survival. What they're really asking you is this: Looking at all of this in hindsight, what did you miss? What were the signs? How can we prevent another kid from going nuts and shooting up the school?"

Helen sighed. She took a long drink from her bottle of water, staring at something just past Larissa.

"There was a lot of discussion about these very things after Columbine," Larissa said.

"I know." Helen's voice was soft. "I read the literature. I wanted to know the same things. That's when we got the metal detectors. And we started urging some kids to get professional help. Parents are averse, you know, but a few listen."

Larissa nodded.

Helen looked at her. "We still missed Leif. I never would have sent a note home to his parents. I don't even remember him."

"I do," Larissa said. "He was in one of my classes. He was having trouble. I was going to talk with him when I got back from my sister's wedding."

Helen gave her a tired smile. "All those things we were going to do. Is there a place for that in your book, too?"

"It would be *our* book, and yes, I think we can have a section about hopes and failed plans. But I think the book itself could be cathartic for the community. I think we need to focus on the event."

"The event." Helen shook her head. "Can we get anymore euphemistic?"

"Whether we like it or not," Larissa said, "these shootings are going to define Manatowa High for years to come. For this group of kids, this will be the center of their high school experience. I don't like it, but it's true. The shootings will be their first and main memory, which will color everything else. And then they'll be able to think about prom or cutting class or their favorite teacher."

"I know." Helen drank some more water. "A book won't change that."

"No, it won't," Larissa said. "But it'll keep things in the open. Like you said in assembly on Monday, talking is important."

"Yeah." Helen put the half-full bottle of water against her forehead. "After the last few days, I'm wishing I hadn't said that."

Larissa didn't know how to respond. So she took a sip of her own water and waited. She had to sell Helen first. Without Helen's support, this project wouldn't exist.

"I still come back to Leif," Helen said. "He was a student here. He had an experience. I don't think we can have a book without mentioning him."

Larissa nodded. She hadn't really thought of that. "I don't feel comfortable asking his parents to write about what he did."

"Me either," Helen said. "But I don't think we can ignore him. If he hadn't snapped, we'd be having a normal school day right now."

Larissa's throat was dry, which was strange considering she'd just had a large sip of water. The top of her head felt like it could float away.

She heard herself say, "I could write that part."

Helen was frowning.

Larissa took a deep breath, and she thought about her statement. Part of her—the subconscious part—really wanted to examine what happened to Leif. Another part was terrified of it.

She recognized the feeling from her last days in the field. Some interviews became more difficult than others.

But they'd turned out better than others.

"I'm the only one with the training," she said, this time from a more centered place. "I know how to interview all kinds of people. I'll talk to his family and the kids who knew him. I'll write this up as interviews, without my interpretations. It might not explain anything, but it will give us his side of the story—and I can guarantee that it would not be the focus of the book."

Helen sighed. Then she finished her bottle of water, put the cap on, and tossed the whole thing at a recycling bin across the room. The plastic bottle landed on top of a pile of others and bounced once before coming to rest.

"You said we could make money," she said. "What exactly are we talking about?"

"At least one-point-two million dollars," Larissa said.

Helen's mouth opened. Then she let out a little laugh. It was a shocked laugh, a laugh of disbelief.

"At least…? Where did you come up with that number?"

"I didn't," Larissa said. "It's the number Jane Sloane got for her book on Manatowa High. I figure we'll get at least that, maybe more, just on the advance. I won't sign a deal without the publishing house contributing some of its profits, and I know my agent will wave part of her commission. If we put something at the end of the book—some kind of appeal for funds—we might make even more."

"At least…." Helen muttered. She got up again and went back to the refrigerator, taking out another bottle of water. This time, she didn't offer Larissa one. "You're sure?"

"I'm positive," Larissa said. "Why give an outsider so much money when we have the real story? Hm? And I have credentials so that we won't seem like some fly-by-night idea. They know they'll get quality."

"God," Helen said, sinking into her chair, "we'd have to set up a foundation, and get lawyers involved, and—"

"Yes," Larissa said, "but you're getting ahead of me here. First we need permission. And we need some ground rules."

"Ground rules?" Helen asked. "You mean like no one talks to the likes of Jane Sloane."

"Actually, no. That'll tip her off. We'll let her know we're working on a book and we'll let people talk to her."

"But won't that interfere with what we're doing?"

"No," Larissa said. "The one thing that she can't know is that the book is through a major publisher and that it'll come out before hers. The rules are simple, though: No one can show her what they've written."

"That many people can't keep a secret," Helen said.

"Then only a few of us will know who the publisher is and when the book is going to come out," Larissa said.

"Wow." Helen opened the second bottle, then closed it, then opened it again. "How fast do you need a decision on this?"

"My agent is the one who pitched it to me," Larissa said. "She says if we wait until next week, we won't get a million, no matter who we are."

"You believe her?" Helen asked.

Larissa nodded.

"I'm not even sure who should approve this," Helen said. "I mean, technically, you can do this without us."

"Technically. It's better to have school approval. Maybe even community approval."

Helen set the water bottle on top of some papers. "I'll call our lawyer. He'll have an idea. He'll probably want to talk with you."

"Stress confidentiality."

"Confidentiality, hell," Helen said. "It's the money that interests me. If we can take some of the burden off these families, then maybe I can sleep at night."

Her breath caught, as if she'd said too much.

Larissa nodded, understanding entirely. "Maybe we all can," she said.

thirteen

i t was 7:30 when Larissa finally left the school. She had already field-
ed two phone calls from the school's lawyer, and she suspected she'd
have more before the night was out.

A few cars still remained in the parking lot, all covered in snow. The
storm had grown worse. The parking lot lights revealed swirls of snow.

She brought her scarf over her face, tugged down her knit cap, and
pulled her purse to her side. She'd decided to leave her briefcase at work; she
wasn't going to grade papers. When she got home, she'd put an old movie in
the DVD player, curl up on the couch, and try to think about nothing.

The snow pelted her. This wasn't a soft flakey snow, but a wannabe
ice storm. The roads would be crusted. She was glad she didn't have to
drive far.

When she reached her car, she tried to scoop the snow off her windshield with her gloves. The snow was frozen on.

She sighed, hating this kind of storm. Just to clear her front windshield, she'd have to turn on the defrost, get her scraper, and spend ten
minutes chipping away. By then, some of the back window might be
melted, but the side windows wouldn't be.

When she was a teenager, she would scrape a small hole in the ice
over the driver's side and drive with limited visibility. Now, as someone
who'd been on the scene of too many car accidents caused by just that

kind of thinking, she would spend the time to clear the windows, even though she only had to drive a few blocks.

She had to tug to the get the driver's side door open. Ice broke in sheets and cascaded down the side, taking the snow with it. At least she wouldn't have to scrape that window.

She started the ignition, turned the front and back defrost on full bore, and grabbed her scraper. She tucked her purse under the seat, then got out and closed the door.

As she started to scrape, she heard another car door open and shut. The sound surprised her—she hadn't heard anyone drive in.

She turned around, scraper gripped tightly, and watched as a woman stepped gingerly over the icy tire tracks.

Larissa's heart was pounding. She was more on edge than she had thought. She was holding the plastic scraper like it was a weapon.

The woman was wearing a fur-trimmed coat and had on a matching Russian-style fur hat. She was walking slowly because her boots had heels so high they added six inches to her height.

"You really are a grade-A bitch, you know," the woman said, and Larissa recognized the voice.

Jane Sloane.

She didn't look as thin wrapped up in that coat as she had in the church. Her hands were gloved, but empty. Still, Larissa knew better than to rise to the bait.

"You're very unoriginal," Larissa said. "You're the second reporter who has accosted me in a parking lot today looking for a story."

"I'm not a reporter." Sloane stopped next to the car and stamped her feet.

"I forgot," Larissa said. "You're what? A TV personality? A talking head? Or, let me see, what do they call that? A commentator?"

"I'm a writer," Sloane said. "Same as you."

"I'm a teacher." Larissa started scraping the windshield hard, letting the sound of plastic against ice substitute for conversation.

"I hear you have a book deal."

Larissa didn't let her surprise show. Word traveled faster than she wanted it to.

"My agent wants me to have a book deal," she said. "I do not plan to write about the shootings."

Which was true. If she did get a deal, it would be to edit a volume and conduct an interview, not write commentary.

"I'm hearing a rumor that you have a deal already in place. Something to do with the community?"

That leak was quick. A little too quick, given that only two other people knew about her plans. Which meant that either someone had told Jane Sloane—which Larissa doubted, considering both the attorney's reaction to her and Helen's—or the rumors were true: Sloane illegally bugged her subjects' homes and offices.

"You do realize that reporters aren't allowed on school grounds," Larissa said.

"And that doesn't apply to me. I'm not a reporter. You can see my lawyer's analysis if you want."

"I'm sure the cops'll want to." Larissa set the scraper on the car's hood, then opened the door and took her cell phone out of her purse. "I'm calling them now."

"I told you," Sloane said. "You're a grade-A bitch. What do you have against me?"

"Just the way you're going to pick this community apart for your own personal gain." Larissa dialed with her thumb. The leather of her glove was wet enough to get traction on the numbers.

"And you're not? That book deal sounds pretty real."

"It's not a deal." Larissa put the phone to her ear. She listened to the rings. When the 911 dispatch answered, she said, "I'm Larissa Johanssen. I'm standing in the parking lot of Manatowa High with Jane Sloane, who is a journalist. None of those vultures are allowed on school property, and I want her to leave."

"We'll send someone," the dispatch said with a quiet anger.

"Thanks." Larissa closed her phone.

If she confronted Sloane directly about the possible bugging, she'd be confirming that there was a book. So she decided to play it differently, at least for the moment.

"I am the journalism teacher," Larissa said. "I am doing some memorials for the students who were injured and who died. But they're going to be locally produced. They're within my job description. I'm not trying to capitalize on other people's pain like you are."

"Really?" Sloane asked. "My source says differently."

"Feel free to call my agent, Tomasina Liu. Ask her if there's a book deal in place or even if there's one in the works. She'll tell you that there isn't. Call now. I'll give you the number."

Sloane's mouth twisted. "I have it."

"Good." Larissa slipped the phone in her pocket. She could see red and blue police lights through the snow.

Sloane saw them, too. "I want my battery back."

"And I want my students to still be alive," Larissa said. "And, since that's not possible, I want you to leave my town."

"That's not possible, either." Sloane waved a gloved hand and tried to pick her way back to her car.

She didn't make it. Two police cars pulled between her and Larissa. Four police officers got out.

"Which one of you is Larissa Johanssen?"

"I am," Larissa said. "And that's Jane Sloane. She's a vulture who doesn't believe the rules apply to her."

An officer came over to her. The other officers walked over to Sloane. One of them started talking to her.

"I suppose you want to file a complaint," the officer said to Larissa, with enough emphasis so that she knew *he* wanted her to file as well.

"Yes," Larissa said softly. "And I have reason to believe that she probably bugged Principal Meiers' office."

"That's a hell of a charge."

Larissa nodded. "There's been rumors about her doing crap like that for years. And she knows some things that she shouldn't."

He glanced over his shoulder. Sloane was gesturing. The other officers seemed interested in what she was saying.

"We'll check it out. We're taking her in. She's the first we've caught violating the injunction so the chief wants us to make an example."

Larissa smiled. "Call the local media."

"Oh, we've already let the locals know," he said. "They'll meet us at the station. We want this heard loud and clear. We don't need no more grief from these people. They're bad enough. Begging your pardon."

He added that last part rather hastily. He must have just remembered who she was.

"No need," Larissa said. "If I believed reporters should act the way she is, then I wouldn't have called you."

He smiled at her. "I'm going to need a statement."

"Just tell me when," Larissa said.

"Tomorrow's fine," he said. "Drop in after school. Until then, we'll use your 911 call as reason to hold her."

Larissa nodded. "What about the bugs?"

"Next on the list," he said. He reached a hand into the pocket of his heavy coat and gave her a business card. "Ask for me when you come."

Two of the other officers bundled Sloane into their police car. Larissa was too far away and the snow was too heavy to see if Sloane was handcuffed.

Larissa hoped she was.

"You gonna be okay?" he asked.

"Yeah," she said.

He touched a hand to his hat, nodded, and headed back to his car. The snow was melting off her windshields. This encounter had taken longer than she thought.

She wondered if she should call Helen and warn her about the possible bugging of her office, then changed her mind. Helen had already left. She would find out soon enough. But right now, she deserved a good dinner and some quiet time.

So did Larissa.

She cleared off the rest of the snow with her hands. Then she got inside her already warm car, and drove the few short blocks to her home.

fourteen

ednesday, the school board met in private session and approved the book idea. Announcements went up all over Manatowa, and the following night, the town council was planning to hold a special meeting about the project.

Larissa's desire for secrecy simply wasn't possible: even though the meetings were closed to the press, word got out anyway. Her phones were flooded with calls that went unanswered. She finally put a message on her voicemail saying that she had no comment now and she would have no comment in the future about anything to do with recent events.

By that, she meant not just the shooting, but also Jane Sloane's arrest. The police found tiny webcams all over the high school. The cams had limited range. Sloane or an assistant had to sit in the parking lot with a laptop to get the feeds from the cams. But her laptop had footage from the principal's office that afternoon—and it was enough to charge her with all sorts of infractions.

The story hit the national news almost immediately, making an instant celebrity out of some poor young reporter from Duluth who had friends in Manatowa and managed to get the best outraged quotes.

Sloane put up bail and hired a famous attorney, then immediately left to do the round of talk shows, defending herself while saying she couldn't comment directly on the case.

She wouldn't be in Manatowa again. The arrest had started one of those publishing scandals that seemed to reverberate through the national media: How many of Jane Sloane's previous books were based on illegally obtained information?

Larissa was willing to bet all of them were. Sloane specialized in comments and thoughts from unnamed witnesses. Those witnesses might have been Sloane herself, eavesdropping on others.

Now entertainment reporters were scrounging through Sloane's books; previous interviewees were checking their homes for bugs and tiny webcams; and the resulting scandal had caused Sloane's books—and a book by some privacy rights advocate who was expressing horror at all of this—skyrocket up the charts.

Half the calls Larissa got were about possible interviews on the Sloane case. One of the things that made it juicier to her former colleagues was that she had called 911 on Sloane. Whenever Larissa turned on the twenty-four-hour cable news channels, it seemed, she heard her own voice, speaking calmly on the 911 transcript:

I'm Larissa Johanssen. I'm standing in the parking lot of Manatowa High with Jane Sloane, who is a journalist. None of those vultures are allowed on school property, and I want her to leave.

A lot of the resulting discussion was about her and her use of the word "vultures." Some so-called reporters expressed outrage at her use of the word when she had once been a colleague. Others agreed, and every single ethics-in-the-media expert who was called onto those shows to give "a different perspective" said Larissa had a point—if the poor schlubs could get a word in edgewise.

She was happy, at least, that some of the pressure on Manatowa had eased. Yes, the Sloane story was connected to the shootings, but it was peripheral, and it didn't require reporters to spend all day in the brutal cold, hoping to get a comment from traumatized students.

Instead, the reporters camped out on Larissa's lawn. A few had tried to run into her garage when she used the garage door opener from down the block. Now she pushed the button as she pulled into the driveway.

She would ease the car into the garage and hit the button again, hoping she wouldn't trap someone inside.

The moment she did was the moment she got a restraining order against her former colleagues for whom, she still believed, the word *vulture* did apply.

Most of her students applauded her actions, although some wanted to know why she was willing to turn in another reporter.

"Isn't it the reporter's job to do everything he can to get the story?" Dave Frent had asked after school on Wednesday. He and some of the other students were working in the computer room. He was downloading video footage he had gotten from two separate sets of parents.

Mandi was leaning over her computer. Her hair was stringy and her skin bad. She had left late the night before and come in early Wednesday morning. She looked like she hadn't slept.

Hannah was also there, viewing some footage on her camcorder before handing it to Mandi. If anything, Hannah's makeup had become even more perfect these last few days. It was as if she needed to look spectacular to hide the emotions inside her.

Larissa would have to step in soon and relieve Mandi—there was simply too much material for one student to cut and assemble. But every time Larissa had suggested it, Mandi had resisted.

"It's important," she'd say. "We have to get it right."

Larissa didn't mind the implication that she would do it wrong. She knew what Mandi meant. Mandi had a vision for the documentary and Larissa didn't. Only Mandi wasn't skilled enough yet to articulate that vision and direct Larissa how to meet it. Which gave Mandi no choice but to do it herself.

Larissa hoped she'd finish before she collapsed or before her parents pulled her from the project. Larissa now had two other projects of her own—the newspaper, which had to come out on Friday, and the book proposal, which was taking way too much of her time.

"A reporter should do everything he can within the law," Larissa said. "But illegal acts in the name of the story belong in the movies, not in real life."

"Didn't Woodward and Bernstein break the law?" Joe Omart was standing near the door. Larissa hadn't heard him come in.

He had stopped wearing plaid and had gone back to his sports shirt and tie. It looked less intimidating with his new wire-rim glasses. Something had changed in his face in the last week; Larissa could get a glimpse of the man he would become.

"I mean, they were looking at classified documents, weren't they?" He crossed his arms and leaned against the door frame. "Isn't that against the law?"

Larissa couldn't remember the details of the Watergate scandal. There were so many details and so much debate about it all.

Most of the time, she just cursed Woodward and Bernstein for giving every succeeding generation of reporters the idea that *they* were the story: after all, reporters had brought down the President of the United States and had somehow convinced wannabes that reporting was easy and glamorous and had nothing to do with good, hard work.

"They didn't steal anything. Nor did they break in anywhere or put up illegal listening devices. They took information given to them and they had to verify it with two other sources or it wouldn't get into the *Post*." That much Larissa did remember. "There's a long way from what they did to what Jane Sloane did."

"No one would've caught her if you hadn't called the cops on her," Hannah said with something like admiration in her voice.

"I just wanted her to leave me alone," Larissa said. "If I'd run into her at a diner, I would have left."

"But you knew she had been listening in," Dave said as he sat down next to Mandi. "That's something."

"She knew things she shouldn't," Larissa said. "She slipped up."

"I thought reporters were supposed to be observers," Joe said. "Shouldn't you have broken the story without calling the police?"

"I'm not a reporter," Larissa said, even though the words twisted at her stomach. She was still a reporter. She just wasn't practicing her craft at the moment. "I called as a private citizen."

"I think we should cover that for the school paper," Joe said. "It's a great story."

"It is," Larissa said. "But Friday's edition is the memorial edition, and there's no room for anything else. On Monday, we'll start covering current events again, all right?"

She'd meant that statement to calm down the discussion, but it seemed to embolden it. The students started talking about where the webcams were discovered—one in the cafeteria, another in the link, still more in various quiet discussion areas, leading Dave to speculate that Sloane had an accomplice, someone who knew Manatowa High well.

Larissa sighed. Even her own students found it easier to focus on Jane Sloane than on the tragedy before them. She was about to shut them down when Mandi slammed her fists against the table.

"Would you people just shut up?" she snapped. "Ga-*ah*-d. How am I supposed to concentrate?"

Everyone looked at her in surprise. Mandi occasionally made sarcastic comments, but never yelled at the group.

"She has a point," Larissa said. "We have a lot of work to do in the next two days. Let's get to it."

Everyone returned to the stories they were working on. Larissa put a hand on Mandi's shoulder.

"Come with me," she said quietly.

Mandi shook her head. "I have to finish this."

She hadn't taken her gaze off the screen. On it was a montage of baby pictures, laughing infants in colorful clothes—one wearing a turban; another in a Santa hat.

"Save it," Larissa said, "and come with me."

Mandi leaned her head against the screen and sighed. She saved the image. Then she grabbed the thumb drive she wore on a string around her neck, pulled off the top, and saved the entire file to the drive.

She put the thumb drive back together and stood, using her free hand to put the computer to sleep.

"I'm okay," she said, as if she knew what Larissa was going to talk to her about.

She probably did. They all did. But Larissa had to. These projects were consuming her, and they were consuming her students.

"I know," Larissa said. "Let's walk anyway."

They left the journalism room, passing Ryan and Tofee coming in carrying take-out menus from various pizza places. Larissa smiled at them, but didn't stop.

She took Mandi down the hall to the link. There she pulled several dollars from her pocket and walked up to the vending machines.

Before Leif had gone on his rampage, the vending machines were what passed for controversy at Manatowa High. The state government said students were getting too fat and needed low-fat options. The legislature, in its wisdom, mandated that all vending machines on school campuses offer "healthful" alternatives. When the school district asked the vending machine operators to change what was in the machines, the operators sued each district for breach of contract.

Larissa thought of those arguments nostalgically, as if they'd happened years ago instead of just last month. She plugged four dollars into the machine, bought a PayDay and a Butterfinger.

"What do you want?" Larissa asked.

"I'm not supposed to eat that stuff," Mandi said, but Larissa couldn't tell if the self-denial came because of the old health arguments or if Mandi's parents truly didn't allow sweets.

"There's some peanuts and an apple," Larissa said. "Just pick. Whatever looks good."

Mandi gave her a sideways smile, a smile that said *it all looks good*, and then pressed the buttons for a Reese's Peanut Butter Cup and the apple.

They came out looking like a mini meal, and made Larissa feel vaguely guilty that she hadn't at least gotten one healthy item.

She got them both bottled water from the other machine, then sat with Mandi on a wooden bench across from the cafeteria.

It probably wasn't the best choice of seating areas. The students who had been sitting here that day had seen Leif go into the cafeteria. At least one—Marcus Aldridge—had recognized the guns, told a friend to call 911—one of the first calls to be received—and had followed Leif inside.

He'd tried to tackle Leif. Instead, Leif turned around and shot him six times, killing him.

Mandi rubbed the apple on her shirt before taking a bite. Larissa opened the Butterfinger. She'd save the PayDay for later.

"I appreciate all you're putting into this project," she said, "but I'm worried. It looks like it's consuming you. Your parents can't be happy."

"No one's happy right now." Mandi took a bite from the apple. She stared at the cafeteria.

Larissa wondered if Mandi had seen the same mental images she had.

"I know," Larissa said. "But I can't work you to exhaustion."

"You're not," Mandi said. "I've got to finish this."

"Let me help."

Mandi shook her head. She took another bite from the apple, then drank some of the water. She set the bottle on the window sill behind them.

Larissa tried a different tack. "Mandi, you didn't want to do this in the first place. You don't have to just because I asked."

"I'm not." She finished the apple and tossed it into a nearby garbage can. "I'm doing it because I have to."

Larissa frowned. "That's what I'm trying to tell you. You don't have to."

"I *do*." Mandi turned the Reese's over in her fingers without opening the wrapping. "It's what I can do. It's the only thing I can do."

Larissa nodded. She'd wanted her students to feel like they were doing something, but she hadn't wanted them to become obsessed with it.

"You have to rest," she said quietly. "You have to eat."

"I am," Mandi said, "and I go to class, too. But we only have until Saturday, and everyone brought so much stuff."

"We don't have to use it all."

"I'm *not*." Mandi set the Reese's down, put her hands on her knees, and turned toward Larissa. "It's just so hard, you know? It's like I'm telling these intertwined stories and they're not going to end well and you told us to be upbeat and it's so hard. I look at those faces, and I remember these guys— we were in school together forever—and I remember how Tonya Rolvaag used to come to school in the same clothes every day before they took her away from her mom and gave her to her dad, and how Milo Valvoulis gave away his only toy truck in the first grade gift exchange because he didn't want anyone to know the family didn't have any money, and how Ione Addonizio got beat up last year and they put the clip on Facebook and her dad made them take it down or he'd sue."

Larissa started. She hadn't known any of those things.

"The picture we got of Marcus is the only one that survived the house fire his folks had six years ago. His grandparents are e-mailing some from Alaska when they get home, but we might not get them in time."

Mandi bowed her head and did that little maneuver with her thumb and forefinger. She sighed again, managing to keep the sound so quiet, Larissa wouldn't have known if she weren't sitting right next to her.

"I can't think of any of the good stuff. I look at Ione holding up that debate trophy and I just remember her saying after the picture was taken how winning those trophies was going to get her into Harvard and I think she's not going to Harvard. She's not going anywhere. And you said we have to make this, y'know, not brutal, and I don't know how to do that and be true to them, you know? Because it's not just about the prom pictures and the debate trophies and the good grades. It's about the Facebook video and the house fire and all the years we knew them. And I don't know how to put that into the montage without making it a downer."

Her voice wobbled by the end. Larissa put a hand on Mandi's back and to her surprise, Mandi leaned into her. They sat, silently, for a long time.

"I've done this before," Larissa said, which was a partial lie. She'd never done a memorial montage of high school students. She'd done a few obit montages of famous people when she'd been working on the weekends and no one else could do them. But she figured that experience would help. "Let me see what you have. We can fine tune if need be."

"I told everybody they have until tomorrow to bring me stuff."

"Then let's work on it tomorrow night. Let's do a mock script."

"A script? For pictures?"

"Yeah," Larissa said. "So we're not keeping it in our heads."

"I thought you have to go to the town meeting thing," Mandi said.

Larissa almost cursed out loud. She did have to go.

"Friday, then," she said. "I'll give you a pass from some of your classes. We'll work during my free hours."

Mandi kept her head on Larissa's shoulder. She said into Larissa's sweater, "I want to direct this, you know? I want this to be what I do for them."

"You will," Larissa said. "I'm just going to tighten. It'll be your vision." Her shoulder was wet.

"If they saw it, they'd laugh," Mandi said. "They'd think it was so stupid."

"Do you think it's stupid?" Larissa asked.

Mandi shook her head. Her hair moved against Larissa's neck.

"Then they wouldn't, either. They know how hard you're working on this."

"They don't know anything," Mandi said. "They're dead."

The statement hung between them for a moment. Larissa couldn't offer another platitude. The students didn't like them—and they seemed wrong, as Mandi just pointed out.

"I miss them," Mandi whispered. "Even the people I didn't like."

Larissa smiled in spite of herself. She'd been feeling that way, only about Walter Haigen, the assistant principal. He'd been hard on her, thinking of her as a celebrity who skated through school instead of a woman who had a teaching degree.

"I know," she said softly. "Nothing prepares you for this."

"Is that why you got mad at your friend?"

It took Larissa a minute to realize that Mandi thought Jane Sloane was a friend of hers.

"I never liked Jane," Larissa said. "But I wasn't mad at her."

Mandi sat up, keeping her head down as she wiped her face with her sleeve. Then she looked at Larissa. "You sounded mad on that 911 call."

"Did I?" Larissa frowned. She remembered being calm. "She was being such an ass."

Mandi laughed at the word. "You got her."

"Not really," Larissa said. "I just made her more famous."

"And stupid. You made everyone know how stupid she is."

"I guess."

"That's why you're doing this stuff, isn't it?" Mandi asked. "You want it done right. Like you teach. You know, with ethics and stuff."

Larissa blinked. That had been her argument, but she wasn't sure she meant it. She was doing it for her guilt, for her penance. Painting the school hadn't been enough.

And she was tired of the lies. She didn't want Leif to be an anti-hero. She didn't want his name to be the one tied to Manatowa High like Dylan Klebold and Eric Harris were tied to Columbine.

She wanted her students remembered—all of them, even if they grew up poor, or had to change custodial parents, or charged into a cafeteria when they should have stayed in the hallway.

"The book sounds cool and all," Mandi said, "but I wish we could make a movie."

Larissa almost didn't hear the comment. It took a minute to filter in.

"That's what the memorial documentary is," Larissa said.

"No," Mandi said. "It's what Hannah said on Monday."

Larissa didn't remember what Hannah said on Monday. She remembered the conversation and how difficult it had been, but not all of the particulars.

"About us having enough stuff for a Ken Burns special. If we can do a book, how come we can't do a Ken Burns special?"

Because, Larissa almost said, only Ken Burns can. But that would trivialize Mandi's point.

"It's a good idea," Larissa said after a moment. "Let's consider it. We have enough on our plate at the moment, but keep your footage, all of it—and not just on the thumb drive. Back it up at home too, okay? But not on some off-site website. You don't want the press to get it."

"Like that Sloane woman."

"Exactly," Larissa said.

"You're serious? We can do this?"

"I didn't say so," Larissa said. "But I want to consider it."

Even though she had already made up her mind. The few images she'd seen were hard enough. She wouldn't be able to do a Ken Burns-style documentary. But she would encourage Mandi to.

Film schools were looking for people just like her. Even though now was not the time to tell her.

Right now was about the memorial and getting through the week.

"Ready to go back?" she asked.

Mandi nodded and stood, grabbing both her Reese's and her water. As Larissa stood, Mandi asked, "How did you do this every day?"

"Do what?"

"Write about stuff like this?"

The question was serious and heartfelt. Mandi obviously needed to know.

But she didn't need to know how sometimes it destroyed the reporter. She didn't need anymore sorrow at the moment.

"I didn't know the victims," Larissa said. "I was just like Jane Sloane. I had no clue these were real people. I was looking for the stories."

"You're not like her," Mandi said.

"Maybe not anymore," Larissa said.

"You never were," Mandi said with a vehemence that surprised Larissa. "You couldn't be."

"I like to hope not," Larissa said. "But that's the easy way."

"What's the hard way?" Mandi asked.

"Looking at those pictures," Larissa said, "and letting the tears come."

Mandi blinked, then looked down. "Why does anyone do this job?" she asked quietly.

"I think we each answer it for ourselves," Larissa said.

"Why did you?"

Larissa hesitated. She'd never entirely examined why she had become a reporter. Reporters were observers; they didn't get involved.

But they also made sure everyone knew what had happened.

At their best, they were guardians of the truth.

"Because I don't like secrets," she said.

Mandi gave her a surprised look. Larissa felt it echo in herself. She hadn't planned to say that.

"I'm not uncovering secrets," Mandi said. "I'm keeping them."

"No, you're not," Larissa said. "You're just choosing to tell the appropriate story at the appropriate time. There might be a later date to tell those other stories, the ones you told me. Just not at a memorial service."

"Or in the memorial edition of the paper."

Larissa nodded. "Or in the memorial edition."

"Wow." Mandi wiped her face with the back of hand. "There's so much to think about."

"Yeah." Larissa didn't know what to add. So many times in the last few days she'd found herself at a loss for words. That was one thing she hadn't learned as a reporter: that sometimes words were inadequate.

She didn't know if her silences hurt or helped. She didn't know if the work she was having the students do was appropriate. She had no idea if they would remember this time with horror or compassion or a real sense of healing.

The fly-in version of these stories—"investigate," report, leave—never really allowed for the feeling of loss. Nor did it show what the survivors went through day to day.

Not even the follow-ups—Columbine One Year Later—really showed how these communities, how these *people* coped. How they'd changed beyond the superficial and obvious. Or if they even realized what was different for them now—deep down.

She still didn't know how to put this all into words. Maybe because she was living through it.

Maybe because there were no words.

Her stomach twisted at the thought. There had to be words. There had to be a way to describe it all.

Or it would prove her grandmother right: the only response to a tragedy on this scale was silence.

Larissa did not believe that.

She could not believe it, even as a small part of herself wondered if it was true.

fifteen

*l*arissa arrived late to the town hall meeting. She had put the student newspaper to bed—content filed, layout complete—but she was letting the students finish the printing. She'd already signed off on the school's copy shop account, and she left the entire staff to wait while an employee printed the run. Then the students would count, wrap, and set aside papers for each homeroom.

She had told them to guard the run carefully; she didn't want any reporters to get an early edition.

Not that there was much newsworthy in this edition. The obituaries were heartfelt and did contain some material that hadn't been in the local and national papers, but they weren't earth-shattering. She figured some of the earth-shattering content would come next week, when she let the staff report on their own.

She had also been helping Mandi splice the video and photos together. Mandi's vision had been a clean one: first she had done a montage of the students' class pictures, which morphed into the baby pictures. Then she did a small photo or video presentation for each student. The students appeared alphabetically.

The adults got their own section, which began with their yearbook pictures as well. The entire piece would end with those same pictures and then fade into the words *In Memoriam*.

It was a lot of work, and Larissa wasn't sure any of it could be finished by Saturday night. But she would try.

Mandi had arranged it all brilliantly so there was no need for a voice-over, which meant that they didn't have to have an official script. After talking with Larissa the night before, Mandi had sketched her ideas onto a sheet of paper, with notations in the margins, and that would have to do.

Once Larissa understood the pattern, she was able to help with the splicing.

Mandi wanted to finish it, though. Larissa was so worried about the amount of time Mandi was spending, however, that she had spoken to Mandi's parents when they picked her up Wednesday night.

I figure it's better than brooding, Mrs. Edwards had said. *Feels like the whole town's doing that.*

There was a bit of judgment in her statement, as if there was something wrong with mourning. Larissa didn't quibble. If Mandi wasn't getting sympathy at home, then maybe working here was better.

But she would get Mandi—and her other journalism students—to talk with the counselors just the same.

The town hall meeting was being held in the largest meeting room in City Hall. The City Hall building had been finished in 1911. It was one of those sturdy stone edifices that seemed indestructible. It had marble floors and granite-colored walls, which someone once assured her had originally been a shade of industrial green. Brass railings ran at waist height and over the years, someone had installed reinforced handrails on all the stairways.

The elevators were original to the building, which was one of the first in Minnesota to have such exotic equipment. They had been revamped in the 1950s and needed another overhaul.

The entire building had been around so long that it smelled of stale cigarette smoke, even though smoking had been banned in public places for more than twenty years.

The large meeting room was on the top floor. It had windows all around. A blond wood dais covered the front, and matching blond tables stood in the back. They had been pushed against the wall to make room for hundreds of folding chairs.

The chairs were full. People sat on the tables, arms crossed, coats draped over their arms. Despite the windows, which leaked air and normally made this room cold, the room was stuffy and too warm. It was not designed for this many bodies, especially on a winter's night when the building's heat was on full.

She had to push past people just to get in the back door. She recognized a few reporters lined up against the wall. They had notebooks and tape recorders. The only video allowed came from a communal camera placed just above the door.

Once this meeting was planned, there was no way to ban reporters. The city had Sunshine Laws that dated from the post-Watergate frenzy of the late 1970s. Honesty in government could only occur under the harsh light of day—which meant that all meetings were open to the public and to the press.

Not always the best way to run a government, but certainly the best way to keep it honest.

Still, she was annoyed that the reporters were here. She had been so successful at avoiding them these last few days. She knew she'd have to register several "no comments" before she left tonight.

Mayor Werner Reng saw her and beckoned her forward. Reng used to be a junior, but he dropped the appellation immediately after his father died. Unlike most juniors, Reng had not bestowed the name on his own son, although the poor kid had gotten the Reng looks.

Those looks were heavy and bony with a strong forehead and a matching jawline. The cheeks were narrow, accenting the large blue eyes and the crooked nose. Reng stayed in shape—Larissa had originally met him on her morning runs—but that only served to accent his strong features. His brother Reinholt, a member of the city council, had gained an extra one hundred pounds over the years that had softened his face and made him seem less like a villain from a 1950s noir film and more like a man who could easily play Santa Claus at the mall.

Reinholt Reng sat at the far end of the dais. On the other end sat his ex-wife, Judith. She represented a different neighborhood and a different political party. Local rumor was that the divorce had come not because they didn't love each other, but because they had such different political views.

Werner Reng sat in the middle, with a gavel in hand. Helen Meiers sat to his right and Rosemary Kriegel, the school board president, sat on his left. The remaining members of the school board and the council were scattered in no particular order along and behind the dais.

There was not an open chair for Larissa.

One of the men in the front row stood and handed his folding chair to a school board member. The woman set the chair next to the mayor. He patted it and smiled at Larissa.

"Here she is now," he said. "Let's welcome Larissa Johanssen."

To her shock, the assembled citizens applauded her. She blushed and hurried the rest of the way to the front.

As she sat, she apologized for being late. The mayor waved her comment aside. He waited for the applause to die down before he added,

"I hope you all realize that she could have written a book all on her own and kept the money like that Sloane woman is trying to do. Miss Johanssen has the credentials and the abilities to do a solid book about the tragedy, but she's the one who came up with the idea of donating it all. I understand you have a presentation for us, Miss Johanssen?"

Larissa did, but she had expected to have a few minutes to catch her breath. Instead, she stood back up, smoothed her hair with one hand, and took the microphone that the mayor handed to her.

This was the third time she'd made the presentation. The conversation she'd had with Helen, as disorganized as it had been, had been the first time. Then she'd made a more complete version to the school board the day before. And now it was beginning to feel old hat to her—she knew which high points to hit, what to stress, and how to create interest even in folks who had none.

Her old reporting skills came in handy here; she could talk and watch the people around her at the same time.

Gavin Quinn sat in the very center of the room. He wore a bulky black turtleneck and matching black jeans, making him look less thin than he had a few nights before. But his face was still haunted. His hair was mussed, as if he'd forgotten to comb it, and he watched her intently.

She had to look away from him. She saw a row of teachers—some of them the crew she'd worked with on Saturday—and a handful of students, many from her English and journalism classes.

Pete Petrovich sat in the back row, his daughter beside him. His son leaned against one of the blond tables, arms crossed. Petrovich was watching Larissa closely too, as if trying to assess what her real motives were.

A number of people had that same look. They were seeing her as an outsider, an outsider who wanted to make trouble for Manatowa instead of solve it.

So she ad-libbed a little.

"I was born in New Lake," she said at the appropriate moment, "and graduated from New Lake High School. When I had the opportunity to come back and teach in Minnesota, I grabbed it. I've been all over the globe, and I can testify that this truly *is* God's country. Let's prove to the world that we're not some crazy place that somehow breeds dangerous children. Let's show them our true character, and use this project to take care of our own."

Some of the expressions relaxed—some of the skeptics caught and accepted the message. But a few others hardened.

A hand went up near Gavin.

"Are we ready for questions?" Larissa asked the mayor.

He nodded. Under his breath, he added, "Go ahead," as if he thought taking questions wasn't a good idea.

But wasn't that the point of a town meeting? To assess the thoughts of the town?

Several other hands went up. Larissa pointed at the one that went up first.

A heavyset woman in a lined flannel coat stood up and immediately stuck her hands in her pockets.

"I don't mean no disrespect," she said, "but where're you coming up with that number there? It seems like dreaming, one million dollars."

"The book deal that Jane Sloane got was for one-point-two million," Larissa said. "I think, and folks I've spoken to agree, that a book written by the people of Manatowa about their experiences directly would be worth more than that."

The woman nodded and sat down.

There were more questions about the money. Larissa explained how book deals worked, and that some more money might come from foreign or film rights, but there was no guarantee.

The town's attorney answered a few others, about the non-profit organization they'd have to set up as the beneficiary of the advance money. And there were quite a few questions about how survivors would get money they deserved.

No one had yet figured out that system, but the attorney and some of the other attorneys and accountants in the room had ideas.

Larissa sat down while they spoke. She caught her breath, feeling the exhaustion of the last few weeks wash over her. As far as she could see, she would be busy—and not in a way she was used to.

Yet she welcomed it. Last week, she might have said she needed the distraction, but it was more than that. She needed to feel useful.

And more than helping the students at school, this project would allow her to feel useful.

The mayor called on a man toward the back. As he stood, he looked around to make sure the mayor hadn't called on anyone else and he was mistakenly taking their place.

"This all sounds good in theory," the man said, "but Miss Johanssen, she talked about how the world would perceive us. When this book comes out, aren't they gonna perceive us as ghoulish, you know, trying to capitalize on our own local tragedy?"

The shame question. The politeness question. Her sister Nadia would call it the Minnesota Dilemma: If there's a problem, shouldn't they handle it among themselves, without talking to outsiders? Wasn't it more polite to fade into the background than to call attention to themselves, good and bad?

Some were reacting to the numbers: a million dollars seemed like a lot of money. Others to the idea of exposing themselves—and the entire community—publicly.

Larissa extended a hand for the microphone.

"Your question is a good one and it has a number of parts," she said. "First, let's talk about the money. I need some help here, from a few folks in the know."

She turned to Helen.

"We have how many injured students?"

Helen had the material before her. She'd compiled it before the school board meeting.

"We have ten injured students," Helen said as she stood. "All have serious injuries. I did some inquiries. Only one is covered completely by insurance. Seven come from families with no insurance at all. The other two have catastrophic coverage, but are looking at bills of several thousand dollars."

"Doesn't the school have to pay that?" someone shouted from the back.

"We have a limited liability," Helen said. "We'll cover some, but not life care, which a few of these students will need. And that doesn't count the mental health costs to many in the student body. Not to mention the costs to the families of the three adult victims, who, in all three cases, lost the family's sole provider."

"What's the bottom line?" the mayor asked.

"There isn't one that I can find," Helen said. "But an educated guess by the doctors involved is that care for these kids will run in excess of several million dollars. This fund for the book is just the beginning. We're going to have to raise more money than that if we, as a community, want to help them."

"At the back of the book," Larissa said, "we'll have the address of the non-profit for anyone who wants to donate. And when we do publicity about the book, we'll talk about the costs of recovery as well."

A murmur ran through the crowd. No one had thought about the publicity. She wished she hadn't mentioned it.

"The other question you're asking," she said to the man in the back before someone could ask the publicity question, "is should we expose ourselves like this? What are we saying to the world about Manatowa? It's not normally our way to ask for help or to expose our problems. So why am I suggesting we do it in a book?"

A few people nodded, as if they'd thought of that question and simply hadn't asked it.

"I'm suggesting it for several reasons," Larissa said. "If we don't write this, people like Jane Sloane will."

"Isn't she a rival of yours?" a man shouted from the front row.

"No," Larissa said. "Some of you seem to have forgotten that I'm a teacher now. If you doubt what I'm saying, read some Jane Sloane books or maybe something by Anne Rule or some other true crime writers. These people write what they see, and what they believe, but they never live in the communities they write about. They miss a lot."

She looked directly at Gavin. He was still staring at her intently.

"If you like the way the media is handling this, then don't participate. But if the current coverage is bothering you—all that stuff about the shooter and this backwater town—then realize that the only way to influence what people think of us is to put out the message ourselves."

She paused. The entire room was silent. Even the reporters were quiet. A few had the grace to blush.

"Is it ghoulish?" Larissa asked. "I don't know the answer to that. I wish I did. I do know the entire community will be dealing with the tragedy for years to come. This is just one small way of putting it into perspective."

More silence.

So she added, "Besides, if you don't want to be part of the book, you don't have to be. That's the other beauty of this."

Then she handed the microphone back to the mayor and sat down.

A woman popped up as if she'd been tossed from her seat. People with their hands up glared at her, but no one told her to sit down.

"You mentioned publicity," the woman said to Larissa. "Aren't we just begging for it? Aren't we keeping the tragedy alive by publishing a book?"

The mayor tilted the microphone to Larissa, as if he expected a short answer like "yes" or "no." Instead, Larissa took it back. She stood.

"You're all aware that I used to be in the media. So let me tell you this, based on my experience. If there's another shooting before the end of this school year, reporters will return for your reaction to it. A year from now, reporters will return to see how we're all coping. If a book comes out, whether it's ours or Jane Sloane's or some general book on school tragedies, reporters will come here and want to talk to the survivors about their reaction to it. We can't stop that."

"So why add to it?" the woman asked.

"If I may." Gavin stood up. He turned around slowly so that people could see him. "I'm Gavin Quinn. I'm a reporter. Some of you might recognize me. I've been doing this a very, very long time."

Larissa remained standing. She also kept ahold of her microphone so that she could shout down Gavin if she had to.

But at the moment, she was curious about what he was going to say.

"If anything, Miz" (and he emphasized that word) "Johanssen is underestimating what the media can do to Manatowa. If you don't do anything, you'll be known for the shooting and nothing else. People with school-aged children won't come from out of the area for jobs here because they'll think it's a dangerous community."

Voices murmured. The crowd stirred in its seat. Surprisingly, at least to Larissa, several people looked away from Gavin instead of at him, as if the very idea he had just mentioned embarrassed them.

Others glared, their disagreement clear.

He shrugged, then opened his hands: a Gavin move, meaning he was going to explain his point. "What do you folks know about Columbine, Colorado? Springfield, Oregon? West Paducah, Kentucky? Only that they're the site of school shootings."

More people looked away.

Gavin turned around again, as if he was trying to see the effect of his words on the crowd.

"Columbine," he said, "is a rich, middle-class area. Springfield is a poor community, very blue collar. Yet we lump them together. Because we know very little about them, except their tragedies. Is that how you want people to think of Manatowa?"

"I don't see how some book'll change that," the woman who'd initially asked the question said.

"It's not the book that'll change it," he said. "It's charity. You taking care of your own. That becomes the story. And now, I hate to tell you, but this town meeting does as well. If you vote against the project, that'll be as big a part of the story as the shootings themselves."

The woman looked at him, appalled. Larissa suppressed a smile. Gavin had said what she couldn't. That because of the public nature of this meeting, the book gained importance whether it happened or not. And if the citizens of Manatowa voted the book down—for good reasons, like trying to maintain their privacy—the media story would be all about how Manatowa couldn't bring itself to take care of its own.

How the lack of charity in this small Minnesota town was probably what caused Leif to lose it in the first place.

Gavin studied the crowd. Then, when he seemed satisfied that no one would disagree with him, he sat down.

The crowd was silent. Even the murmuring had stopped.

After a moment, Larissa sat, too, handing the microphone back to the mayor. Gavin had said what she wanted to say, only better.

And he wouldn't get in trouble for it, because he didn't live here.

The mayor clutched the microphone for a moment. He glanced at Helen, then at Rosemary Kriegel, trying to see if they wanted to speak, but they were looking down.

Most everyone in the room was looking down.

Gavin had shamed them.

Finally, the mayor sighed, then tilted the microphone toward his mouth. "Ultimately, the power to decide this matter lies with the city council. Normally, I'd say let our representatives do the job you hired them for. But these are extraordinary circumstances and this is an unusual proposition that will require full cooperation from the community. So we want to know where you stand on this matter."

He glanced at the entire panel, leaning forward so that he could see his brother, and then turning so that he could see his former sister-in-law.

"I'm told that we need to move quickly on this project if we're to get the kind of funds Miss Johanssen talked about. We have a lot of steps before we can even offer up the project to some New York publisher. We have to form a non-profit or some kind of legal trust to handle the monies. We have to—"

A woman waved her hand from the audience, then stood.

The mayor sighed loudly into the microphone. "Ma'am, we're pretty much through with the debate."

"No one declared it done," a man shouted in the back.

"We didn't do Robert's Rules," the man sitting next to Larissa said softly to the mayor.

"Crap," the mayor said, and the microphone amplified the word slightly. "All right. One more comment, and then I want to close debate."

"I move that after one comment the debate is closed," said the man next to Larissa.

Someone else seconded, and the group shouted "Aye" without the mayor calling for it.

Then he leaned forward. "You wanted to say something, Ma'am."

"Yes," she said. "How're we gonna divide up the money?"

It was the word "million" that had probably gotten to them. Larissa tried not to take offense at the question, because she had been expecting it, but she still felt a surge of irritation.

"That's why we need a non-profit." The mayor managed to answer without showing the irritation that caused the hand he had on his lap to clench into a fist.

The problem was the way the woman had phrased the question. "Divide up" made it sound like everyone was getting a windfall.

"It would be based on need, I'm sure," he said.

"We can't divide up nothing if we don't have nothing!" someone yelled. "Let's vote."

"Yes," the mayor said. "Let's vote."

Larissa's stomach twisted. She wasn't quite sure how she wanted the vote to go. If the community supported the project, she would have a lot of work and more weeks like this one. If the community didn't support the project, then Gavin was right: They would seem selfish.

Maybe they were. And maybe there was nothing wrong with that. There was a tendency to hunker down after a serious trauma, to move inward, to shut off.

Her family had done that.

And she was still paying for it.

"We're going to have a show of hands," the mayor said.

The crowd groaned. Voice vote was easier, and a bit more private. Sure, the people on either side of you would know how you voted, but no one else would.

With a show of hands, anyone could turn around and see you expressing your opinion.

"All those in favor of this charitable book project, raise your right hand."

Larissa raised her hand. So did the mayor and Helen. She couldn't see anyone else at the dais without looking either direction.

Besides, she was more fascinated by the crowd.

The sea of hands was overwhelming. Larissa expected half, maybe less. But this stunned her.

The community wanted to do the project.

Part of her—the cynical old reporter side—thought the community wanted to do the project so that they could "divide up" the spoils. But she knew better.

Maybe the people in those seats wanted something to do, the way she had when she returned from Hawaii.

"Got a count?" the mayor said to someone on his other side. Apparently the answer was affirmative, because he then said, "Hands down. Now I want to see the hands of those opposed."

Even Larissa could count those. Fifteen. And she suspected that two of those votes were from people who had voted both yes and no. But she didn't say anything.

"Well, then," the mayor said. "It looks like this meeting has pointed a clear direction for the council. I want to thank you all for giving us your time. We're going to take half an hour to empty the room, and then the council will meet in closed session."

The conversations started immediately. People stood and faced each other, talking about what just happened. Some grabbed coats, others took their purses and knapsacks. Some came to the dais.

"Do you still need me?" Larissa asked the mayor. "I've got students at Kinko's."

The mayor held out his hand. "You did a spectacular job. You and your friend are exactly right: This will show the nation what Manatowa is made of. We're not a community of Leif Soderstroms. We're good folk at heart."

She didn't need the speech. But she smiled and took his hand anyway.

"As soon as the legal wrangling is done, we'll be in touch," the mayor said, dismissing her without actually saying so.

"Remember, we need to move rather quickly on this," she said.

"I think we're all aware of that." He turned away from her as several people on the floor below called his name.

She folded the metal chair someone had given her and started to carry it away from the dais. A man took it from her hands and stacked it against the wall.

She slipped on her coat, put her purse over her arm, and looked for a side exit. She wanted to stay away from those reporters—and some of the locals.

Particularly if most of them thought, as the mayor obviously did, that she and Gavin had double-teamed the crowd.

She had almost reached the door when Gavin caught up with her. He pulled her into the hallway, his fingers digging into the skin of her upper arm.

As soon as she got free of the crowd around her, she shook him off.

"What was that?" she asked.

He frowned. "I was just getting you out."

He seemed to understand that she didn't want time with the other reporters. Of course, anyone seeing him with her would think that he was interviewing her.

"I could've gotten out on my own," she said, "but that's not what I'm asking. What was that comment in the meeting?"

His eyebrows went up, then his eyes crinkled on the side. Gavin always had the ability to smile without smiling, something she had once admired.

Now she saw it as a way of remaining hidden, the way he always remained hidden.

"I thought it might be good if an outsider talked to them." He shrugged. "It seemed to work."

Whether it worked or not, it angered her. She didn't need or want his help. She didn't need anyone's help.

"I think they would have gotten it without you," she said.

People were pushing by and some watched the interchange with interest. A few headed through the exit doors, their boot strikes on the stairs echoing in the wide stairwell. Everyone else crowded outside the elevators.

"Now you make me feel like I should apologize," he said and this time he was smiling—that charming, oh-so-carefree smile that he rarely used. When he did, it always had an impact.

Or at least, it used to.

"It wasn't your meeting," she said. "It really isn't even your kind of story."

"Maybe it is," he said, "now that you're involved."

A headache built between her eyes. "What does that mean?"

"You're a celebrity. People like celebrity. If the brass is going to demote me to national trauma stories—or more to the point, if I accept

it—I can still chose what kind of reporter I want to be. I can be an Anderson Cooper, filled with outrage and politically correct posturing—all
pretense of objectivity thrown to the wind. Or I can show that my years
of experience will get me the outside angle, the one no one else has."

The anger that she had felt toward him a little while ago returned
with such force that her breath caught. She made herself inhale.

"I am not an angle," she said.

"You know damn well you're an angle," he said, "and now you're part
of the story."

"No," she said. "*You're* part of the story. If the single camera caught
your good side, you can even show yourself making your little speech as
a way of telling the American public how empathetic you are."

"I made you angry," he said flatly.

"You think I'm happy about this?" she asked. "You think I'll just
waltz out of here with you and give you an interview for old times' sake?"

"Since you won't talk about old times or past problems, sure," he
said. "That would be a good change of pace. An interview, and we'll call
it even."

Her face heated. "Even. You think we can call everything that happened 'even.'"

The smirk left his face. She had confused him.

"You remember how you've been feeling lately—why you're here in
the first place?"

"The story," he said, glancing around to make sure no one else was
interested.

"Why they sent you on this particular story? What you told me
about that?"

"This isn't the place to discuss it, Lissy." He glanced pointedly at an
up-and-coming network reporter who was watching them with a little
too much interest.

"Oh, I think it is," she said. "Because when I felt like that, and I
turned to the person I cared about, the person I thought cared about
me, he patted me on the shoulder and headed off to Eastern Europe on a

story. Suddenly wouldn't take my phone calls or answer my e-mails. He was too damn busy."

"Lissy," he said. "That's past. I'll apologize for that. It was boorish of me—"

"Boorish?" She shook her head. "It wasn't boorish. You were protecting yourself. Even I understood that. But now, you're not protecting anyone. You're flailing all over the place, talking about reinventing yourself, and you're going to hurt people along the way. Stop talking about being even. We were a good team, and then we weren't. It's over and I, for one, don't want to revive any part of it. Including drinks and interviews, and conversations ostensibly about stories that always lead to something else."

He opened his mouth, but she wouldn't let him say anything.

"And for the record, this was a town hall meeting. The only people who were supposed to participate were the members of the town. You're not one of them. I am. No one appreciated what you had to say, Gavin. You just showed people why they need to control the media. Because it's full of insensitive assholes like you."

The color had risen in his cheeks. "Look, Lissy, I didn't mean—"

"Yes, you did," she said. "An apology won't do it. Just leave me alone. Leave my students alone. Leave my town alone. It might be better for all of us—including you and your damn career—if you got out of here. Get that therapy. Take some R&R. Just get the hell out of here."

His eyes glittered, and he didn't blink. A reporter's trick. Her words had brought tears to his eyes, and if he blinked, they would trail down his cheeks. He wouldn't be able to blink until people stopped looking at him.

Until she stopped looking at him.

Her heart constricted. She had hurt him. She had meant to hurt him, but not that badly. Not bad enough to bring tears to his eyes.

She shook her head and pushed past him toward the stairs. Damn him for making her angry. Damn him for being here. Damn him for making her feel anything toward him.

Especially compassion.

sixteen

*a*s she hurried down the stairs, she heard footsteps behind her. They were heavy—a man's footsteps—and they were getting closer.

She turned, ready to tell Gavin to leave her alone, and saw Petrovich. He took the last few stairs in one big step and reached the landing at the same time she did.

"Where're your kids?" she asked, trying to sound normal. Calm. Not nearly as shaken as she felt.

"They're taking the elevator. They're going to meet me in the lobby." He smiled. His smile was softer than Gavin's. It wasn't a weapon to be taken out and used only when needed. "Even if we stop and talk for a while, I have a hunch we'll beat them. That elevator line is long."

"Yeah, I saw." She headed across the landing and to the next flight of stairs. "I have to get back to my students. We're putting the paper to bed tonight."

"Busy." He was keeping up with her.

She nodded. "It's certainly not what I would have expected a few weeks ago."

They reached the next landing and he put out a hand, touching her gently. They were the only ones in the stairwell now.

"Listen, I saw you with that reporter." Petrovich seemed uncomfortable. "He's not...harassing you, is he? I mean, that looked pretty heated, and all."

Her cheeks grew warm. She knew others had been watching, but hadn't realized how they might interpret it.

"If it's none of my business," Petrovich said, "just say so. I'll butt out, but I was kind of worried, especially the way he looked at you during the meeting…."

Larissa frowned. "How did he look at me?"

Petrovich shrugged. "He was just…staring…you know."

She hadn't realized that Gavin had been staring at her, but it didn't surprise her. Gavin *focused* on people. That was one way he got his stories.

And like it or not, he'd made it clear that she was part of the story now.

"We used to be involved." Now it was her turn to be uncomfortable. "He expects me to give him an exclusive."

Not until she got the words out did she realize how silly the sounded. Most people who had once been involved used the word "exclusive" to mean that they didn't date anyone else.

Reporters used to it to mean that they wanted a part of the story that no one else had.

"I mean, an interview," she said. "An exclusive interview."

Petrovich nodded. "I know what you mean. It just seemed a little more intense than that."

Larissa started down the next flight of stairs. "It was. It had all that history involved in the discussion. You know. Old relationships. You can't just talk about one thing. There's always a subtext."

"Yeah." Petrovich wasn't looking at her. "It must be hard for you."

"What?" she asked. "This week? No harder than it is for everyone else. Easier than it is for some."

"I didn't mean that," he said. "I meant, you know, given that you used to be one of the media. Calling the police on Jane Sloane—"

"She's an idiot," Larissa said.

He grinned at her, obviously surprised.

She smiled in spite of herself. "I have no idea how many of my colleagues would have loved to do the same thing, but didn't have the chance. And couldn't if they wanted to keep their jobs."

He chuckled. "Okay. Not her. But everyone else. I've seen the news footage. They hound you. They speculate on why you're not talking to them."

They'd reached the next landing. This time, Larissa didn't stop. "I'm not talking because if I did, the discussion would be just as heated as it is with Gavin. They don't get it. Hell, *I* didn't get it. This isn't a story. These are people's lives."

"Yeah." He didn't say anything for most of the flight down. When they'd reached the small corridor that led to the first floor, he stopped.

"You think this book is a good idea?"

"I wish it wasn't necessary," she said. "But better us than the Jane Sloanes of the world."

"You could do it, couldn't you?" he said. "Just you. You obviously get it now. You'd do just fine."

"It's not about me," she said.

"I know, but—"

"If I write the book," she said. "It becomes about me. My impressions. My thoughts. My feelings. That's the beauty of this thing. It's not about me. It'll be about Manatowa."

He gave her a half smile. It was as warm as his full smile, but a bit rueful. "My daughter wants to know how to write for the project. But my son, this whole thing makes him angry."

"Angry?" Larissa hadn't expected that. "Why?"

Petrovich shrugged one shoulder. "I think he just wants to move on. I think he believes this'll get in the way."

"There's something to be said for moving on," she said.

"And something to be said for examining how you feel." He pulled open the door for her. Instantly, voices overwhelmed them.

Half of the crowd that had been in the upstairs hallway was now on the main floor. A few reporters hovered near the door. One of them stepped forward and shoved a microphone in Larissa's face.

"Larissa, how did it feel to call the cops on Jane Sloane?"

Like it would feel if I slugged you in the face.

"This is my cue," she said to Petrovich. She meant that she was going to go down the stairs to the parking garage, but she changed her mind. Instead, she pulled him back into the stairwell and slammed the door.

Someone tried to pull it open, but she held it closed.

"What are you doing Sunday?" she asked.

That flush returned to his cheeks. "Sunday?"

"Afternoon," she said.

"Um…" he frowned, as if he couldn't quite figure out what she wanted.

That was when she realized he thought she was asking him out.

"I realized tonight that I'm being a hypocrite," she said.

His frown deepened.

"If I'm going to force people to write about what happened here, then maybe I should look at what happened to us. When we were kids."

He swallowed. For a moment, he looked disappointed. Or maybe that was relief. She couldn't quite tell.

"Or maybe," he said, "that would be too much to handle right now."

"If you don't want to dig out the clippings," she said, "I can go to the library. I'm sure—"

"It'd be easier if I gave you what I have." He smiled again—a soft smile, reassuring. He had a repertoire of smiles, unlike Gavin, who only had the one. "Come on over Sunday afternoon. I'll have some coffee and we can look at the clippings."

"Or I can just pick them up," she said. "It's just that I don't have much time between now and then. That's the first available moment."

The person outside the door tugged again. She had to pull hard to keep it closed.

"I think it might be better we're both there. I can explain it." He bit his lower lip. "I've been thinking about showing the kids, too."

"Your children don't know?" she asked.

"They know. They've known for a long time. But they've been asking a lot of questions this week. Maybe this'll help them know that the past is survivable."

She nodded, even though she wasn't sure she agreed. Was the past survivable? Or was it something that one simply got through? Was "getting through" surviving? Or was it something less, something like living a half a life?

Something like reporting an event rather than living through it?

The door banged open. Larissa got a glimpse of several faces before she was able to pull it closed again.

"I think you should probably go up a flight, and then take a different group of stairs down," she said. "Otherwise they'll mob you and want to know why we were in here alone so long."

He stuck a hand in his pocket and pulled out a business card. "How's two?"

It took her a moment to realize he was referring to Sunday. She took the card. "Two's great."

He grabbed the door, his warm hand brushing hers. "I'm going to hold this for a few minutes. Go. They'll have no idea where you went."

She slipped her hand from his. "Thanks."

Then she headed down the stairs to the garage. The door banged a few times as she went down, and then she was in the garage itself.

Except for a few cars, it was empty.

For the first time in what seemed like years, she was finally alone.

seventeen

*t*he next morning, Tomasina called. Larissa didn't pick up on her drive to work. She silenced her phone for class and forgot about it for most of the morning.

The newspapers got delivered during homeroom. On her way back to her own classroom, she glanced through the windows in the doors of various rooms. Usually students read the paper, or marked on it, or tossed it away.

This time, they stared at it as if it frightened them. It was yet another reminder of all that they'd lived through—all that they were living through.

Her newspaper team met back in the journalism room. Instead of the usual high fives when a paper was successfully completed, they took their own copies, set them on their desks, and then went back to the computer area.

The video was almost done. Mandi only had to compile a few more things. Last night, the students had asked Larissa about the book, and she couldn't tell them much.

This morning, they didn't seem interested. They were wiped out— emotionally and physically. And they still weren't done.

"I don't think we should have credits on the memorial," Ryan said as Larissa came into the room.

"First no VO and now no credits? Is this a j-project or not?" Hannah crossed her arms. She was leaning against the table, her copy of the newspaper next to her purse.

She was trying to sound cool by using jargon. She had been disappointed that she couldn't narrate the voice-over. Now she was complaining about not having her name on the finished piece.

"It's not a for-glory project," Ryan snapped at her. "It's not about us."

Some of the other students closed their eyes. The group was tired of the arguing, tired of the constant debates.

Larissa was, too. She felt like she'd been talking and defending herself and her projects all week long. She wondered if everyone else was as short on sleep as she was. She hadn't made it through an entire night since she'd seen the news report in her Hawaiian hotel room.

"Mandi's been struggling with the credit issue." Larissa nodded toward Mandi, who looked even more tired than Larissa felt. "As Ryan said, credits are about the makers, and this film is not about those who created it."

"No credits? C'mon, Miz Johanssen. We have to put our names on it." Hannah bumped Drew with her elbow. He actually looked away from her, as if this argument embarrassed him.

He'd gotten quieter and quieter all week, partly as the extent of his injuries became public. A lot of well-meaning kids had asked him if he would ever get use of his hand again. The sling he wore now had a large handmade sign on it that said *I don't know. Stop asking.*

He'd point to it whenever someone brought the injury up.

"I didn't say no credits." Larissa had to work to not snap at Hannah as well. "But we don't want this film to be about us. Taking credit at the end would make our names the last thing the mourners at the service will see."

She immediately regretted the use of the word "mourners." That single word was a painful reminder of all they were doing—and the reasons for it.

"Should the credits be at the beginning?" Kaitlyn was sitting on top of one of the desks. Instead of making her look larger, the defiant act accented her small, malformed frame.

"I think so," Larissa said.

Mandi started to protest just as Hannah did, but Larissa stopped them by putting up her hand.

"Let me finish," she said. "I think we should run the title—*Memorial*, the one Ryan suggested, which is a good one, I think—and then we put something like 'prepared by' and follow it with all your names."

"But Mandi's doing extra work," Kaitlyn said. "Shouldn't she get extra credit?"

"Memorial," Drew said softly. "Directed by Mandi Edwards. Compiled by…and then our names."

"Compiled by? It sounds like we didn't do anything," Hannah said. "I still think we need a VO."

"And you think you should do it." Joe grinned at her. He was sitting two seats down from her, one of the newspapers rolled in his hand as if he were holding a club.

"Well, someone should," Hannah said, but she preened as she did so.

"We don't need a voice-over." This from Tofee Grice. "If we talk, we'll sound stupid."

"Some of us will sound stupid," Hannah said.

The fight was going to escalate. Larissa was tempted to let it do so. It would blow off some steam. Or it might escalate into something ugly, given how frayed the students were.

How frayed they all were.

"No voice-over," she said. "I like Drew's suggestion. We can use the word *written* instead of *compiled*."

"We didn't write," Joe said. "We gathered. I like *compiled*."

"Me, too." Several others agreed in chorus.

"Then let me suggest this," Larissa said. "Just the words, in a nice white font against a black background. Then we fade out. Then the piece starts with that great opening that Mandi designed."

"I don't have time to do some stupid font thing," Mandi said. It was her way of saying she didn't approve.

"I'll do it," Drew said.

"Like you can," Hannah said. "You need both hand…"

Then her voice faded out. She realized she had finally crossed a line.

Drew stood up and walked a few seats forward. He didn't look at Hannah. He didn't look at anyone except Larissa.

"I can do it, Miz Johanssen. I'll work with Mandi to find the right font. We'll do something appropriate, then you can approve it."

His cheeks had two spots of color. They seemed to be his only reaction to Hannah's words.

At some point, Drew was going to have to stop holding in his feelings. The boy had to be furious.

And terrified.

Remember, a counselor's voice said in her head, *I'm here if you want to talk.*

Half a memory—the counselor's office in a school just south of Manatowa. The counselor, a woman, looking at Larissa with a mixture of compassion and frustration.

At some point, the counselor said, *those emotions will surface. Better to bring them out now.*

"Miss Johanssen?" Drew said. "Is it okay if I do that?"

"It's fine," Larissa said. "It's good, as a matter of fact. And I'm not going to be the only one to approve this memorial video—"

The bell rang. None of her students moved.

She waited until the clanging stopped before finishing her thought.

"I'm afraid I'll need all of you after school. And Drew, I'll need you to design that frontispiece sometime before the end of classes."

"Okay." He went back toward Hannah. She gave him an apologetic smile, but he didn't lift his head to look at her. Instead he scooped up his books with his good hand.

The other kids stood. They all watched Drew leave before they started to file out.

He was gaining a special status with them. An important status, as if he had an extra patina of charisma that he hadn't had a month before.

They didn't seem to feel sorry for him. They acted as if he had achieved something more than they had, as if he had come out of this more honorable than when he had gone in.

Mandi was the last to leave. She had to pack up her books, which were scattered around the computer.

"What else do you need me to do to finish this?" Larissa asked. She'd done a few things over the past few days, but not as much as she had wanted to in order to keep the burden off Mandi.

"If you could put his front on the piece," she said. "I'd appreciate it."

"You don't want to work with Drew?"

"I'll help him with the fonts and stuff, but I don't want to lay the credits in. Can you do that?"

Easily, Larissa thought, but didn't say. It was one of the easiest jobs they had. Mandi had done so much more than that already.

"You really don't want them on, do you?" Larissa asked.

"I think it's wrong to have our names on it at all." Mandi shoved her books in her backpack.

"How about we run it both ways after school? Principal Meiers is coming, and we can have her make the final call."

"I think we should make the final call," Mandi said. "It's our project."

"Yeah," Larissa said, "but it affects a lot of people."

"Just Hannah," Mandi said.

Mandi had misunderstood Larissa. "That's not what I meant. I meant that a lot of people will have a reaction to what we've done. We want to make sure this is in the best taste possible."

"No names," Mandi said. "That's respectful."

"What you and the others have done, that's respectful. Signing it is just a matter of opinion. I think it's always good to know who did something. To have the piece be anonymous is almost as if we don't want to claim our emotions."

Mandi's eyes filled with tears. She tilted her head back, blinked, then angrily wiped at the handful of tears that escaped.

"I don't want to answer questions," she said. "How come we used that picture and not this one? How come we spent thirty seconds more on Mr. Haigen than we did on Miz Winter? How—"

"Did we?" Larissa asked.

"No," Mandi snapped. "We spent a lot more time on everyone except Miz Winter. She doesn't have a family and no one knew her very well. Kaitlyn had to look really hard just to find pictures."

Larissa suppressed a sigh. She hadn't realized that Mandi was trying to equalize time as well as the beauty of the imagery. The girl was thinking of everything.

"People forget credits that run up front," Larissa said. "They may try to remember, but they won't. Especially after something this emotional. If you want, we don't have to put you down as director. We can just run a list of names. But you've done such an amazing job. I do think you should have credit for it. You've thought of everything."

Mandi wiped at her face again. "I don't want credit. Just put me with the *compiled by*."

Larissa nodded. "I'll tell Drew when he comes in."

"Thanks." Mandi stepped past her. "I'm going to be late."

And as she hurried out the door, the second bell rang. Larissa stepped after her, but couldn't stop her to give her a pass. She would ask later if Mandi needed one.

Some teachers had reacted to the crisis by demanding passes from every tardy student. Some had become very *laissezfaire*, not wanting any paperwork for anything, figuring that the students needed time—even between classes—to deal with their grief.

Larissa went into the main classroom. It was empty. Suddenly, she was by herself. It felt odd after all those days of running from place to place.

For the first time since she'd been back, she had third period off. Just like she used to.

Before the shootings.

Before the shootings, she used to go to the cafeteria to see if any of her students having lunch needed some extra help. She'd spoken to Leif there just before she left for Hawaii, asking him if he wanted some tutoring when she got back.

He hadn't answered.

She wondered if he'd been planning his attack even then.

She shivered, grabbed her bag, and remembered her phone. She pulled it out, saw that she had missed six calls, and pressed the missed-call button.

All of the calls had come from Tomasina.

Larissa leaned against her desk, sighed, and let the phone dial the number.

Tomasina answered on the second ring.

"It's about time," she said.

"I'm working today," Larissa said. "I've been with my students."

"You could've called last night. I saw the news. Your city council approved the book project. I've been fielding calls all morning. Everyone wants to buy this thing. I think we'll make a lot more than that idiot Sloane woman."

Larissa didn't care about the money. She was about to say that when she realized she was wrong. She did care, but only as a way of helping her students and this town.

She hadn't been like that a few years before. Then the money would have been a way to keep score.

"It was on the news?" she asked.

"You and Gavin giving speeches—who knew he actually cared about such things? Which reminds me. *Are* you an item again?"

It was the emphasis on "are" as if this were part of another discussion, one they'd had earlier, that started an ache in her heart. Someone remembered, and was speculating if Larissa and Gavin had double-teamed the people of Manatowa. The talking heads were probably all over it. Maybe even the entertainment programs.

"The news talked about me and Gavin?" she asked, her voice cracking.

"Not the news-news," Tomasina said. "But the entertainment news, sure. And everyone is talking about the way you sold this thing to the town and how it might actually be worth a lot more than one million dollars. Some folks are talking movie, others are talking a series of books."

"Tommi." Larissa had to stop her from continuing.

"I've been fielding calls all morning. *Everyone* wants to make a deal, Larissa. And *everyone* wants to offer more than everyone else."

This was probably better than Tomasina had imagined. It would certainly bring up the price for the volume.

But that news didn't cheer Larissa. It made the ache around her heart grow.

"This isn't about the money," Larissa said.

"Sure it is, honey. You said it yourself. Some of those kids are seriously injured—"

"Sixteen are dead," Larissa snapped.

Tomasina must have heard something in Larissa's tone because she stopped speaking.

After a moment, she said, "All right. I'm being insensitive, I know it. But you know that this will help your community. And you didn't call me when the project got approved."

Tomasina was trying to apologize. But Larissa didn't want to acknowledge it. Not yet. Maybe not ever.

"Because we don't know who you're making the deal with. The lawyers are trying to figure out whether a non-profit is appropriate or a limited trust or something else. There is no legal entity yet, Tommi."

"But there's a vague idea, right? We can hold drawing up the contract. But let me negotiate, all right? Everyone wants this thing. Let's strike while the iron's hot."

Now Larissa knew Tomasina was excited, because she rarely spoke in clichés. "I can't authorize it," Larissa said. "I'm not in charge."

"You're the editor."

"Yes, but I won't be involved in the business side in any way. You'll have to wait."

"Give me the names of the lawyers," Tomasina said. "We need to do something."

"It's Friday," Larissa said. "No one's going to offer until Monday, earliest, and maybe not Tuesday. Let these people have time to work."

"I'm getting offers now, and I want to set a floor and a timeline," Tomasina said. "We still have half a business day left."

"And we have a city-wide memorial service tomorrow. No one is thinking about book deals."

Larissa caught her bottom lip between her teeth. Her tone had been brutal. She never spoke to anyone like that, at least she hadn't in years, not since those final broadcast days when she kept assuring her producers she was fine.

Tomasina said nothing for several long minutes.

Larissa bit back the urge to apologize. No one was thinking about this town. They were wondering if Larissa and Gavin were lovers again, if the tragedy had brought them closer. If the unusual book deal would happen—not because it would help Manatowa, but because it might make millions. No one wanted to know how the families were doing. They wanted to see someone cry on camera.

She rubbed her forehead.

Her grandmother clutched Larissa to her side. Nadia and Ric followed. The reporters crowded them, shouting questions.

—We're going to a fucking funeral, Ric yelled.

Grandmother shushed him.

He glared at her. —It's a goddamn funeral. They should leave us alone.

—Language, Grandmother said, as if the shouting were his fault. —Watch that language.

"Give me the names of the attorneys," Tomasina was saying in a tight voice.

Larissa had to focus to hear it. "They won't know anything today."

"I'm pretty smart about legal matters myself," Tomasina snapped. She was clearly angry. "That's what you pay me for."

"I thought we weren't paying you on this one," Larissa muttered.

"Names," Tomasina said.

Larissa sighed. It took her a moment to remember—her mind had been lost in past for a second there—and then she gave Tomasina the names.

"I don't have phone numbers."

"I'm sure I can find them," Tomasina said. "I'll let you know when we have a deal."

"You talk to them about it," Larissa said, but she was talking to silence. Tomasina had hung up.

Larissa flipped her phone closed and put it in her purse. Then she rubbed the bridge of her nose. She was exhausted, so exhausted that the past was breaking through to the present.

It had happened twice in the last twenty-four hours. She couldn't have that happen. Not before the video was done.

Not before the memorial service.

If she was smart, she'd cancel that meeting with Petrovich on Sunday. It would only bring up more of the past.

She grabbed the phone, and was about to call him when she stopped. She stared at the empty display.

Mandi hadn't slept in days. Drew was forcing himself to work with one hand to get the video right.

Even Hannah, with her fragile but inflated ego and incorrect views, was trying her best to face the tragedy she had just lived through.

Larissa had asked them all to do more than she had ever done with her own past.

Which, she knew, was why it was breaking through.

It was time to show as much courage as her students were.

Past time, really. She should have shown that courage a long, long time ago.

She closed the phone, but kept it clutched in her right hand.

Thirty years ago, her father had murdered six people in New Lake's First National Bank. He had gone into his place of employment as if it were a normal day of work, then pulled out a gun, and terrorized everyone inside.

He hadn't asked for money. He hadn't asked for anything.

He just shot as many people as he could before shooting himself.

And her mother, unable to face the news. Her mother...

Larissa squeezed the phone so hard that it beeped. She put it to her forehead.

It had been a normal school day. He'd walked her to the bus.

It'd been a Saturday. She had been in the bank.

She had been studying fractions.

She had been hiding under a desk with Pete Petrovich.

Her grandmother had picked her up from school.

Her grandmother...

Larissa shook her head. She didn't remember it. She truly didn't remember how she had gotten to her grandparents' house that day, not if she hadn't already been in school.

Had she inserted false memories for the real ones?

Or had she inserted real memories for the emptiness—the temporary amnesia—so many trauma victims suffered?

The cell phone was warm against her forehead. She let her hand drop, and as she did, the phone rang.

She must have switched the phone off silent mode when she squeezed it.

She was shaking.

She looked at the display. Tomasina again.

Larissa flipped open the phone and listened to her voice tremble as she answered it.

"Your lawyers gave me a go," Tomasina said. "We'll worry about the legal entity next week. I thought you should know."

"Thanks," Larissa said. Her voice sounded normal this time.

"I didn't want to leave it with you like that. I'm trying to balance all this, Larissa. I have no idea what you're going through, but I'm trying to help. Honest to God."

"I know that," Larissa said.

"So let me call you when this happens. You know more about it than the suits do."

"They're not suits," Larissa said. "They're parents and siblings and former students of this school. They've—"

"Point taken," Tomasina said. "I'll do the very best I can to be a sensitive soul. But I'm going to fail. I'm still going to get you and those kids the most money possible. Okay? I'm not doing it for my fee or for the fame. I'm doing it because it's right."

"I know that, too," Larissa said.

And she did. She knew this came from Tomasina's warm heart. The entire town would be helped because Tomasina had had one of her typically brilliant ideas.

"So this weekend," Tomasina said. "My prayers are with you. I mean that. I'll be thinking of you the whole time."

"Thanks," Larissa said.

"Friends?" Tomasina asked.

"We never stopped, Tommi." Larissa's voice was trembling again. Her eyes hurt. She blinked hard, felt her lids scratch against dryness. How could her eyes be dry when her heart ached so badly?

"You hang in," Tomasina said. "And when I call you, it'll be with great news."

"All right," Larissa said. "I do appreciate it."

"I know, kiddo," Tomasina said. "And I know right now that you all are in hell. We're just trying to make it a little less painful around there."

"Thanks." Larissa flipped her phone shut. She couldn't talk anymore.

She couldn't think anymore.

She glanced at her watch. Her break was almost over.

Third period was almost over.

And she hadn't even gone to the cafeteria.

She had a hunch it might be a while before she did.

She glanced at the door. The students were going, every day. But she hadn't.

It was the clippings or the cafeteria during third-period lunch.

She couldn't do both. She couldn't face both.

She shut off the ringer on her phone, then dropped the phone back in her purse.

Clippings. She was going to face those clippings first.

Then she'd go to lunch with her students.

All of them. The budding failures, the sad-eyed ones, and the survivors.

She was going to reclaim her life—one difficult moment at a time.

eighteen

Saturday she put on a black silk dress she hadn't worn since her brother's funeral. The dress had a traditional A-line that fell below her knees. The collar poked out of the sheer overcoat that covered a very black, very beautiful interior sheath.

She remembered buying the dress for cocktail parties, thinking it would look sophisticated. It hadn't been in her closet a week when her brother had killed himself.

The family curse, Nadia had said, as if Ric had done something inevitable.

Larissa hadn't said anything, but she remembered feeling numb and unwilling to face the empty church, the handful of mourners—most of whom were friends of Nadia or Larissa, not people who had known Ric—the sympathetic but clueless minister. Neither Nadia nor Larissa would tell him about Ric's past, claiming they didn't know much.

They felt—or Larissa felt, since she hadn't talked to Nadia about it—that Ric's past wasn't suitable for a memorial. He hadn't led a happy life. He had become defiant and angry after their parents' deaths. Then he moved to reckless, sleeping with everything that moved. Finally, he had stopped talking with the family altogether.

When they'd gone to clear out his possessions, it was the emptiness of the apartment that made Larissa almost physically ill. No family photos.

No personal mementos. Nothing but some clothing and a television and some food and an uncomfortable chair.

Nothing that made Ric's home any different from any other single guy's. Except that his interests weren't in it.

Or—worse—maybe they had been.

Maybe he had replaced that anger—that grief—with nothing at all.

Larissa stroked the sleeves of her dress. The sheath didn't go down the arm, so the sleeves were sheer, turning her skin a dark, fleshy color.

She had put on the dress for Ric's funeral like soldiers donned armor.

Her grandmother used to say that if a woman looked beautiful, she could get through anything. Much as Larissa hated the superficiality of the advice, in times of crisis, she lived it.

She was trying to be beautiful now as she got ready for the memorial service. If she had her way, she would skip it. But she had to be there for her students.

She would field the questions people might throw at them, the questions that Mandi feared. Larissa would talk about the decisions, the lack of information on some and the wealth on others.

She would be as diplomatic as she could, and as protective as she needed to be.

And for that, she needed armor.

A black silk dress, Ferragamo shoes, and a matching purse. Her hair pulled into a chignon and a light dusting of makeup, something she rarely wore in her new role as Minnesota high school teacher.

When she looked in the mirror, she saw her old self, the broadcast self, the one who told people the facts as she saw them—right or wrong—but always with great authority.

And that was how she went into the Regent's ballroom. It was the largest public space in all of Manatowa—or at least, the largest space that wasn't a theater. A theater was the wrong venue, someone had decided. People needed to be able to mingle and talk.

The Regent hotel was in the center of town, not far from City Hall. It had been built around the same time, so the hotel had that early twentieth-century majesty, an opulence that modern hotels lacked. The stone cornices outside were decorated with cheerful gargoyles. The doors were heavy oak decorated with the original stained glass—images of the railroad and the river that had once made Manatowa one of the most important communities in the Midwest.

The ballroom was on the second floor. Two grand staircases curved toward it. She could see the open doors from the entry, and catch a hint of the people milling inside.

The air smelled of perfume, coffee, and food. An elderly man—someone she didn't recognize—stood in the coat check window near the main doors. Usually the coat check was manned by a beautiful young girl—shades of the past—but all of the beautiful young girls were in the ballroom, mourning their friends.

Larissa took off her black wool cape and her leather gloves, handing them to the elderly man, along with a five-dollar bill. He looked surprised and then grateful, which made her uncomfortable.

She still wasn't used to a world where five dollars seemed like wealth.

He gave her a ripped ticket, and then she headed for those magnificent stairs.

She had come as close to the beginning of the actual service as possible. She didn't want to talk to too many people. If asked, she would say she was trying to avoid the press, but really, she was trying to minimize her time here.

She'd already lost her morning to this tribute.

The hotel's tech guru had agreed to meet her at nine. She'd been on time, but he'd been late. By then, she'd already inspected the ballroom's media capacity. The room was so large that it actually had a small engineering booth, which allowed the person inside to run sound and lights, as well as project images onto a large screen.

The screen ran on remote control. She could tap a button and the screen would descend. Then she could tap another button and the film would start.

Only she didn't have a film. She had a homemade DVD.

For a while, she thought she'd have to jury rig something herself or head to the school and dub the entire thing onto videocassette (she had found an ancient videocassette recorder under the sound deck).

Then the tech guru showed up. His name was Rowan, and he seemed too young to be out of high school. He was skinny, and had bed hair as well as a rather pathetic stubble along half of his chin. His faded black t-shirt advertised a ten-year-old U-2 concert tour, and his black jeans had holes in both knees.

Not work attire, at least not to her mind. But he was coming in on his day off—or so he had told her on the phone the day before—so maybe he was trying to make sure no one asked him to stick around.

He took some state-of-the-art equipment from a locked storage room and proceeded to set up her "show," as he called it, despite her corrections. He arranged everything so that it would work at the touch of a button. No cues necessary, which meant she didn't have to be up here during the ceremony.

She still wasn't sure if she was relieved or disappointed about that.

Someone had volunteered to run the sound and the lights—she didn't know who—and those people had come in shortly after she left. She had gone home, taken a long bath, and then gotten dressed, slowly, discarding every other black dress she owned until she found the one that had served well and faithfully before as battle armor.

When she reached the ballroom itself, she was glad she'd worn the armor. The room was stunning. It had two levels—the second with a balcony that circled the entire dance floor. That level, she had learned earlier, would be opened if enough people came so that they needed the room.

The hotel had put out chairs, all of them facing a small stage up front. Behind the stage, the screen was already down. Some cameras pointed at the podium in the center. The speakers would be broadcast larger—simulcast, as some venues called it—while they spoke.

Larissa was glad she wasn't on the list.

Lilies, roses, and carnations lined the floor in front of the stage and ran all the way along the sides. Some of the flowers had banners with the words "In Memoriam." Others had tiny cards stuck among the leaves.

People were wandering the sides, reading the cards, probably to avoid conversation.

In the back left corner, tables set with silverware, napkins, and coffee cups waited for the plates of food that wouldn't arrive until a designated time just before the formal service was over.

There was no room for reporters or camera crews. The hotel manager had told her earlier that anyone who worked as a journalist who had no connection to Manatowa or the lost children (his words—"lost children"—and they twisted her heart more than any previous euphemism had) would not be allowed through the door.

He had staff near the stairs who had a list of allowed reporters. Equipment would be confiscated.

She felt then as if he were telling her that as a preemptive strike—so that she wouldn't bring her own camera along.

As if she wanted to cover this.

All morning, she'd been regretting her decision to help with the book.

She slipped inside, and immediately Mandi found her. Mandi was wearing a dress—a wrinkled cotton thing with ruffles that looked like it came from someone else's closet. Mandi's hair was pulled back, too, and someone had given her lipstick in a shade that was too light for her skin.

"I forgot to ask," she said without a hello, "can I be the one to make sure the vid works okay?"

Larissa put a hand on her arm. Mandi's skin was cool through the cotton. "I had a run-through this morning. Everything should be smooth."

"I think we should have someone in that booth—"

"She doesn't want to be here." Her mother had come from the side. She was wearing a similar black cotton dress, but on her it looked appropriate and hung in the right lines.

"I think we all wish the last two weeks hadn't happened," Larissa said, deliberately misunderstanding. "Your daughter did a tremendous job on the memorial video. We couldn't have done it without her."

Mandi flushed and stepped back. She moved slowly until she was out of her mother's sight, and then she hurried down a row toward Kaitlyn, who had put her coat on one chair and her purse on another, obviously saving places.

"This video project was a lifesaver," her mother said. "I don't know what she's going to do now. She's terrified, you know."

Terrified? In spite of herself, Larissa looked at Mandi. She seemed so calm as she talked to Kaitlyn.

"She never was very popular. He turned that gun on her, but something distracted him, and now…"

Her mother shook her head.

"I shouldn't be telling you this. But she's having nightmares when she does sleep. She got beat up a few years ago, by the girls, and then this. It's been all I can do to keep her in school."

Larissa's stomach tightened. Mandi? Mandi who had worked with such focus all week?

"Your project got her out of bed every day. I'm not sure what will now."

Larissa sighed. It wasn't her problem. All of the kids were having trouble. She knew that, and yet…they couldn't lose someone like Mandi.

"You can't get her to the counselors, can you?" Larissa asked in as non-judgmental a tone as she could manage. She'd tried as well.

"She doesn't want to talk to strangers." Her mother glanced down the aisle at her daughter, still talking with Kaitlyn. "And Kaitlyn—that girl's hardly said a word in the past two weeks, and before then, I couldn't shut her up."

Larissa started. She hadn't noticed, but Mandi's mother was right. Kaitlyn used to be the bright lively center of the classes that she had with Larissa. Now Kaitlyn sat toward the back and worked on her assignments, rarely speaking unless spoken to.

"We have to give them time," Larissa said lamely, and in her own words, she heard her grandmother, talking with her grandfather at the kitchen table.

They'll get past it. They have to. Life goes on.

Her grandfather had shook his head. *Not after something like this. Hell, Marja, I'm not sure I can get past this. When I think of what our L'issa went through, what he did, that morning—*

Her grandmother had shushed him. *Pavel, the children.*

Maybe if they could talk, he said, *it would help.*

Nothing can help, her grandmother had said in a bleak voice. *Except God. And time.*

Mandi's mother was saying, "You don't expect this. When you send them to school. You expect everything else—the teasing, the fights, the worries—but not this."

Larissa nodded. She was out of her depth. She'd never had children. She'd never had these kinds of worries. Not for anyone.

Not even, at times, for herself.

Mandi's mother put a hand on Larissa's arm, just a gentle, almost tentative touch.

"Thank you," she said softly.

Larissa nodded, not really wanting to take credit. All she had done was her job in the best way she knew how. She had product to produce, classes to run, and she had known that the week after—the first week classes started again—would be a problem, so she was creative.

She didn't say any of that, though. She just put her hand on Mandi's mother's for a brief instance, then moved away, out of conversational range.

It wasn't until she was heading toward the tables that she realized she had slipped back into celebrity reporter mode. She had learned in those heady days that a smile and a brief touch were often enough to keep people who had to speak to her happy.

She hadn't been trying to keep Mandi's mother happy—just to move away from the awkward conversation.

A hotel staffer stood in the shadows behind the table, arms crossed, watching everyone. He was probably stationed there so that he could slip out at the last minute, to warn the kitchen staff that it was time to start serving.

She nodded toward him and continued down the side, pretending to look at the flowers like everyone else.

But she wasn't looking at the flowers. She was looking at the people. Jessi and Dave were standing arm in arm. Jessi was wearing a black dress, obviously new, that accented her athletic form. Dave's suit fit him perfectly—clothing for the young man who was going somewhere.

Most of the other students, particularly the boys, looked out of place in their suits. Some of the suits were too small, although most were too large—either belonging to their father or another male relative, or bought a bit too big to accommodate the way that teenage boys grew.

Some of the girls' dresses were too frilly—fancy wear or prom wear that got dragged out for this occasion. Some weren't dressy enough. A number of girls wore black jeans and black sweaters, trying to look dressed up even when they couldn't afford to be.

Larissa wasn't sure how she had missed the town's impoverishment before. Mandi had mentioned it as she worked on the video. It had come up in the news in the coverage that Larissa had watched obsessively on her long trip home:

In this formerly bustling railroad and logging community, residents scrambled for a handful of high-tech jobs only to see them get swept overseas. Families that once had enough to support a house, two cars, and a middle-class lifestyle, now scramble to pay the mortgage. It was from just such a family that Leif Soderstrom...

She shook the name out of her head. This wasn't Leif's day. Yes, they wouldn't be here if he hadn't gone crazy, but he wasn't what the day was about, anymore than he would be the center of that book she was doing.

She hoped no one would mention him, not even in passing, throughout the entire service.

"Hey." The voice beside her was soft.

Larissa looked to the right. Robyn Frye stood beside her. She wore a black sweater dress that minimized the weight she'd gained from her two children and highlighted her naturally light blond hair.

"I'm sorry about last weekend."

Last weekend felt like a hundred years ago. Larissa was surprised she felt no resentment for all the horrible things Robyn had said to her.

"We all have had difficult moments," Larissa said.

"I sit in the house, and I'm relieved, you know? That I'm not doing what you're doing. I can't go back, Larissa."

Larissa remembered that sense of relief. She remembered feeling it in her New York apartment when she knew she didn't have to go on the air again.

And she had felt it on her first day of graduate school, when she realized she was not in charge of the narrative. Someone else set the curriculum. Someone else chose the books.

Someone else figured out what they were all going to think about.

"It's okay," Larissa said, and meant it. She found it miraculous that she could show up for work this week.

She hadn't resented it once. She hadn't clutched her pillow and wondered if she could fake sick, just to keep from going out her front door.

She hadn't faced each day with courage, but she hadn't once thought of staying home.

And that was different from how she had been before.

Very different.

Maybe she was getting better.

Or maybe those coping skills she'd learned from her grandmother had actually worked in this instance.

"You have to take care of yourself first," Larissa said.

"And my kids. They can't sleep."

Larissa was beginning to believe no one in Manatowa was sleeping. And she really didn't want to talk about it.

How come she was becoming everyone's counselor? Because she had seen things most others hadn't? Or was it just a skill she had unknowingly acquired when she got her journalism training? A vibe she sent out that said, *Talk to me. I'll listen.*

"Is Neal here?" she asked, trying to change the subject.

Robyn nodded. "He got us seats. He doesn't want to talk to anybody." She lowered her voice. "He's talking about homeschooling the kids."

It would keep you busy, Larissa almost said, but somehow managed to stop the words before they came out. And the words that followed, which would have been a statement of shock: *Are you kidding? Why? Everyone else has come back to school.*

Robyn's daughters were six and eight. By the time they got to high school, this would be lost in the deep, dark past.

"What do you think about that?" Larissa asked, using a tried-and-true avoidance answer. How to seem interested without stating an opinion.

Maybe she should teach her students that technique.

"How can I have our girls go to school when I can't?" Robyn's voice broke. "I hate this."

Larissa put a hand on her friend's back. There were no words—not for any of them—and there didn't seem to be right answers, either.

"My mother-in-law wants me to go to counseling," Robyn said, with no sense of irony at all. She'd been so dismissive of therapy just a week before. "Neal thinks it's a waste of money."

"The school is providing counselors for free," Larissa said.

"For the kids," Robyn said.

Larissa shook her head. "For teachers and administrators, too."

Robyn frowned. Then she glanced over her shoulder at her husband. Larissa did, too. Neal was as blond as his wife, and going just as round. He sat in the exact center of the room, his posture perfect as he faced the stage. He seemed to be willing the service to begin just by the force of his stare.

"Are you going to the counselors?" Robyn had lowered her voice even more.

None of Larissa's answers were good ones. *I was too busy* sounded vaguely judgmental. *I had decades of counseling* a little too needy. Besides, Robyn had used that against her last Saturday, lashing out sarcastically when Larissa suggested she talk to someone: *How does talking help? I mean, how many shrinks have you gone through over the years?*

"I haven't gone yet," Larissa said. "But I plan to."

A bit of a lie. More than a bit, really. She was done with counselors. She'd had too many of them, and they'd pushed too hard. She knew what her problems were and she knew she had to face them.

She was going to face them, just tomorrow.

Sort of.

She probably wouldn't go deep like a counselor would want her to. All that denial her grandmother had taught her had gotten her through the week.

It would probably get her through this service.

And even though it meant that she couldn't report on other people's crises, did that really matter? How many people could, after all? Wasn't it a specialized job for specialized people?

Even Gavin was breaking under the strain.

"You think they'd be mad if I went to the counselors but didn't teach?" Robyn was asking.

"No," Larissa said. "I think they understand that you might need the time with a counselor so that you can teach."

Robyn slipped an arm around Larissa's back and pulled her close. "I was mean to you before."

"It's okay."

"It's been haunting me all week. We learned this month how things can change in an instant, and there I was, being the bitchiest woman on the planet—"

"Hush," Larissa said, sounding just like her grandmother, striving to keep the harmful words inside. She swallowed, then forced herself to put her head on Robyn's shoulder. "We'll always be friends."

She wasn't sure if that was a lie, too.

It probably was.

Larissa didn't keep friends. Especially if they had intentionally hurt her, like Robyn had.

"I hope so." Robyn squeezed, then let go.

Larissa lifted her head.

"Sit with us?" Robyn asked.

"I need to be near an aisle in case the memorial film we prepared screws up."

Robyn nodded. Then she headed back to Neal.

Larissa let out a small sigh. This was as hard as she thought it would be. Harder, maybe, than her brother's funeral.

She didn't remember her parents', although she remembered going into the church for her mother's ceremony—all the reporters, her brother swearing, her grandparents looking alarmed.

But the actual ceremony itself was long gone.

Except that the casket was closed.

She never saw her mother again.

"Those must be unusual flowers." Helen Meiers had come up beside her. "You've been studying them for a while."

"I'm just trying to get ready for this."

Helen looked at the flowers, too. As she did, Larissa saw them—truly saw them—for the first time.

A spray of calla lilies—expensive and hard to get in the Midwest at this time of year—with the tips dyed black. Nineteen of them, one for each of the dead, surrounded by a bit of greenery, and tucked into a large green glass vase.

"Did you want to say something?" Helen asked.

For a moment, Larissa thought she meant now—did she want to say something *now*—and then she realized that Helen meant during the service.

She swallowed her immediate response—*Good God, no*—suddenly grateful for all the on-air training. Thoughts crossed her mind loud and clear before they reached her lips, and she could refine them into something acceptable.

"I'm no good at this sort of thing."

"I don't think anyone is." Helen sighed. "Except maybe Ted Kennedy."

Larissa gave her friend a sideways look. The exhaustion that was showing on Helen's face two days ago had become deep lines around her eyes and mouth. Larissa wondered if they'd be permanent.

"I'm sure that's a skill he never wanted to cultivate," Larissa said.

Helen nodded. "I can empathize. And, oddly, you do get better at it, even if it doesn't get easier."

She would know. She had spoken at every funeral. Even though she hadn't known all of the students personally, they had belonged to her. They were part of her school, her tribe, her responsibility.

Larissa had never asked her how she felt. Helen had told her bits of it. The frustration, the anger, the sadness.

But never that sense of responsibility, that deep-seated worry: *Could I have done better? Could I have found a way to stop this?*

Larissa had felt it when she heard Leif's name on the news.

But it had been a lesser version of what she had felt at Ric's funeral, when she had gotten up to talk.

Only a few people had been in that church. Nadia and husband number—what? Two? Larissa couldn't remember. Nor could she remember the man's name. Then there'd been the minister, his wife, and the church deacons who acted as pallbearers.

A woman had come in and sat in the back. She'd been so thin that Larissa could see the bones in her arms from the lectern, and she had had the horrible pockmarked skin of a meth addict.

At first Larissa had thought she'd come in to get warm, but she'd stayed and cried, and when it had come time to walk to the front and say good-byes to the casket, she had stood alone beside it for the longest time.

Larissa had given her the room to be alone, figuring she could talk with her graveside.

But the woman hadn't shown up graveside. Larissa never saw her again, and could only guess at her part in Ric's life.

"I guess I have to get this started," Helen said. She looked toward the front, her shoulders slumping down. "You think we'll ever be normal again?"

CNN anchor Aaron Brown, after 9/11, had coined a phrase—*the new normal*—which he used repeatedly on his newscasts in the year that followed. *This is what we should expect in the new normal,* he'd say in that slightly patronizing tone of his. *This is how governing happens in the new normal.*

But no matter how patronizing he'd seemed, no matter how much the phrase had grated, he had been right. America had moved into a new normal.

Like Larissa had moved into a new normal when she moved in with her grandparents. When her brother committed suicide. When she could no longer stand before a microphone and trust herself to speak coherently.

But she couldn't use the phrase with Helen. It was too patronizing, too wrong.

"I'm not sure we should strive for normal anymore," Larissa said. "We're living in extraordinary circumstances. I think we have to acknowledge them."

And that, she knew, was different from what her grandmother had wanted. Her grandmother had wanted to recreate as much of the world before as she could.

She had even tried to get the children to call her Mother, not Grandmother, as if she could erase the memory of her own daughter, and pretend she was starting anew.

But the three of them were too old. It felt wrong to use their beloved mother's name for their not-quite-as-beloved grandmother.

In the end, even her grandmother, the Queen of Denial, had given in to a new and different reality. One none of them really wanted to accept.

Helen didn't answer Larissa, merely touched her arm, then headed toward the stage. Larissa watched her walk, threading her way through parents and teachers and students, uttering a kind word to each of them.

Maybe she should have said nothing, just let Helen vent for a moment.

She wondered if she offended, if she had said the wrong thing. She used to do that all the time.

Then, for a while, she hadn't cared. She hadn't cared about anyone or anything or how they reacted to her words.

On-air training had changed that. Each word measured, each word important. Use the word *allegedly* even when she knew that someone had done the crime; use the softer *person of interest* when she knew the police actually meant *suspect*.

Focus on the subject's tears or laughter or anger—any sign of real emotion. But she couldn't show real emotion. She was a reporter, a conduit, an information source only. Not an arbiter of reactions.

Reactions belonged to someone else.

Never to her.

She walked to the back of the ballroom and took a seat near the door leading to the stairs. She wanted to be ready to bolt up them if something went wrong with the video, not that she expected it to.

She rather hoped it would, getting her out of the throng and away—maybe even able to leave early without committing some sort of social sin.

Music started behind her, and it took her a moment to realize it was live. Like the rest of the mourners, she turned and saw the school's choir in their Columbia-blue-and-white robes—the school colors—singing some sort of classical piece.

She wasn't good with classical music. She knew this was churchy and old and if she had to guess, she suspected it was Bach—something religious that the school board would allow without claiming that it favored any particular denomination.

And then she heard the words—*requiem aeternum*—and a shiver ran through her.

These were the words for the Catholic funeral mass. She'd first heard them as a young reporter, covering the funeral of an important Catholic bishop. She'd asked another reporter to translate for her.

Requiem aeternum: Give them eternal rest.

She hoped the director wouldn't do the entire requiem or if she did, that hardly anyone understood it.

Because the next section, *Kyre eleison*—Lord have mercy upon us—was appropriate, but the section that followed was too accurate for a service that was supposed to leave the mourners with a feeling of hope.

Dies irae: Day of Wrath.

Day of Wrath. It was what they had lived through, what Leif had accomplished.

What Larissa's father had accomplished.

And like her father, Leif's day of wrath would have consequences that reverberated down the generations.

I am standing here today, in front of a nearly empty church, she had said all those years ago, *because I can't let Ric go without some words from someone who knew him, someone who remembered when he was a laughing boy with a light in his eyes. Someone who saw that light go out. Someone who always hoped it would rekindle, and now mourns that it will not have the chance.*

Her father's actions—her father's murders—continued long after her father was placed in his grave.

Unshriven. That was what her grandmother had said with an amazing amount of venom in her voice. She'd said it to Ric on the day of their mother's funeral.

When's Dad's funeral? Ric asked.

They buried him already, Grandmother had said.

Without us? Ric's voice had trembled.

Of course without us, Grandmother had said. *You don't hold a funeral for a man like that. You put him in unconsecrated ground and make sure that he meets his maker unshriven.*

What does that mean? Larissa asked her brother as Grandmother walked away, effectively ending the conversation. *What's "unshriven"?*

Her brother had looked at her, his eyes holding the emptiness that she would never get used to.

Damned, he said. *She made sure he was damned.*

Hmm, Nadia had said, surprising both of them because she had been paying attention. *You'd think he'd already done that to himself.*

Nadia's last words ever on the subject of their father.

From that point on whenever his name came up, she'd say, *You don't really want to talk about him* or *Let's not waste our breath.* Or as she got older and more sophisticated, she'd simply change the subject with such a smoothness that you wouldn't even notice until hours later when you were alone—if you'd notice at all.

As the choir reached the end of the *requiem aeternum*, a long line of people mounted the stage. Larissa knew some of them and could identify others by their clothing. Mayor Reng led, followed by the community's religious leaders, and members of the school board as well as Helen Meiers.

Maybe it had been a mistake to keep the reporters out. They'd have seen something they wouldn't have believed because out-of-town reporters rarely took the time to research their subjects.

They would have seen the amazing diversity that Manatowa had cultivated.

When she was a little girl, Manatowa was the big city, the place where she went for dress clothes and school supplies, but where she never stayed because it was "weird." Unlike New Lake, which kept itself as isolated as it could, Manatowa had always brought in refugees, survivors, and outsiders.

Sometimes it happened through the town's only synagogue, as it had before, during, and after the Second World War. Families fleeing the Holocaust had a place to come, and then survivors had a place to call home. Even now, there were elderly members of the community who had a black number tattooed on their forearm—numbers they used to keep covered, and now showed with—not pride—but acknowledgement. Acknowledgement of what they had gone through.

Acknowledgement of all they had survived.

Others had come with the aid of local churches, like the members of the now rather large Hmong community. And some had come to work in the fields in the summers, had stayed and been sponsored for citizenship, and then had brought their own families up from Mexico and South America.

And now it was the local mosque bringing people in from the Middle East, refugees from Iraq and Afghanistan, and some from Africa as well, trying to survive all kinds of genocide and that lovely media euphemism "sectarian violence."

The mosque here had originally been an offshoot of Chicago's Black Muslims, but had become something more. And now Manatowa—small as it was—represented most of the world's largest religions.

They sat behind the podium—Catholic and Buddhist priests side by side, an imam next to a rabbi, several ministers (half of them female), and one Wiccan leader whose white robe seemed as formal as the black robes on the Protestant leaders.

Of course, Manatowa's diversity was evident too in the faces on the video that her students had prepared. Leif hadn't picked one race or type of student.

He'd shot indiscriminately.

The faces on that video were black and Asian and Hispanic. There wasn't even a preponderance of the Nordic blonds that still dominated the community. Just a few, just like there were a few children of mixed race—children whose heritage wasn't obvious in their faces like it had been in the faces of their parents.

Maybe it shouldn't have surprised her that the community had voted to do the book. She hadn't realized herself until she was sitting here, listening to a shaky-voiced choir sing a mass for the dead, that this community had a long history of quiet but appropriate charity.

Which made Gavin's words the other night all that much more fatuous.

She felt a surge of anger, clenched her fists together, and willed it back. Anger could wait. Anger didn't belong here, not in the memorial, not when everyone else was grieving.

Mayor Reng stood and said a few introductory words. Then the lights went out, and in the silence, the video began.

It surprised her. She had thought they would run the video at the end. She found herself longing for a voice-over (maybe Hannah had been right after all) or some music, anything to take her mind off the stark images before her.

Faces of the dead. Nineteen faces. Sixteen of them still so young that their features weren't completely formed. The remaining three looking harsh or sad or a little put-upon in their yearly yearbook shots. The annual photographs that kids usually like and the adults who worked in the school hated.

The adults saw the passage of years. The kids saw only the photographs themselves—good, bad, indifferent. *Was my hair combed well? Did I have a zit? Does that shirt really look that bad on me?*

She remembered those days and those feelings, and she also knew how it felt to sit in front of the photographer as an adult, to have yet another portrait taken, this one not all that different from the one from the year before.

She tried hard not to look annoyed during her photo session. But she hadn't realized, until now, that that was the most recent photograph taken of her.

It was probably the most recent non-candid photograph of the three dead adults as well.

Mandi's vision for the video was excellent. Her execution had been superb. She had gone in alphabetical order. She let the year-book photos revolve, then she moved in for a close-up on one, and used the photographs the student reporters had gathered tell a small story.

Not the whole story, which had so frustrated Mandi. Not the poverty or the abuse or the speech defect. Not the occasional cruelties from the straight-A student, or the football player's penchant for slamming smaller kids into a locker.

But the upbeat story of a life shortened. The grinning infants, the smiling parents, the family portraits. The tiny achievements, from a bowling trophy to a ballet recital. The prized possessions scattered around a now-empty bedroom.

And then she'd focus in on that last photograph again, that high school portrait, and slowly it would recede, until it became part of the grouping. The grouping would turn, and another face would take its place.

The video seemed to last forever. It hadn't seemed that long when she'd screened it before. They hadn't used the full fifteen minutes that Helen Meiers had given them. They hadn't even come close. The final runtime was a little more than half that—about eight minutes.

Eight minutes that had gone fast in the classroom on Friday afternoon, and seemed just as fast this morning when she had made sure the equipment worked to her satisfaction.

But now, in the darkness, with the occasional sob around her, those eight minutes seemed like eighty. Nineteen lives reduced to photographs and one dubious connection:

They would always be tied together in death. Just like Mandi had tied them together in that revolving image.

Larissa hadn't realized how much it looked like the old westerns that had been on television when she was a child, when the bad guy would get the heroes in his sights. Faces would cover the bullet chambers, and then revolve as the six-shooter searched for its intended target.

She shook the image out of her mind. Surely no one else had come up with that.

It wasn't an image from now, anyway. It was an image from then.

From those days after her parents died.

Westerns had been banned in her grandparents' house. Westerns and detective shows and late-night violent movies.

Anything with a gun.

The sound of a gunshot would always make Larissa cry. Nadia would watch in rapt fascination, and Ric would cover his face.

But Larissa would sob uncontrollably, and it was her reaction—not theirs—that led to the banned programs.

Her siblings had resented it.

She had felt mildly relieved.

She wiped at her face now and took a shaky breath. She looked away from the images on the screen, focused on the stairway door, and reminded herself that she hadn't had to go up there. Her part of the ceremony was done—had been done before the ceremony started.

Now all she had to do was make it through the speeches, have a little conversation, and go home.

To a silence that she'd cocooned herself in.

To help her feel safe.

nineteen

the service was interminable, and the gathering afterwards even more so. Larissa found herself in high demand, with people she didn't even know stopping to tell her their ideas for the book.

She had slipped away from those conversations, only to find herself in others, less annoying but a bit too maudlin for her tastes—what someone had last seen a victim do or how a victim had done something nice.

After a perfunctory fifteen minutes, she walked out the side door, down the hall, and dipped into the ladies' room. Then when the women near the sink cleared out, she left as well.

Instead of going back to the ballroom, she went down the stairs, collected her cape, and disappeared into the night.

For once, there weren't camera trucks everywhere. Maybe the media had finally gotten it, although she doubted it. Some of the lack was probably do to hotel security—it had been so fierce that she'd heard a lot about it after the service. But the rest could be attributed to the way the news cycle worked.

Reporters had probably gathered as close to the hotel as they could or used an establishing shot or maybe even some footage previously taped of the ballroom itself. Then they'd stood outside in the bitter cold, and pretended they were about to go into the service, talking about how it started, how each person would be remembered, and what the itinerary was.

The only reason no one waited for the service to end was the time of night. It was past prime time in the East Coast, and no one wanted to provide footage to the local network news broadcasts without using it first themselves.

Since CNN had cut back its late-night coverage, and FOX focused everything on its talking heads, and MSNBC's budget got slashed, no one ran news after the East Coast's golden hours.

That forced a heavier reliance on the BBC for 24-hour cable news stations (especially during breaking international stories) and accidental celebrity for whomever was the prettiest or most telegenic news reporter in the building when something national broke between eleven and four EST.

Larissa gathered her cape around her, unable to believe she was thinking about the news after that long and sad service. Then, as she stepped outside into the deep cold, she realized her focus made sense.

The news had always allowed her to distance herself from something emotional. She didn't have to feel anything if she was thinking about how to cover an event.

Her car was in the hotel's parking lot, illuminated by a giant street light. The lot was packed, and still she saw no reporters.

The snow squalls from earlier in the week had ended, but the cold continued. It felt deeper than before—or maybe that was just the wind, blowing across the hidden prairies with nothing to stop it.

She got into the car and shivered, but didn't bother to blast the heat. The interior wouldn't even be warm by the time she arrived home.

That was one of the benefits of living in a small town.

How her perspective had changed. Manatowa had been the big city when she was a child. When she moved here after all those years of traveling, especially after the last few years of living in New York City, Manatowa had felt unbearably small.

Now she took pleasure in those small things, like the way it took her only five minutes to get from the center of downtown to her home.

As her car's lights brushed her front yard, she made out a car parked in front of her unshoveled sidewalk. The sidewalk was just a formality this winter anyway; the reporters had trampled the snow so badly she doubted she would have a lawn come summer.

Her shoulders tightened as she turned the corner into her driveway. She didn't want a confrontation—not after the emotions she'd already spent (and buried) during the long evening.

A man sat on her front porch steps, a grocery bag beside him and pizza box warmer covering his lap. He wore a parka with the hood up, so she couldn't see his face.

She went into the garage and closed the garage door so quickly she nearly dented the back of her car. Then she waited a moment before getting out—she wanted to make certain he hadn't snuck in somehow.

He hadn't. She was alone. The car's engine ticked, the only sound in the silence. Then she got out, slammed the door, and the bang echoed.

Before he could try to get into her garage, she hurried to the side door, unlocking it, going inside, and locking the door closed behind her in movements so rapid they almost seemed like one.

The doorbell rang. She sighed in exasperation. She should have expected it.

She had installed an intercom—like the one she used to have in her New York apartment building—by the front door.

She pulled off her gloves, then pressed the talk button. "I'm not giving interviews. Not now, not later, not ever."

The sound clinked off, then a hiss let her know that the person outside pressed that intercom's talk button. "I'm not asking for an interview. I'm a geek bearing gifts."

"That's Greek to me," she muttered before she punched the intercom. Her shoulders relaxed though. The joke was an old one—a private one that only she and Gavin had shared, and only when they were lovers.

She pressed the talk button. "What kind of gifts?"

"Only the best. Chicago-style pizza, which I must say is pretty good considering the size of this burg, and the appropriate accompaniment—beer."

Beer sounded good. Beer was an indulgence for her, one she didn't always enjoy. But on nights like this, beer felt like decadence.

She undid the house's security code and unlocked the front door from the kitchen. Then she pressed the intercom button.

"The door's open."

She could hear it click and squeak, then the sound of stomping feet before the door snicked shut.

"That's not very safe, you know." Gavin came into her kitchen, carrying the pizza in one hand like a waiter, the beer in the other. He still had his parka hood up, but he had taken off his boots.

His socks had grayed from too many washings, and they stretched thin across his bony feet.

She took the pizza from him. The bulky warming bag was actually hot to the touch.

"You just got this," she said.

"Guilty." He pushed back the hood, set the beer on the counter, and unzipped his coat. "The radio said the service ended about ten, so I figured you'd get here as soon as you could."

"There was a wake afterwards." She didn't know what else to call it. Gathering, which she had used privately, seemed too informal.

"And that's just not your thing, is it, Lissy? Anymore than funerals are. You used to make me cover the bloody things."

His British affectations no longer annoyed her. They were welcome tonight.

He hung his coat on the back of one of her chairs. With one hand, she picked up the coat and stashed it in her closet.

"I don't recall you being a neat freak," Gavin said.

"I don't recall you being around after I bought my first place." She unzipped the warmer. A logo for the best pizza place in town covered the box inside. "How'd you know I needed this?"

"Funerals for the last ten days and then this, the mother of all memorial services? Hell, you should go on a bender, not just eat Chicago Stuffed." He grabbed paper towels from her paper towel holder and put them on the kitchen table. "I hope you're not going to force me to use a plate."

Normally, she would. But he was right; she didn't need any more ceremony tonight.

She rooted in the bag. "What kind of beer did you buy?"

"I was thinking St. Pauli Girl, just because—you know—we're in Minnesota, but there's a hell of a brew pub not far from here, and I brought the stuff they bottle. The six dark are for you. I found myself piss water."

He remembered all their old jokes. She loved dark beer, having learned to drink in England on an assignment. Like most Americans, he got his start with Millers or Coors or whatever the local 7-Eleven had on sale on a Friday night. He'd developed a taste for American beer. She always thought it tasted like spoiled milk.

She'd told him that once, and he said that he preferred piss water—which, when challenged, he claimed to have tasted. Hence the joke.

"These are some digs," he said as he took the pizza box to the kitchen table. "They pay teachers good here. I didn't think any American public school teacher got something resembling a salary."

"I get a salary and some pretty good benefits. But I don't need them. The books gave me more than enough to live on if I decide I don't want to work again."

"Which is why you're forgoing your fee on this one?" He made the question sound casual, but she felt the blood rush to her face.

"If this is just a ploy to get an interview—"

"No ploy," he said. "Old friends. If I use any of this in anything I write, you have my permission to sue me and my employer for every last dime."

She took a bottle of the dark beer, opened it, and carried it to the table. Then she sat across from him, her eyes narrowing.

"You don't have an employer, do you?" she asked.

"As of Thursday, no," he said. "I told them to piss off."

She pulled a piece of pizza from the box. The pizza was still so warm that a string of cheese stretched from the pie to her paper towel. She wrapped the string around her finger, yanked, and the string broke. Then she pulled the string off her skin with her teeth.

"I told you to go back and see their shrink," she said.

"And I found myself asking what kind of job is it that snaps you into a thousand pieces then asks you to reassemble? What kind of job is it that requires you to be dead inside, except when you're trying to show your sense of outrage or injustice? Yet if a little boy loses an arm five feet from you—collateral damage from a roadside bomb—you get fired if you drop your camera and staunch the bleeding, running him to the nearest military doctor to save his pitiful little life."

She set the pizza down. "That's why you're not overseas anymore?"

He shrugged. "I broke the camera."

Then he took a large bite of pizza. Hers no longer looked quite as tasty.

"I thought in this day and age an heroic reporter is precisely what they're looking for."

"Not if he has the balls to report that what they thought was a road-side bomb was an unexploded American grenade. Not if a reporter covers not just the violence on the ground, but the friendly fire incidents—the ones that haven't been cleared by the military brass. Not if they think you're 'making trouble,' which really means that you're pissing off their advertisers and corporate headquarters."

"So work in print," she said.

He raised his head. The bleak expression in his eyes made her think of Ric for a brief moment. Then Gavin smiled ruefully.

"I don't write well enough."

"*The Times* turned you down?"

"And *The Post*—that's *The Washington Post.* I'm sure *The New York Post* would love me, and my political bent."

She smiled in spite of herself. Gavin was as far to the left as a reporter could be and still consider himself middle-of-the road.

"Even *USA Today* told me I had to brush up on a few skills. What did their international editor say? 'Hmm, Mr. Quinn, I'm rather stunned to see how many ills the force of a man's personality can cover.'"

She took a sip from her beer. Gavin had been like Mandi when Larissa met him. He'd been all intuition and vision. Apparently that had gotten him to the top of the on-air live reporting. But he'd never learned the writing skills. He never needed to.

Ah, love, he used to say, *just let's talk it through and then film me while I give it my best, what do you think?*

Hiding his lack of skills. Or using the skills he had to the best of his ability.

"So what are you going to do now?" she asked.

"Drink myself to oblivion in your kitchen." He lifted his beer bottle in a salute, then took a long drink.

"Six bottles of beer are not enough for you to reach oblivion," she said. "Unless you've lost your edge."

He set the bottle down. "Lost the edge and lost the desire. Young men can get stinking drunk. A man my age regrets the excess in the morning."

She finally took a bite of her pizza. It was good, all cheese and tomatoes and sinfully delicious homemade sausage.

"What are you going to do now?" she asked.

He had finished his first piece. He took another. "I could go back for my teaching degree, but I bet they want you to write."

She said nothing, just sipped her beer. It wasn't the best she'd had, but it was rich and thick and bitter, perfect with the pizza. Perfect for this moment.

"Or I could write a book." Then he grinned. "Whoops. There's that 'write' word again."

"That really hurt you, didn't it?"

He raised his eyebrows. "I seem to recall a dinner with a woman who was fried that *The Times* had deigned to ask her for a writing sample. And she got the job."

She *had* been angry. She thought she had proven herself. But later she understood. It was a different medium.

"You can get a teaching position without going back to school, you know."

"Ah, the celebrity journalist sinecure thing," he said. "Visiting guest lecturer, the once-famous reporter who can no longer get work. No thank you."

"Or you can freelance."

"I'm thinking documentaries," he said, swigging his beer. "You think you can show me how to make something as compelling without a voice-over as that piece your students did?"

She flushed. "You lied to me. You *were* in the hotel."

She had let him into her home. She was having pizza with him. She had *trusted* him, and she had misplaced that trust again.

Her words clearly had a bite to them, because he held up his hands.

"Think for a minute," he said. "If I had been in the hotel, how did I get here with a pizza before you?"

"You left before me," she said.

"I could have, I suppose, but I didn't. I helped set up this morning. I watched the trial run of that documentary or whatever you want to call it. That's not your style. One of your kids edited it, didn't he?"

"She," Larissa said.

"That's some talent. Think she'll work for scale if I go freelance?"

Of course she would. It would be a dream for any of Larissa's students. But the question was a flip one. Gavin didn't really mean it.

He was trying to change the subject, and she wasn't going to let him.

"Why were you there this morning?"

"Honestly," he said, "I hoped I'd run into you."

If what he was saying was true, he had just missed her. She had no idea how she would have reacted that morning if he had come up to her.

Probably rudely.

"Then," he said, "I finally decided on the direct approach. I figured pizza, beer, some conversation. We might reestablish the friendship."

He had been trying to find her. Just like he had been trying all week.

She still wasn't sure what he wanted. Just a chance to talk about his career?

It seemed so like Gavin and so unlike him at the same time. All he ever focused on was his career, and yet in the past, he rarely spoke of it, thinking that no one else would understand both his level of ambition and his need to prove himself.

Or did he want back into her life? And if so, why? She wasn't an ambitious young reporter anymore. She wasn't the star celebrity journalist, either.

She was a high school teacher who had just been to a memorial service for sixteen students.

Eight of whom she'd known well.

Her heart twisted.

Not to mention the shooter. She thought she had known him well, too.

But that wasn't the first time she had been mistaken about hidden violence in a person she knew.

It probably wouldn't be the last.

"I'm not sure I want to reestablish the friendship," she said. "I'm afraid of the cost."

"Yeah." He didn't look at her. He set the empty beer bottle down, reached for another, and then stopped himself. "I suppose bottled water is too much to ask for."

She paused. It seemed like such a non sequitur. But really, all he had meant to do was shut down the discussion of their past.

That, too, was just like Gavin.

"I have some bottled water in the fridge," she said.

He got up, and got himself one.

"No more beer?" she asked.

"Naw," he said. "I'm tired of pretending I'm tough and jaded and talented."

"You are tough and jaded and talented."

"I'm not tough or jaded and apparently I can't write."

"Who needs to write when you can narrate clearly without a script?"

He looked at her. "You don't think I should have quit."

"If they were sending you places like this, yes, I do," she said. "At this point, Manatowa is a baby reporter's paradise. Everyone knows how these stories go. Some poor kid shoots up a school. People suffer. Other kids die. A community is torn apart, and then attempts to reassemble itself. A reporter with brains can do the story without leaving the office."

"Now who's cynical?" he asked.

That flush returned. Maybe she'd had too much beer. It had been a long time since she had any, and this single bottle was hitting her hard.

Or maybe she just needed an excuse to say what she thought.

She hadn't done that for a very long time.

"I'm just saying that this story doesn't play to your strengths. You're investigative. You're able to get into parts of the world no one else can. You can see things with a clarity that's rare, even for the most learned observer. And you're letting the suits kick you around."

"Suits pay my not-so-measly salary."

"Most of which you've invested because you were never home long enough to spend it," she said. "Use some of it. Take a financial risk for once. Lord knows you know how to take to take other risks. But you've never been very courageous financially."

"Hey," he said, about to contradict her.

But she grabbed a second piece of pizza and shook it at him. Cheese-covered onions toppled off the side.

"Make a documentary. Hook up with the *Discovery Channel* or *WGBH* or the Annenberg Foundation. Get them to fund your dream project. You have a dream project, right?"

"Dream project," he said, sounding a little stunned.

As if he'd never heard those two words in the same sentence before. He twisted the cap off the bottled water, then studied the rim of the bottle as if it held the secrets of the universe.

"Dream project," he repeated. "Do you have one?"

"We're not talking about me," she said.

"I'll bet it's not editing some book project written by a bunch of amateurs. Have you thought about the copyediting you'll do? Have you thought how awful that thing is going to be?"

She had thought of it, and it had made her cringe. But she knew it was surmountable.

She wasn't sure this conversation was.

"Do you," she repeated slowly, as if she were talking to a very stupid child, "have a dream project?"

He shook his head, then took a swig from the water bottle.

"Imagine," she said, "if you had the funds to do the story you've always wanted to do, the story you thought everyone should know. What would that story be?"

"What wouldn't it be?" he asked quietly. "God. There are so many."

"Like?"

"Like you," he said, and there was so much passion in his voice that it stunned her. "What the hell are you doing here, teaching kids? You're the best producer I've ever known and you're a hell of a writer. You're a dynamite reporter too, although you tend to avoid the tough interviews. But you're a journalist through and through, and you're here, burying yourself in Mayberry."

"This isn't Mayberry," she said before she understood that he was changing the subject again.

"I'd love to explore what it is that makes people like you—people with real compassion—leave our profession."

"Examine yourself," she said. "Aren't you the one who just quit?"

Her heart was pounding. She was feeling manipulated. Had he just quit? Or had he come here to interview her all along? Did he already have funding lined up for a documentary on failed reporters? Or was he just thinking aloud?

"You did *just* quit, didn't you?" she asked, her tone pointed. "Or was this all a ruse to get me to talk to you?"

He licked his lower lip, one of his few tells. And what it told her was that he had been lying to her.

"Dammit," she said. "You're not here for the shooting. You're not here for some network. You're here for me."

"Yes," he said, setting the water bottle down. "I had no idea where you were until this thing happened."

He was trying honesty now. If she wasn't so pissed off, she could make a list of the various ways he would manipulate her to get the story.

Although he'd done a great job already. He'd gotten her to give him some lectures. He'd seen her work the room at the town council. He'd seen the student documentary.

And he'd come here, with pizza and beer, and talk of growing older. Only he wasn't trying to figure out his own future.

He was trying to understand what had happened to hers.

Which was why he had switched from beer to water so early on.

"Are you taping this conversation?" She tossed her half-eaten piece of pizza back into the box. Then she slammed the box lid closed and picked the box up. She carried it to the warmer on the counter and shoved the box inside.

Then she went to the closet, got Gavin's parka and tossed it at him.

"You can get out," she said.

"I'm not taping anything," he said.

"But you'll make notes."

"I'm trying to understand," he said. "Okay. Here's the truth. I am doing a piece—a long piece, actually, and if it's as good as I think, it'll air over some successive nights. If it doesn't do well, then it'll go into journalism schools, so that they can start teaching how to prevent this."

"What is this?" she asked.

"The loss of great people like you."

"And like you, if you're doing documentaries."

"I'm doing documentaries because I don't want to be embedded, and I don't want to be marginalized," he said. "If I get my own stuff, no one will air it. I have to go through approved channels. You want me to expound on the corporatization of American news? How the Reagan Administration's gutting of FCC protections destroyed American journalism? Because I can. I can go on for hours. Which is how I got this gig in the first place."

He was breathing hard, and his eyes glinted.

"You *were* fired," she said with a touch of surprise.

"I quit," he said.

The wounded tone in his voice told her more than his words had. "Because they gave you an ultimatum."

He folded his coat over his arms. "Fucking suits."

"So you bitched to all your colleagues," she said.

"Every chance I got."

"And finally someone hired you to do this."

"Hell, no." His face flushed. "I took your advice before you gave it. This is my baby. I went after the financing. I'm devoting all my waking hours to it. I'm the one who succeeds or fails because it's my goddamn project, not because some suit ordered me to cover a story."

She nodded. Which was why his grandstanding in front of the town hall meeting didn't matter. Why he could be wherever he wanted, not in the pack of reporters.

Why he was sitting with her now.

"So, I was right," she said quietly. "You did lie to me. You never had PTSD."

"Ah, hell, Liss. Why do you think I'm stateside?"

"Because you wouldn't embed," she said.

"Yes," he said. "Because the only way to deal with PTSD and still be a reporter is to go to a situation where anxiety is fucking *normal*. Don't you get it? Some of us can't retire because if we did, we'd go bug-fuck crazy."

"So why isn't your documentary about Rwanda or Afghanistan or maybe a trip down the Amazon following the drug trade?"

He plucked at the fur around the hood of his parka. "Because, when I couldn't find you, I did some research."

"Which was how you knew I was in Manatowa," she said, not quite following the logic here.

"No," he said. "When I got diagnosed. The only other reporter I knew who had the damn thing was you. And I wanted to talk to you, and you vanished."

"And you, being a world-renowned investigative reporter, couldn't find me."

He sighed. "All right. So I didn't look that hard. It felt like crawling. It still did, that night last week by your car."

"When you were conning me."

"I wasn't—" He stopped himself. "When I wasn't telling you the whole truth."

"How Gavin Quinn of you, not to tell the whole truth."

"I tell the truth when I'm reporting," he snapped. And that was true. He did tell the truth in front of a camera. "Nothing I've told you is a lie except the timing. I did apply to *The Times*. I did get turned down for my lack of writing skill. I did look at all the other options, including working for a less prestigious network, like Dan Rather is doing, and decided none of that was for me. I wanted to do my own work."

"So why are you here, lying to me now?" she asked. "You *are* doing some puff piece for money. Is *Access Hollywood* going to pay you the big bucks for exclusive footage of me at the memorial service?"

"*No*," he said. "I don't know how many times I can reiterate that. No."

She walked to the kitchen table. She wasn't ready to throw him out anymore, although she was still considering it.

She wished she hadn't packed up the pizza. She was still hungry.

"Contrary to what you seem to believe," he said, "you're not that big a celebrity. The producers want you because you're the closest thing Minnesota has to a celebrity except Garrison Keillor. That's all. Someone the press knows was near crisis. 'Oh, shit. We can make the story personal.'"

She flushed again. "I know that."

"Well, then, you should know that I couldn't sell a documentary about you."

She knew that too, but the news still surprised her. He had led her to believe that whatever he was doing *was* about her.

"Then why are you here?"

"Because you went through it," he said. "You quit. You're the other choice."

"What?" she asked.

"After you burn out, there are still a bunch of choices you can make if you want to spend your life reporting—real reporting, not that talking heads crap. First, you can go into the war zones and the danger areas until you can't anymore. Then you become an anchor or a talking head or a columnist or something. Or you downsize, go to a lesser market, become their star."

She gave up and went back to the warming bag. She pulled out the box, got a plate out of the cupboard this time, and plucked two pieces of pizza on it. Then she shoved the plate into the microwave.

"Or you keep going, you keep reporting, until you literally lose your mind. Or die."

She grabbed a fork and stood there with it in her hand like a weapon. Gavin didn't seem to notice.

"Or," he said, "you go in until you break, take some time, heal, and go back."

The timer dinged. She took the plate out. The bottom was too hot, but she didn't move her hand. Instead, she set the plate on the counter, and proceeded to eat standing up.

"Or you quit. You teach. You join the Foreign Legion. I don't know. But you're done reporting. You, L'iss, represent that category for me, because you're one of the living breathing people who has actually walked away from the job *voluntarily*. That's an important point, you know. Most of the folks who leave the profession don't do it voluntarily. They get fired and they don't want to claw their way back so they do something else. Although…"

He stood and grabbed some pizza for himself. He cupped one hand under the piece so that he wouldn't get anything on her floor.

"…none of them," he said with great emphasis, "no one else has gone on to teach high school in some Podunk town. And I do gotta ask—not on the record, because tonight, none of this is on the record—what the fuck? Why here? Why not the University of Minnesota if you have to be in the stinking Midwest or the University of Chicago or Northwestern, which, for God's sake, has a real journalism department. Why here?"

"Why not?" she asked. Her fingers ached from the hot plate, and she was angry. Underneath it all, she was furious at him for making presumptions about her.

"It's a waste of your skills," he said. "What are you teaching these kids? How to be 'real reporters'? Are you teaching them how to compromise their ethics? Are you teaching them that the corporations rule? Are you teaching them the importance of advertising and how the advertisers can control content?"

She didn't want to answer any of that, and she didn't want to yell at him—not yet, anyway. So she changed the subject.

"I'm more curious about who kept going back in," she said. "I don't know anyone. Not even you, because if you were going back in, you wouldn't be here. You'd be doing some Katrina exposé or getting yourself and a camera locked in a maximum security prison or something."

"My documentary is historical as well as contemporary," he said with some pride.

She cut into her piece of pizza with a fork, not looking at him. She didn't want to make fun of his project. "My documentary" indeed. Historical and contemporary. As if that had never been done before.

"For example," he said, "one of the people who went back into the fray was Ernie Pyle."

"You're saying that because he got killed covering World War II, he had PTSD and should have gotten out?"

"Have you read his work?" Gavin asked.

"Yes, and he was fine. Healthier than all of us put together," Larissa snapped. She cut another piece of pizza, bigger this time, and crammed it into her mouth like a recalcitrant teenager. She didn't want to think about this.

He shrugged as if he didn't care if she disagreed with him.

"Then," he said, "there's Martha Gellhorn. She always went back in."

"Hemingway's—what, second?—wife? Her?"

"You get anti-points," he said. "I thought you were a feminist."

"Feminist is an old-fashioned term," Larissa said crankily.

"She was a better reporter than Hemingway," Gavin said. "She was not as good a novelist, but she was a great reporter. Hemingway only covered World War II because she was already there, sneaking up to the front lines and getting stories that no one else was. Everyone asked him how he could stay away when his wife was there."

Larissa shook her head. "So?"

"So Gellhorn would go into a difficult situation, cover it with aplomb, then 'retire' to write a novel. And then a few years later, she'd go back to reporting. She covered everything from the Spanish Civil War to Vietnam."

"Bully for her," Larissa said.

"L'iss," he said. "You can find all kinds of stuff if you just look. For example, I think the ultimate quitter was Edward R. Murrow."

That got her attention. "Murrow? The reporter's reporter?"

"War correspondent in the 1940s, didn't cover Korea. Fled from Vietnam. His war in the 1950s was against the suits and McCarthy, and that was accidental. He was still selling himself short by doing celebrity interviews. When he couldn't fight the suits anymore, he quit."

"I thought he got sick," Larissa said.

"And what's illness?" Gavin asked. "PTSD by another name."

"I think it was cancer," Larissa said sarcastically.

"At the end, yeah. He smoked like crazy. But he gave up reporting and went to work for the USIA—the ultimate propaganda machine— long before he was diagnosed. The great defender of the First Amendment quit."

"Or was a sellout," Larissa said.

"You don't make money working with the government. He'd've made more if he stayed in TV and did puff pieces."

"Point taken," she said, "but I don't fit into your patterns. I did quit—"

"And you have PTSD. You admitted it to me."

"—but not why you think," she said.

He froze. So did she. She hadn't meant to admit that. She didn't want him looking at her too deeply. She had never told him about New Lake or her family.

She wasn't about to now.

She tried to back up. "Why did you become a reporter? Some great search for truth, right?'

He shrugged.

"I think we're all trying to find an excuse for observing and not acting on what we see. Or trying to understand the world by putting it into words. I could've kept reporting," she said. "I would have had to do some really intense therapy, but I could have."

"You chose not to."

"That's right," she said. "I chose to come home."

Her breath caught. She hadn't admitted that before. Not to anyone, not to herself. In fact, she couldn't remember ever referring to Minnesota as "home" before.

He was watching her, his head tilted. Her heart pounded. She had just given him an opening.

She didn't want to.

Nor did she want to talk about the decision to come here. She had choices—she could have taught college, just like he said. Or she could have gone to a job at a prestigious private high school in San Francisco. She'd had an offer from an arts high school in Georgia.

She'd turned all of them down, putting herself in the pool, knowing she'd end up in the Midwest.

Altruism, she'd told herself.

But really, it was just a way to come back here with a sense of permanence.

Even if she did promise herself she could quit if she couldn't hack the work.

"Home?" he said. "You're from Manatowa?"

She shook her head. "The Midwest. I just wanted to stop roaming. And I didn't want to do local news. I didn't want to write. I wanted to think about all the important stuff, like why I did what I did. Kids make you do that. They ask tough questions. They expect answers."

"So," he said, folding the remains of his pizza into small squares. Tomato sauce dripped on the floor but he didn't seem to notice. "You had walked into an idyll until some kid shot it up."

I'd walked back into hell. Leif just confirmed that's where I was, she thought. But she didn't say it.

"How come you didn't collapse when you heard the news?" he asked. "This should've triggered the PTSD, especially since you had to have the students write about it."

The moment passed. He hadn't realized how close he had come to getting a different story for his documentary. Imagine how he would have done it. A woman who had lived through the New Lake shootings (and suffered PTSD for them) had returned to the Midwest only to go through another random shooting.

She was glad her grandparents had insisted on the name change. It protected her from becoming a sound bite.

She wondered if they had realized it when they made the decision.

"I like what I'm doing here," Larissa said—and that was true. "I like the kids. I care about this school and this community. I'm not shut off anymore, Gavin."

Or, at least, she wasn't as shut off as she had been before.

"So you cried," he said. "You've grieved and yelled and sobbed and hit things and went through all the Kübler-Ross stuff."

She took another bite of pizza so she didn't have to answer him immediately.

She hadn't cried. Not the way he was talking about. And while she had felt some panic and a bit of fear, there had been no real anger.

No real emotions. Not the way he was talking about.

But they lurked beneath the surface.

Making her faint.

Making her think about the news coverage instead of the memorial service.

Making her hold up the dam inside herself with both hands so that it wouldn't burst.

"I mourn those kids," she said softly. "I mourn all of them, including Leif, because we didn't get to him in time."

"We?" Gavin wiped his hands on a napkin. It turned red from the sauce. "You think you could have helped that kid?"

She shrugged. "I don't know. None of us know. We have no idea why he turned like that—and all the superficial news stories in the world won't tell us."

"Superficial?" Gavin asked.

"Oh, hell, Gav, you know what I'm talking about. You guys'll pick Leif's life apart. You'll see if he was abused as a child, if he visited bomb-making websites, if he wrote scary essays when he was in the third grade.

You'll find out if he had a pet and how that pet died. Every act of cruelty he committed, every nasty word he said, every defiant utterance, will become a sign of the way he was going. Signs that this community ignored."

"Someone should've seen it, L'iss," Gavin said.

"Maybe someone did," she said. "I haven't been reading the reporting on Leif. I've been dealing with kids in mourning, injured kids, kids who can't focus on their school work because the goddamn building terrifies them."

"Does it terrify you?" he asked.

The question stopped her. It was a legitimate question, and one she'd never asked herself.

"No," she said after a moment. She saw the school as a place that had transformed. Before she went to Hawaii, Manatowa High School had been the place she taught. Then she had come home to a place filled with history. History of fear and terror and attempted mass murder.

A place she still recognized, but no longer one she understood.

"So how do you feel about it?"

"The school?" she asked, knowing he was grilling her. On this, she didn't care.

"Yeah," he said.

She shrugged. "It's the place where I work."

She wasn't going to give him more than that.

"What I want to know," he said, "was how come this event didn't trigger your PTSD when covering shootings in other towns did. This is so much more personal."

It did trigger, but not badly, and only when Petrovich brought up the New Lake shootings. She hadn't realized that before. Maybe she was better. Maybe she had learned how to cope.

Or maybe she had simply been too busy to collapse.

But that didn't seem right. She'd been busy before, and on things she cared about.

When she didn't say anything, Gavin added, "You remember. I was with you in LA when the SWAT guys got those bank robbers."

Her entire body froze. She had to will herself to breathe. Of all the incidents for him to remember, the bank incident was the worst.

She had made it on the air, but she hyperventilated between takes. Her crew wanted to take her to the hospital—hell, Gavin (who was there for another network) wanted to take her to the hospital—but she wouldn't let them. She finished the task before her, but not without some price. The nightmares alone plagued her for months.

"You remember?" he said, pushing harder than she liked. What was he trying to do? See if he could force her into an episode?

She didn't move. She watched him as if he had a hidden weapon.

"Those serial bank robbers," he said, "the ones that had so much fire power? About ten, twelve years ago? It looked like an honest-to-God movie shootout in the streets of downtown LA—"

"I remember," she said, mostly to shut him up.

And she did shut him up. He stared at her as if she were an experiment, wanting to see if she got trapped in the memory.

She couldn't help that. He had pushed hard enough. The memory came.

The serial bank robbers had been a local LA story until someone realized they were carrying more firepower than the average army—and that they'd made off with more than ten million dollars from three heists.

Her producer had sent her to Los Angeles with a full crew, not wanting to trust LA's local reporters—who got cute on air after too many hours.

Larissa had arrived thirty-six hours before the next robbery, and had heard the first acknowledgement of that robbery on a police scanner she'd been listening to in the KTLA newsroom while waiting for a video link.

She canceled the link, rounded up her crew, and left before the KTLA crew knew what was happening.

She was the first reporter on scene, closest to the action, and she saw—through the shaded glass windows of the bank—the exact moment when the first robber's head exploded.

He had been shot with a high-powered weapon.

One moment, he had a head, encased in a black ski mask.

The next the ski mask, the head, everything was gone.

Except for the blood and brains splattered all over the window she had been staring through.

The pizza threatened to return.

Gavin tilted his head slightly. She wasn't going to give him the satisfaction of covering her mouth.

She swallowed hard, keeping the pizza down, and hoping that he hadn't seen that tiny movement.

As she did, the anger she felt at him earlier returned. She wanted to say *of course she'd had a reaction*. Banks. Blood on the windows. The police storming in.

Dead people along the floor.

But if she spoke, she really would lose that pizza.

Like she had lost her breakfast after she had gotten footage—illegal footage from using the zoom on a camera—from the interior.

Thrown up after she'd finished ten minutes live. She gave the signal to cut, then leaned over and vomited all over her own purse.

"Wow, you got pale," Gavin said. "Or is that green? What happened that day, L'iss?"

She swallowed once, twice, and then a third time. It was a struggle to keep the pizza down.

He could see it now. No need trying to hide it.

"I'm not doing your goddamn documentary," she said. "I'm not relevant. And, I suspect, neither are the people you named. It's all speculation."

"L'iss—"

"I don't trust you anymore, Gavin," she said. "I'm not sure I ever did. You'll ambush me like you just did—"

"That proves you have PTSD. Just the memory made you ill—"

"I saw the interior of that bank," she said with a little too much heat. She wasn't sure which bank she was referring to. Her father's bank? That bank in LA? She had no real idea, and she had to be careful not to reveal too much or Gavin really would do a news story on her.

Hell, she would, if she were still reporting.

"Yeah," he said. "So did I. I saw worse in Bosnia."

"Yeah," she said. "Bosnia. Where there was a fucking war going on."

"Genocide," he agreed cheerfully.

It was the cheerful tone that got to her the most. He didn't have PTSD. He had lied about that. And she had given him credit. Had thought he was one of those reporters who kept his soul.

But he no longer had compassion. No one said the word *genocide* with that much good cheer in his voice.

No one except a calloused reporter who'd seen too much and decided the only way to cope was to feel nothing.

"Get out," she said. "And I mean it this time. Don't come back."

"L'iss—"

"I'm not doing your documentary. I'm not having another conversation with you. And if I watch the goddamn thing and it so much as mentions my name, my lawyers will be all over you—and whatever network airs the thing. I may not win any suit, but I'll make sure your documentary career is done."

"L'iss—"

"I mean it, Gavin. Get out."

He put on his parka. He was frowning at her, as if he couldn't understand the change that had come over her.

"L'iss, honestly, I didn't do anything here. The bank—"

"—happened twelve years ago. It was disturbing. It's still disturbing. Human beings get upset when they see the results of violence, unless they've inured themselves to it. Like you have. You've become one of them, Gavin. You're one of the walking dead. And like the rest of those ghouls, you don't even know it yet."

"L'iss—"

"If you don't get out, I will call the police."

"Like you did on Jane Sloane?" His voice dripped with sarcasm. Calling the police once made Larissa sound like a heroine, especially with someone as unpopular as Jane Sloane was, even among her colleagues.

Twice would make Larissa look like a woman with a vendetta against her old profession.

Or worse, like a crazy woman who couldn't cope with the stresses that were once part of her life.

"Yeah," Larissa said. "Just like Jane Sloane. I don't have a reputation I need to care about any longer. But you do. Imagine the speculation if I have the police haul you out of my house. A former lover. What did he try to do, anyway? It would be pretty clear to anyone who was paying attention that you've been stalking me ever since you arrived."

He stood up. "I have not."

"Standing by my car until I need it? Showing up at meetings you don't need to be covering? Sitting on my porch until I get home from a *memorial* service? Whose reputation will be destroyed, Gavin? Certainly not mine. At least, not in this town. And oddly enough, to me these days, this town is all that matters."

"You have gone wack, you know that, right, L'iss?" He was backing toward the door as he spoke. "You used to help colleagues."

"I still do," she said. "I'm a teacher, remember. You're no longer a colleague."

"L'iss—"

"Gavin, for the final time. Get the hell out of my house."

He did. He went out the front door, slamming it behind him. She locked it, then set the alarm system, including the perimeter alarm, something she hadn't done since the month after she moved in.

Then, through the window, she watched him hobble through the snow to his car. He paused as he got in, looking at her house. When he realized she was watching him, he shook his head, very slowly, as if to say she was crazier now than she had ever been.

She let the curtain drop and sank into a chair near the front door.

She didn't feel crazy. She felt saner than she had in years. The insane pressure of national-level reporting was off her shoulders. Until the last few weeks, she got eight hours of sleep at night. She ate regularly. She even had time to work out.

She cared about things—about her job and the school—and most importantly about the people around her.

She hadn't been lying to Gavin when she told him she mourned those students.

But more than that, she mourned the ones who survived.

They would be scarred like she was. They would have this black bruise on their souls that would get brushed every now and again, and unless they learned how to cope, extreme pain would radiate outward.

Like it had for her after the LA bank robberies.

After Ric's suicide.

After Nadia's second wedding, when she married the man who looked just like their father had the morning he'd left for work.

The morning he'd tried to slaughter everyone he saw.

A weekday, Larissa had thought. A weekday where she had been safe at school.

But Petrovich had said it was a Saturday, and he had no reason to lie.

Yet she misremembered.

Why?

Why couldn't she remember pushing him under the desk in the bank?

The logical answer was that she wasn't there. He interpolated her into the scene just the way she had exchanged days of the week.

But that made no sense.

If she was home that Saturday, wouldn't she have been with her mother? And didn't parents who committed suicide because they couldn't face what was coming—like her mother had when she heard the news—didn't those people kill the children, too? Because any thinking parent knew that future would be worse for the child, the survivor.

The one who would be forever linked with a man who murdered six people in a bank.

Her father.

Everyone would be watching her, waiting for her to lose control just like he had.

He snapped, her grandmother said, as if that were an explanation.

Larissa had snapped that morning of the Los Angeles bank robbery. But she hadn't killed six people. She had vomited all over her purse and was so traumatized that she could barely work for weeks afterwards.

That was snapping.

Not killing people for no apparent reason.

Like her father had.

Like Leif.

She closed her eyes and leaned her head back against the chair. Tears burned against her lids but didn't fall.

Her editor at *The New York Times* repeatedly said to his staff of reporters that if you took on the problems and emotions of the world, you would never be able to get out of bed in the morning.

That was how reporters coped—by seeing everything as a *story*, not as real life, not as something that could worm inside and twist the heart.

But none of them, not a single "story" was a *story*, not really. They were events. Tragedies, usually, something that harmed existing lives or transformed them or ruined them entirely.

She was—and forever would be—the daughter of a man who had murdered six people.

Her students had lost sixteen friends and acquaintances. Most of her students had *witnessed* that loss.

She had been at a memorial service today—a tragic and exceedingly sad memorial service—in which people told stories about the sixteen dead souls.

Stories. Upbeat usually, but stories.

Memories.

Stories that would become static. There would be no new stories about those sixteen people. No new observations, no new witticisms, no new *events* in their lives.

Their lives were over, cut short by a boy with too many guns.

His story was over too, just like her father's. Her father had taken his gun—he'd had only one—and when it became clear that he wouldn't get out of the bank alive (or maybe this had always been his intent), he turned that gun on himself.

His story ended along with everyone else's.

His life had ended.

Larissa's had continued.

Stunted somewhat. Emotionally scarred.

But she was here, in this chair, on this evening, after having tossed an old friend who apparently no longer knew the meaning of the word "friendship" out of her house forever.

Out of her life forever.

Because he didn't understand the difference between *stories* and *events*. Between tragedies and theories. Between loss and the discussion of loss.

He hadn't helped her mourn. He hadn't done anything except made her angry.

Or actually, if she was going to be honest with herself, he hadn't done anything except help her channel anger that was already inside her.

Anger at Leif for "snapping."

Anger at herself for being gone during the crucial week.

Anger at the kids who died for leaving—and the kids who lived for expecting her to help them cope.

Anger at her own inadequacies.

She of all people should understand what her students were going through. Not just the ones who had to "cover the story," but the ones who had been in the cafeteria that morning.

The ones who had survived.

She hadn't talked with any of them about the pain of survival, and she was uniquely qualified to do so.

But she wasn't sure she could.

She wasn't sure she had survived—at least not intact.

She had surrounded herself in sheaths of glass. She could see through them—she could observe—but any time she tried to feel, any time she tried to break the glass, it got tougher, thicker, and harder to see through.

A therapist—she couldn't remember which one—had told her she had to shatter before she could rebuild. That therapist had said that Larissa had never allowed herself to shatter, and Larissa had responded that she never would.

Shattering terrified her. She wasn't sure what lived inside the glass. But whatever it was, it seemed very distant from her. She was both the observer and the observed.

Even now she knew what she looked like in this chair. She knew that she seemed relaxed, maybe even asleep. She knew that the tears pressing against her lids would never fall, nor would they show up in redness or blotches on her face.

She knew that she would get up, clean up her kitchen, and go about her evening as if nothing had happened.

She also knew that was wrong. But she didn't know how to act right—and she comforted herself by wondering if anyone knew how to act after a memorial service for sixteen people who had done nothing more than go to school one morning.

But it was cold comfort.

It was an observer's comfort—something a reporter or a talking head or a old friend would say upon hearing a sad but disturbing story.

It wasn't the response of someone who had known all sixteen people, however casually.

It wasn't the response of someone who *cared*.

She opened her eyes. Gavin's car was long gone. She hadn't even heard it drive away.

She got out of her chair and went to the kitchen. He'd left a hell of a mess, tomato sauce on the floor, pizza and a lot of beer on various counters.

Slowly, she cleaned it up, wishing that she knew how to do something else.

Wishing she knew how to react like a human being, instead of like a creature encased in glass.

twenty

S unday dawned clear and cold, the first clear day since she had come home from Hawaii. Minnesota's winter sun always seemed thin to her, but this morning, as it shone on the ice-covered snow, it had a sparkle that belied her mood.

She was exhausted, mentally and emotionally. She had gotten maybe four full hours of sleep. But they hadn't felt like full hours. They'd felt like moments of inattention. She'd only known she'd been asleep because of the nightmares.

They came one right after the other, and they were all old.

Oddly enough, the first was the newest. Ric, in his empty apartment, sitting in the one comfortable chair, twirling their father's gun in his hand.

It's inevitable, he said in his teenaged-boy voice, the one that went deep and then broke like someone about to cry. *So I figure why fight it. The Mueller family curse. Have you looked at the history of suicide in our family, L'issa? Not just Dad, but two great-uncles, a great-grandfather, some cousins. It's only a matter of time. So I figure why spend years fighting when I'll only lose?*

She reached for him, but his head exploded, like the robber's head exploded, like...someone else's...head exploded, only she couldn't reach that someone else, only the impression of that person, standing, alive, and then, headless on the floor, blood and brains sprayed upon the... wall?...cabinet?...door?

She woke from that, gasping and terrified, with that tantalizing sense of something so close and yet so far out of reach, and like she had, ever since Ric's death—ever since the bank robbery, which added that cruel twist to the dream—she walked it off, pacing her house as if it were a place she had never seen before.

And eventually, when she had enough courage, she went back to bed, only to be plagued by older dreams. Nightmares of running, of having her hand grasped so hard she thought the bones would break, of a gun waving in her face, and her father sobbing, and of her grandmother, coming to school to get her, and finding her already in tears.

She walked off each of the dreams, and finally watched the sun rise, weak and pale, over her back yard. The snow started to glisten the moment the light hit it. She watched as a succession of newspaper delivery boys (girls? She couldn't tell) tossed folded newspapers from the passenger window of a passing car, and she decided there was no point in trying to sleep any longer.

She was just torturing herself.

Maybe she would be able to sleep dreamlessly that night, considering how exhausted she already was.

Over peanut butter-slathered English muffins and hot coffee, she picked up the phone to call Petrovich. She was too tired, and not in any kind of condition to talk about the past.

She had his number half-dialed when she hung up in disgust. Now was the best time. She had already decided, if not for herself, then for the kids.

Or maybe for the nightmares. Maybe confronting the past instead of running from them would finally shut them off.

She prepared to go to Petrovich's house like she had prepared for the memorial service. She spent nearly an hour in her closet, trying to find the right clothing. Armor, much needed, even if no one else noticed.

She also knew she didn't dare be too dressed up—she didn't want to give the wrong impression. Some of her clothing was too formal, other pieces too businesslike, the rest too flirty.

She finally decided on a pair of beloved jeans, a tad too tight after the Minnesota winter, and a thick cable-knit sweater that made her look like she were about to fish the mighty depths of the ocean.

The sweater gave her armor—its bulk protecting her heart—and the jeans made her feel young, not like a teacher or a journalist or a professional woman, but like a person, a young person with her whole life ahead of her, instead of one who had such a tattered history behind her.

Her coat spoiled some of the illusion—the only coat she had that was big enough to accommodate that sweater was an ancient wool coat she used to wear on assignment. She countered the formality of the coat with tennis shoes and her only pair of mittens, grabbed a purse that had only the essentials, and drove herself to the southern part of town.

This part of Manatowa looked like the neighborhoods of her childhood. Ranch houses, which had once seemed so big, now looked tiny on their oversized lots. Built in the day when garage doors faced the street, and large houses were for rich people, these ranches had come back into style just recently as part of a return-to-the-fifties trend.

Petrovich's house was at the end of a dead end. The house had once been a split-level ranch but had clearly been redesigned and expanded. The old split-level was visible in the bones—but the house was now large enough to have two wings.

The garage had vanished, probably made into part of the living space. Instead she had to follow a circular drive that went around the house and led to a parking area in the rear.

If houses in Manatowa hadn't gotten so big during the nineties, she would have thought of this as a mansion. But it wasn't a mansion. It wasn't even a McMansion. It was just an old house, lovingly remodeled into something else.

Something she hadn't quite seen before.

The garage was a separate building tucked against woods that seemed to vanish in the distance. She parked in front of one of the garage doors, hoping she wasn't blocking anyone in. The house was to her left, and through the driver's side window, she could see the back of the house, windows catching those thin rays of sun.

Petrovich stood behind the glass patio doors and watched her pull up. The patio doors opened onto a real patio, with one of those giant gas barbeques built into the concrete, and a swimming pool—empty and covered for the winter—as the focal point for the entire living space.

It had to be pleasant here in the summer, even with the extended parking so close by.

She got out of the car and wrestled with the hem of her coat, which had gotten stuck on her seatbelt. Her face was red when she finally freed the material. She slammed the door, turned, and saw Petrovich had let himself out onto the patio.

He was wearing jeans, a plaid shirt with rolled-up sleeves, and thick white socks. No shoes. The wind ruffled his blond hair, and for a moment she could see how he must have looked when he was a teenager, remarkably like the son who bore his name.

"Get inside," she said, looking pointedly at his feet. "You have to be freezing."

"Ah, Minnesotans are hardy souls," he said with a smile. But he crossed his arms and shivered, then hopped over the threshold so that he stood on thick pile carpet.

She walked around the pool—it was good-sized, not usual wimpy cooling-off pools she'd seen in Southern California—and stepped inside the house.

The patio doors led directly into the kitchen, dining room, and family room. The kitchen had clearly been redone. It was large, with an island, a flat-topped ceramic stove, and a refrigerator that looked like it could stock enough food for an army. Dishes covered the area near the sink, but not a lot of them. Just the breakfast and lunch dishes, as if someone were waiting for a dishwasher load before cleaning up.

The Sunday paper sat on the end of the island, the pages messed and clearly read. The dining room table still had placemats but they were scattered as if someone had forgotten to pick them up after the last meal.

On the large-screen TV in the family room, basketball players in their loose uniforms vied around the basket. The word "mute" ran along the bottom of the screen.

It took her a moment to realize the players were girls, not boys.

The family room itself was remarkably clean, and it didn't look like company-clean, but everyday-clean. Blankets draped over the couch, and one was scrunched on a La-Z-Boy on the side of the room. Some video game consoles sat on the coffee table, but weren't being used, along with some soda cans and three romance novels, all of which were open and turned upside down.

"Welcome to my humble abode," Petrovich said.

Larissa smiled a little self-consciously. He had watched her take in each detail, and hadn't said a word.

"It's not so humble," she said. "You have an east wing and a west wing."

He shrugged. "I practice here before I try new stuff on clients. So we've added a few things. The place belonged to my folks, and it was paid off when we got it—my wife and I—as a wedding present. Ever since, I've added to it, seeing if I could do half the things I thought I could do."

"Can you?" she asked.

He glanced over his shoulder. "I finally had to hire out the pool. Those things are tricky, especially outdoor ones that have to adjust to extremes of heat and cold."

"Why not build an indoor pool?"

"Would have loved that," he said, "but split levels have 'daylight basements' and no room for swimming pools."

"So you had to practice the indoor variety somewhere else," she said.

"I swore off pools after that monster," he said with a smile. "Toss your coat anywhere."

She pulled off the coat and set it on a footstool near the patio doors. She put her purse there, too, and her mittens.

He padded into the kitchen. His socks, white on top, were brown on the bottom. Apparently he lived in his stockinged feet.

"Coffee?" he asked.

"I'd love some," she said.

"I also have some peach cobbler that P.J. needs to practice for the home ec bake-off next week. It's not pretty, but it tastes good."

It took her a moment to remember that P.J. was Petrovich's son, and not his daughter. Things had changed a lot since Larissa was in school.

"That sounds good, too."

Petrovich took plates from a cabinet, then removed the cobbler from the refrigerator. He cut pieces and brought the plates to the table. Along the way, he grabbed two forks and a pile of napkins.

"Where are the kids?" Larissa asked. Her stomach was already in a knot. She had wondered how Petrovich would handle showing her the clips with his newly traumatized children around.

Or maybe the kids already knew and were inured to the clippings from their father's past.

"Diane has basketball practice. They have to make up for the past few weeks." He looked down as he said that. "And P.J. went to the movies with some friends."

She smiled, feeling a bit of the knot loosen.

Petrovich went back into the kitchen, poured the coffee, then held up her mug. "Cream, sugar? I'd offer brandy, but I'm not allowed to keep the hard stuff in the house."

He said that last lightly, but she remembered him mentioning a twelve-step program last weekend. So she smiled just to be polite. "Black is fine."

He brought both mugs over and sat down near her. "I feel like I coerced you into looking at these clippings," he said.

"Maybe at first." She pulled the cobbler toward her. P.J. had gotten something wrong in the sauce. It hadn't set properly, and juice ran all over the plate. "But I've been thinking all week about the discrepancies between what you remember and what I remember. I figured I may as well take a look."

"It won't be easy," he said.

"Nothing's been easy lately." She gave him another smile, but it felt as pale as the sunlight.

"Which is exactly why this can wait if you want it to."

She shook her head. "I'm here. Let's do it."

Her voice sounded confident and sure, even though she didn't feel that way. She knew that if she didn't look at those clippings now, she might not ever be back.

Petrovich pulled open a drawer in the dining table itself, which meant that those place mats hid an antique. Tables with drawers were rare now. No one thought to store their silver in the tables themselves any longer.

He took out a thick red file folder and set it next to his cobbler.

"I don't know why I kept all this stuff," he said, placing his hand on top of the folder. "I started the day I got out of the hospital."

Larissa felt the knot return. "I thought you weren't shot," she said before she could stop herself.

I thought you said that I saved you from being shot was the sentence she prevented from coming out of her mouth. She was back in reporter mode, and she hadn't even realized it until this moment, although she should have known when she absorbed each and every detail of the house as she walked into it.

"I wasn't," he said. "But I was near a window when the shooting started and—well, look."

He pushed his left sleeve up even higher. He leaned toward her and pointed a series of white scars that covered his skin from his shoulder to his elbow.

"My God," Larissa said. "All glass?"

"A three-hour surgery to get it all out. And for months afterward, bits of glass would work their way out of my skin."

She shuddered. "I had no idea."

"Why would you?" he said. "You said your grandmother protected you from the coverage. Believe me, after these past two weeks, I understand that. I wish I could do that with my kids."

You could, she almost said, but did not. It would have been hard, particularly with that school assembly and the memorial service.

The world had changed. It now forced people to deal with things, whether they wanted to or not.

"It's better this way," he said, but he didn't sound entirely convinced. He ran his hand over the file. "What is it about this part of Minnesota? You'd think something like this wouldn't happen twice in my lifetime."

"Things like this happen everywhere," Larissa said.

"If they happen everywhere, they wouldn't be newsworthy."

"They're not," she said. Then she swallowed, realizing how that sounded. It sounded like she was trivializing the last week. "The school shootings still are newsworthy, although there's debate about whether or not to give them too much coverage. Teenagers are notoriously suggestive, and if one was already suicidal or wanted to go out with a blaze of glory, some argue that such coverage only guarantees more shootings in the future."

"Do you believe that?" He looked at her, his expression impassive.

She shrugged. "I don't believe you can stop someone bent on destruction."

Her words hung between them for a moment. Then he squeezed the folder, but didn't pick it up.

"Yet you say these things aren't unusual." He was looking at the folder's faded cover. She looked, too, saw some words scrawled on it, but she couldn't read them upside down.

"Do you listen to the news?" she asked.

"Headlines," he said. "When I'm driving or on a job."

She nodded. "Every day, someone goes postal. Sometimes he gets caught. Sometimes he doesn't harm anyone—it's just a hostage situation."

"Just a hostage situation," Petrovich muttered.

She felt color warm her cheeks. She wasn't trivializing. She was explaining. He had asked, after all.

"Sometimes," she said, "he shoots someone before turning the gun on himself. Only the cases that are prolonged, or happen in a famous place of business or have high casualties, make the national news."

Petrovich shook his head. "You sound so matter-of-fact."

Those glass shields had their uses. But she didn't say that. She shrugged. "I am matter-of-fact. I've covered too many homicides to treat them like a strange occurrence. Yet each one is personal and devastating."

Just like she'd been thinking the night before. Only her tone was calm today. Would she be judging herself as harshly as she had judged Gavin, if she had heard herself use this tone of voice before?

"I don't know how anyone can get used to murders," Petrovich said. "Single or multiple."

"I didn't say I was used to them," Larissa said. "Only that they weren't unusual."

This time her voice shook. He looked at her. His eyes were a deep shade of blue. They had laugh lines around the edges, and the beginnings of sun wrinkles along his cheeks and down to his mouth.

But even after all he'd been through, the lines weren't making his face sad. His features were pleasant, and would become more so with the passage of time.

He slid the folder toward her.

"The clippings are in chronological order," he said. "You can take the whole folder if you want."

She shook her head even before she had a chance to consider his offer. If she took the clippings, she would never look at them. She would always intend to look at them. They would sit on a counter or a table and taunt her. But the folder would never be opened, and one day she would give up, bringing it back to him and lying about how she felt about what she had seen.

"I'd prefer to look here, if that's all right," she said.

He nodded.

She didn't offer an explanation and he didn't ask for one. Instead, she pulled the file closer, set the cobbler aside, and opened the folder.

The clipping on top was a banner headline from the New Lake Herald: *Six Dead in Bank Shooting*. And beneath it, *Gunman kills six before turning weapon on himself.*

Seven dead. She'd always heard six. But that made sense. Six innocents had died. And then her father had shot himself in front of the survivors.

Cause a Mystery said one of the subheadings. The story covered the entire page above the fold. And there was a photograph of the demolished bank—the shattered front window, the overturned desks, and splotches of what could only be blood.

Larissa stared at the photograph for a long time. She didn't remember the bank like that. She remembered it the way she had seen it when she went in with her father on weekends. The smell of heat or air conditioning, the slight scent of money, the rubbery odor of the artificial plants near the door.

The desks were all made from some kind of plastic made to resemble wood, and the chairs were lightweight, too, as if the bank itself wasn't permanent. Only the teller cages were made of real wood. They had been taken from the original bank downtown and placed in the "new" bank, the one built at the beginning of the 1970s, in the height of the post-modern movement.

Her finger touched the image of the shattered window. "You were here?" she asked.

"Yeah," he said. "Waiting for my dad. I was watching something down the street. The first shot missed, and shattered the window."

But that couldn't be right. Because if the window shattered from a gunshot fired from inside, the glass would have gone outside.

She nodded, though, and forced herself to look closely at the clipping.

Six people were killed and six others seriously injured when a gunman opened fire in New Lake First National Bank on Saturday.

Saturday. Petrovich had been right. Why hadn't she remembered it that way?

Larissa put a hand to her forehead and continued reading.

Conrad Mueller, the bank's assistant manager, opened fire shortly after he entered the bank. He shot security guard John Anderson, teller Mavis Berg, and trainee Anna Guterman in rapid succession, then called for bank president Davis Wolters. Wolters had barricaded himself in his office and was on the phone with police.

When Wolters did not appear, Mueller fired random shots into the crowded lobby, injuring LaVerne Zimmerman, Jack Olson, and his young

*son, Jeffrey. Peter Petrovich, Violet Hughes, and Walter Perry later died
at the hospital. Edwin Steers tackled Mueller from behind and attempt to
disarm him, but Mueller shot him in the face. Ruth Hultman ran for the
exit and Mueller shot her as well. Finally, Mueller shot Stephen Ferguson
before turning the gun on himself.*

*Police arrived on the scene just as the shootings ended. Cruisers were
used to take many of those with minor injuries to New Lake Hospital.
The seriously injured were stabilized at New Lake, then driven to Duluth
by ambulance.*

Two died along the way.

*The First National Bank shooting is the worst violence New Lake has
ever seen....*

She stopped reading and rubbed her eyes. She didn't remember any
of this. She didn't remember being in the bank. Nor did she remember
her father losing control like that, even though she knew he had.

But it was an intellectual remembrance—a knowledge, not a memory.

Or at least, that was what she had believed. Maybe it was what she
still believed.

How come she couldn't remember any of this?

She read through the next clippings both from the day after, one
from the *Minneapolis Tribune* and the other from the *Duluth News Tribune*, but they added little to the facts that the New Lake reporters had
uncovered.

Then, from Monday's paper:

Gunman Murdered Wife Before Bank Shootings

"What?" Larissa muttered. Her head ached. Her mother had killed
herself. Her grandmother had said so. Her mother hadn't been able
to live with the shame, so she had taken one of their father's guns and
turned it on herself.

But where would she have gotten that gun? It would have been evi-
dence in the bank shooting. All of his guns would have been.

Maybe Larissa had remembered that detail wrong.

"You okay?" Petrovich asked.

Of course she wasn't okay. She was reading about the central event of her life, one she obviously did not remember.

One that had caused her to quit jobs, lose control, and stay in bed for days at a time. One that had kept her from marriage, from children of her own.

From banks, for God's sake. She preferred automatic tellers. She preferred automatic tellers in malls and gas stations and grocery stores.

She tried to avoid the inside of banks whenever she could.

She made herself read the story before her.

According to the reporter, Conrad Mueller had had breakfast with his wife and youngest child. His son had gone to a friend's on his bicycle before Mueller awoke, and his eldest daughter had been at a slumber party.

How come Larissa didn't remember this? Although it made sense. Nadia was never home in those days. She was boy crazy and she lied about everything.

Or at least, that was what her grandmother had said.

Her grandmother, who hadn't spent a lot of time with them until after the shootings.

The murders.

She had to use the correct words now. They were murders.

She blinked and forced herself to read again. It took great concentration for the words to penetrate her brain.

To get through that glass shielding.

The report continued: Mueller finished his breakfast and grabbed his briefcase. In a calm voice, he asked his youngest if she wanted to go to work with him, as she often did on Saturdays.

She agreed.

He then took his gun, shot his wife, and dragged his youngest daughter by the arm out of the house.

Larissa frowned. He hadn't shot her. He hadn't shot Larissa. But he had shot her mother.

He had loved her mother.

He had bought her that hat.

Larissa rubbed her eyes again.

"Hey," Petrovich said. "Maybe this isn't a good idea...."

But she didn't look at him. She didn't answer him.

She made herself read.

The reporter had gotten a great deal of information, and he must have gotten it from Larissa even though she did not remember the interview.

Or the events.

She didn't remember the events either.

Apparently, her father had dragged her that mile to the bank. He hadn't driven. He had walked, daughter in tow, briefcase in the other hand—was he clutching the gun? Was he brandishing it? Or had he hidden it again?

Then he walked through the glass doors into the airlock...

...and nearly slipped on the marble floor.

"Told them they should have a mat in here," he said as if his face weren't speckled with blood. His grip on her arm was so tight that her fingers tingled.

He pulled her forward. She dug in her heels, but it did no good. The floor was slippery and she slid after him. As he reached for the glass interior door, she wanted to yell.

She wanted to tell someone—Duck!—or Look Out! Or even something as simple as "He shot my mommy!"

But the words didn't come out. She opened her mouth, and she was silent. She couldn't say anything.

If she said something, he might remember he had her and he might shoot her with that same empty look in his eyes that he had when he shot Mommy.

He pushed open the interior door, and Mr. Anderson, the big fat man in the too-tight uniform who smelled of vanilla pipe tobacco and sometimes gave her candy, said, "Why, Mr. Mueller. We weren't expecting you today."

And instead of answering, Daddy shot him.

Shot him, right in the chest, right next to his ID plate and that fake badge Mr. Anderson wore that he sometimes laughed about.

Daddy shot him and Mr. Anderson reached toward the gun. But behind him, blood had spattered all over the desk and Miss Lund, Daddy's secretary, who let out a tiny scream and backed out of her chair.

Someone else screamed and Daddy fired a shot into the air and everyone looked at him. Then he opened his briefcase and took out another gun. He had two now, and another tucked into the waistband of his pants. Larissa could see its bulge through his suit coat.

"Mr. Mueller," said Miss Berg, the nice teller who sometimes showed Larissa how to use the adding machines. "Don't do this. Just set the gun down and we'll get Mr. Wolters and—"

Daddy shot her. She let out a small eep! And the lady next to her, a lady Larissa had never seen before, she yelled, "No!" really loud and Daddy shot her, too.

And somebody—some man who was in line—he said, "Tell us what you want."

And Daddy didn't say anything. He turned toward that man, and that was when his hand slipped off Larissa's wrist and she ran for the desks, careful not to hit anything because if she hit something, she might make a noise, and if she made a noise, he'd remember she was there, and if he remembered she was there, he'd shoot her like he shot Mommy, and her face would go away, and her blood would spatter on the cabinets, and she would be like a gory movie creature and not like a Mommy at all.

Larissa hadn't screamed when Daddy did that. She hadn't even got sick, because something blocked her throat. It was real tight.

She wasn't even sure he knew he'd grabbed her. He just took her hand like any other Saturday, like he took the handle of the briefcase, and then he'd walked too fast, and she'd kept up because she knew if she said anything…

If she said anything…

If she said anything, she would die.

She would die just like Mommy or Mr. Anderson or nice Miss Berg or that stranger lady who had screamed.

Larissa ran for the desks and other people were running, some had fallen flat, and there was this boy in the middle of it all, screaming at a man on the ground, a man with blood instead of a neck, screaming at him to get up.

Larissa grabbed the boy around the middle and pulled him down.

"Shut up," she said. "Shut up, shut up, shut up."

But the boy kept screaming, so she put her hand over his mouth.

But it wasn't enough. Daddy had come over. He was looking for the screamer, she just knew it.

He was looking, and she couldn't let him find that boy. Grown-ups—they should know how to deal with other grown-ups—but this boy, he was screaming because his dad was hurt, like Larissa wanted to scream about her mom, and he didn't know what danger he was in, screaming like that.

She pulled him under the desk, shoved him all the way to the back even though he was bigger than she was.

"Stay here," she whispered. That lump was still in her throat, but she could whisper. She was surprised he could hear her with all the moaning and the shouting and the sirens in the distance.

"What about you?" The boy didn't know how to be quiet.

God, she'd seen him before. He was the cute kid in school. One grade up. The one she'd giggle about with her friends. The one who looked at her just last week and she mooned about it for days.

"What about you?" he repeated.

"He won't hurt me," she whispered, then crawled to the front of the desk. If Daddy did see her and did remember who she was, he'd shoot her, but he'd never see the cute kid. He wouldn't know someone else was back there.

He wouldn't know.

The sirens were getting closer, but they didn't make her feel better. The gun went off again, then one more time.

She leaned out just a little.

Daddy turned and turned and turned, as if he was seeing everything for the first time. He had blood on his shoes and bits of skin and his pants were covered in stuff like he'd been walking in the mud.

His face was still speckled with Mommy's blood but his eyes weren't empty anymore. They were filled with tears. The tears spilled over and ran through the speckles, turning red as they dripped off his chin.

"Jesus," he whispered. "Holy Jesus, what have I done?"

Then the sirens were right outside. Through the window, she could see the police cars—more than she'd ever seen—all pulled up across the street, the lights still flaring and men pouring out like in the movies.

Daddy saw them, too. He blinked, shook his head once, and looked at the gun in his hand.

Then he brought it to his head.

"No!" Larissa screamed.

His eyes—his tear-filled eyes—met hers and his mouth moved, but nothing came out.

Then everything exploded. The world exploded. Daddy exploded.

And the boy pushed past her trying to get out and she fell against the floor and there were more explosions and then it was raining glass.

Raining glass and the police were yelling and someone—a woman—inside was yelling back.

"It's okay. He's dead."

It's okay. He's dead.

But that wasn't okay. That was her daddy. He couldn't be dead. Anymore than her mother was.

This was all a dream and she would wake up in her bed and her mommy would laugh and her daddy would be holding a special box and her brother and sister would be looking on, and they would all be waiting for Larissa to join them.

She would wake up and everything would be right.

But someone picked her up and brushed the glass off her and asked her who she belonged to.

And when she pointed at what was left of Daddy, they covered her face and led her outside.

She sat in a car for a very long time. A police car. It had no handles on the back doors and a plastic window on top of the front seat. The window was scratched and so old that it didn't reflect anything.

Not that she wanted to look.

She'd seen enough.

Then a lady got into the back, a police lady she said, and said it would be okay, her grandmother was coming.

Larissa knew better than to ask for her mother.

Then the lady said, "If you tell us what happened, you'll feel better."

That was a lie. Larissa knew it from the start.

"Just pretend you're giving a report," the lady said. "You know, like in school. Pretend it's about somebody else, and you'll remember. It'll be easy."

"Why?" Larissa had said.

"So we know the truth." The lady took Larissa's hand. "The truth's important, don't you think?"

Larissa didn't know. But she made a report.

Her first report.

And she told the truth because the lady thought the truth was important.

Larissa needed something important right then.

Because everything else that was important had suddenly disappeared.

twenty-one

*P*etrovich had his hand on her shoulder. He was holding a glass of water.

"Larissa," he was saying. "Come on. Have something to drink."

She looked up at him and saw relief in his eyes.

"You vanished for a while," he said. "You were staring at that article and you just vanished."

Vanished. Yes, that made sense to her. She had gotten lost in her own past. She had—what was the word?—recovered it. As if it had been lost.

And it was, to her. It had been lost.

Or misremembered.

Or covered with another story, one her grandmother wanted her to believe.

To protect her. Her grandmother had been trying to protect her.

Larissa took the water and drank it. It soothed her parched throat, and somehow swept past that lump. Had the lump always been there? Or had it appeared the day her mother was shot?

The day her father murdered her mother.

In front of her.

She got up and walked into the kitchen, still carrying the glass. Then without asking permission, she filled the glass again and drank it down.

Petrovich touched the article about her mother, then he looked at her.

"Jesus," he said. "You didn't know that either."

"My grandmother said she committed suicide. She heard what he did and killed herself." Larissa filled the glass a second time. "I always wondered why she left us when we needed her the most. Why she *chose* to leave us. But she didn't."

"No," Petrovich said softly. "She had no choice in the matter."

Larissa nodded, but the movement felt reflexive. "How come suicide is better than murder? Why would my grandmother lie like that? How come she would think we would want our mother to be a coward?"

"Maybe she didn't see it that way," he said.

"She left us when we needed her the most!" The words were child-like. The voice was childlike, and it had escaped from her. She never let voices like that escape from her. She always had the blocking mechanism. Her voices had layers of glass to get through, so they wouldn't—they couldn't—come out.

Only this one did.

She turned around, filled the glass a third time, and drank some more. Then she made herself set the glass on the counter.

"Do the articles say why he did this?" She couldn't face anymore of them. She'd had more than enough truth for one day.

Petrovich kept his hand on the clippings. "It took a while for them to find out, but they did. He'd been embezzling. Him and the bank president, Wolters. Only the auditors figured it out and Wolters blamed your dad. That was Friday. Saturday he shot up the bank."

She leaned against the sink, both hands behind her, holding her upright.

"Why would he think that was a solution?" she asked.

Petrovich shook his head. "You're looking for logic."

"Yeah, I guess so."

"These things aren't logical."

She of all people should know that. In fact, she would have said that to anyone who asked about Leif. Or about any of the other spree killers she had covered.

She'd even interviewed the school shooter from Oregon, Kip Kinkle, and although he had been planning the shooting for a long time, he said he had no idea—not really—why he had picked that day, that moment, and why, on the way to the school, it had seemed like the right thing to do.

He'd been such a little boy. A scrawny young thing with tears in his eyes.

She'd *liked* him, for God's sake. He'd seemed so nice, that boy who had killed his classmates and his parents. He'd seemed so sad and so full of remorse.

She had *liked* him.

She had loved her father.

That day, in the bank, her father's lips had moved when his gaze met hers.

His father's lips had moved.

They had formed the word "Sorry."

He had been looking at her.

He had seen her.

Because she had yelled. She had *screamed* despite the lump in her throat. She had screamed at him, and he had seen her, and he had come back into his eyes.

He had come back.

Maybe if she had spoken before, he would have come back sooner. Maybe all those other people would be alive.

Maybe her mother would be alive.

Larissa slumped against the sink.

"Come on." Somehow Petrovich had reached her side. He put his arm around her and led her to the couch. He moved some of the bunched up blankets and helped her down.

The basketball game still played silently on television. One team was winning by ten points. Tall, sweaty girls high-fived each other, their ponytails swinging.

"Maybe this was a mistake," Petrovich said. "Maybe not knowing—"

"No," Larissa said. "It's just a lot to take in."

It wasn't news to her. Not really. She'd been there, after all. She'd lived through it. Just like he had.

But she had covered the experience with layers of lies. Of stories. Of ways to get past it.

Her mother had committed suicide, her grandmother said, so they couldn't go back into the house. Grandma had gotten their things. That was when Grandma had come for her in school. With a car full of clothes and toys and books, and Larissa was already crying.

It seemed like she always cried in those days.

Her mother had committed suicide, her father had snapped, and six people had died. (Seven! her mind shouted. Seven when she included her father. And shouldn't they include her father? He was part of the casualty list, after all.)

She changed her name, became Larissa Johanssen and pretended that no one remembered. But how could they not remember? Her father had killed their fathers or their mothers or shot their sisters or their wives.

Her father had shot Petrovich's father.

In front of Petrovich.

"How can you be nice to me?" she asked in that little-girl voice. It embarrassed her. She wished it away, but she didn't want the lump back in her throat.

"What do you mean?" Petrovich asked. His arm was still around her. She was grateful for the human contact. The warmth.

She couldn't remember any warmth after her folks died. Her grand-parents—neither set—touched anyone. Maybe that was why Nadia slept around, why Ric always sat in a chair with his arms wrapped around his own torso, why Larissa carried tiny stuffed animals in her purse until she was through college.

Substitute warmth.

"My father," she said. "He killed your father."

"And you saved my life," Petrovich said.

She had. She remembered that now. She had pulled him under a desk. He was smart enough to figure out that her father would have shot him for screaming. Her father had shot everyone who talked.

Or touched him.

Or so much as looked at him wrong.

Petrovich—Pete—had been the only one who hadn't fallen to the ground when the shots started.

Because he froze.

"My father didn't shoot out the window," she said.

Petrovich looked at her sideways, a frown creasing his forehead.

"The police did. After he killed himself. They didn't know he was dead. They were coming in. That's why the glass went inside, not out."

She touched the ridges on his arm.

His mouth was open slightly, looking at her fingers on his white scars.

He made a small "huh" noise, as if he were filing that piece of information away.

"That makes sense," he said. "I always remember him being dead when he shot out the window."

She swallowed. *Him being dead.*

He had died, hadn't he? Her father. He had destroyed her entire world that day, and somehow she had survived.

She had built a new one.

But it was amazing that she had survived. Not just because he hadn't shot her.

But because of the shock.

Within the space of an hour, she had gone from a sheltered child to one who had witnessed the death of both parents in front of her, and watched as others—people she liked—had died as well.

Horribly.

The way kids had died in the cafeteria just two weeks before.

How many people had she seen killed over the years? Two dozen? Three?

And each time, she told the truth about it.

Because the truth was important.

She was even planning to tell the truth now in that small book she would edit.

No wonder she had collapsed when she tried to continue reporting.

You could only tell someone else's truth for so long before you had to examine your own.

She used truth to justify her own silence. That lump in her throat. The glass that surrounded her.

The feelings she'd hidden so she wouldn't upset her grandmother, her grandfather, her siblings, or her friends.

She had gone back to school a few days later with a new name and a new identity and pretended to be someone new. And everyone had gone along with it because it was easier than talking about what had happened.

The way Manatowa High was doing.

They were talking.

Her students were talking.

Because it was better that way.

But it didn't make the memories go away. It didn't even make them easier to deal with.

It just kept them accessible.

Maybe that was how to fight PTSD. Maybe that was how a person remained functional after great tragedy.

Maybe it took nothing more than a willingness to face the facts of what happened head on.

"I take it, then, that you remember," Petrovich said.

She nodded. "He brought me with him."

Petrovich watched her, keeping his hand light on her shoulder.

"He held onto me while he shot Mr. Anderson."

"The security guard," Petrovich said.

"And then he forgot about me."

"I don't know about that," Petrovich said. "You were convinced he wouldn't hurt you."

"Oh, no, I wasn't," she said. Her voice was breathless, still young. Not reporting at all.

"But that's what you told me. You said he wouldn't hurt you."

"I lied," she said. "I put you behind me under that desk. I figured he wouldn't see you."

Petrovich let go of her shoulder, then sat forward so that he could see her face without crowding her.

"You *were* protecting me." He sounded surprised.

"Yes," she said.

"Why?"

She smiled. It was a fond, almost rueful smile, directed at her young self, at a person she had lost that day as clearly as she had lost her parents.

"You were the cute one."

"What?" he asked, confused.

"I recognized you, standing there. You were the cute guy who had talked to me the week before. I had the biggest crush on you."

He ran a hand over his mouth, shook his head, and then leaned back. "You wouldn't talk to me afterwards."

"You knew who I was," she said.

"Everyone knew who you were," he said.

She nodded. "But my grandmother made me promise not to say anything about it. And what else could I talk to you about?"

He shook his head.

"She was trying to protect me," Larissa said.

"She did," He said. "Look at you. You're doing fine. Better than fine. You're—"

"Oh, no," she said. "I fell apart. We all fell apart, trying to live her way. Ric—my brother—he couldn't pretend anymore. Or maybe he just couldn't shut out the memories. He killed himself."

"Jesus," Petrovich said.

"And my sister, she marries anyone who even remotely reminds her of my father. Then she gets scared of him and divorces him, and moves onto the next one."

"And you?" Petrovich asked.

"I couldn't tell other people's stories anymore," she said. "I broke."

Shattered. Only it wasn't sudden like that window. Or like her father's "snap."

One crack appeared. Then another, and another, until finally she couldn't support all her glass shields. She had to protect herself differently.

She had to take the shields away from situations that would shatter them.

Like crime scenes. Like war zones.

Like murder.

"Then you came here," he said.

"And oddly," she said, "it felt like home."

It was home. From the horrible weather to the pretty house to the nice people, it was home.

And the shooter. The shooter—Leif—showed the poison that still existed.

"I told Robyn to go to the counselors," Larissa said. "Guess I should, too."

Only this time, she wouldn't pretend nothing was wrong. She wouldn't hide behind those glass shields. They were gone. The last of them had vanished this afternoon as the memories broke through.

"Yeah," Petrovich said. "I've been talking to my therapist. And the kids've been going, too."

"That's doing it right," Larissa said. "My grandmother, she had no idea what *right* was."

"Imagine what she went through. Her son-in-law didn't just murder six random people at a bank—he also killed her daughter."

"Her only daughter."

"And then she had to raise his children."

"Her daughter's children," Larissa said. "We weren't allowed to talk about him."

Stuffing it all down. Putting it all away. Like an ugly picture or a ruined piece of clothing. Just something to forget.

"I couldn't imagine," Petrovich said. "It was hard enough when my wife died. And these are my children, and no one was murdered."

"But I'm sure it echoed," Larissa said. "Losing her. It probably echoed with losing your father."

"Yeah." He spoke softly. "These kids, they're going to echo like we do, won't they?"

She nodded. She'd been thinking about that all week.

"And we can't prevent it."

"What's done is done," she said, using another of her grandmother's phrases. "But we can help them with the echoes. We can let them know that flashbacks are normal."

"Fear is normal," he said.

"And survival is possible."

He took her hand. His skin was so warm. She couldn't remember ever touching skin that warm before.

"We did survive, didn't we?" he said.

"Some better than others," she said.

"You did all right."

"I think I'll do better now," she said.

It was strange that a second tragedy would bring back the first. And treating this tragedy differently would help her. The way the town was talking about it.

Hell, the town was going to write about it, and she would make sure that the words got into print.

Without telling the stories herself. She would tell her own story.

All of it.

From her father to Leif. From Ric to Gavin. From the cute boy to Petrovich.

She'd tell what she remembered, how she felt, and how she survived.

She didn't regret having those glass shields. They got her through.

And now she had to learn how to live without them.

That was why she thought she should visit the school counselors, maybe find one of her own here in Manatowa. She would need the support while she read the rest of the clippings, and while Petrovich was a good man, he didn't need her leaning on his shoulder while he had to be there for his children.

"Don't be afraid to talk to me," he said as if he were reading her mind. "We share some strange experiences, but we share them. We should be able to talk about them."

"Without accusing each other of false memories," she said. "I'm sorry about that."

"I startled you."

"You did," she said. "You still do."

His gaze met hers. His eyes were warm. She felt no guile from him. He wasn't lying to her to get a story. He didn't care about stories.

He cared about her.

"You're still the cute guy," she said, and he laughed. It was a deep guttural laugh.

It took him a moment to catch his breath, but when he did, he said, "At least you're talking to me now."

"Thanks to you, I can," she said.

He shook his head. "That's all you. Nothing happens that we're not ready for."

"Oh, that's not true," she said. "I doubt we're ever ready for the Leif Soderstroms of the world."

She almost said her father's name, but she wasn't quite ready to do that either. He had had too much power over her life as it was. Lurking there, a snap and then a destroyed life.

She had been afraid of snapping like he had. Or like Ric.

But she hadn't. And she wouldn't.

She was the strong one.

Now she had to teach her students how to be strong. Without lying to them. Without pretending things were better than they were.

Without telling stories.

That female police officer had been right so long ago. The truth was important.

When it was your truth.

You had to look at it for all that it was, good and bad. And then you had to use it as a stepping stone to move forward.

She was finally moving forward.

Building a life.

Her own life.

For the very first time.

about the author

KRISTINE KATHRYN RUSCH, a former journalist herself, has won dozens of awards for her writing. Her mysteries (written as Kris Nelscott) have been nominated for the Edgar Award, the Shamus Award, and the Oregon Book Award. Her short fiction has appeared in many prestigious markets, including *The North American Review* and the Best American series as well as 18 other year's best volumes. Her novels have been published in 14 countries. For more information about her writing, go to www.kristinekathrynrusch.com.

www.ingramcontent.com/pod-product-compliance
Lightning Source LLC
Chambersburg PA
CBHW020051180626
46812CB00006B/2275